TORTUROUS TREK

TORTUROUS TREK

Max Brand®

Published in 2018 by Blackstone Publishing

Printed in the United States of America

ISBN 978-1-4708-6108-7
Fiction / Westerns

1 3 5 7 9 10 8 6 4 2

CIP data for this book is available
from the Library of Congress

Blackstone Publishing
31 Mistletoe Rd.
Ashland, OR 97520

www.BlackstonePublishing.com

CHAPTER ONE

Nagle's Bar in Circle City was one of the best; certainly it was the most democratic, for it offered three grades of whiskey. There was a whole keg of each on tap.

One was sold at twenty-five cents the glass. On it was a sign that read: THIS LIQUOR IS FOR STRONG MEN. ARE YOU STRONG?

On the second keg, which retailed at fifty cents a drink, was the legend: THIS ONLY HURTS YOU NOW AND THEN.

On the third keg, the price of which was seventy-five cents, or six bits in the vernacular, was the following: YOUR OLD MAN DRANK THIS; WHY NOT YOU?

The answer of one wit to this was: "Because the old man didn't last long."

However, as has been pointed out, Nagle's Saloon offered two drinks—of a kind—for half a dollar. And Sammy Day, when he stepped into Nagle's place, unheralded, unannounced, had fifty cents and a great thirst.

He looked at the legends over both of the cheaper kegs and then turned wistful eyes upon the higher-priced stuff. He was one who liked quality and never objected to high prices, if he could pay them. However, on this occasion he was limited to the half-dollar. He did not even have an overcoat to pawn, though the temperature outside was floating around zero. He had had an overcoat and plenty of cash the evening before, when he arrived by forced marches from the southland. Tonight he had nothing except the clothes he stood up in. Some $2,500 had slipped away across this bar and at the poker tables in the next room. He had no regrets. But at this moment, he wanted a drink.

The philosophical man adapts his desires to his pocketbook. But Sammy Day was not philosophical. He always acted as though he had a million in his pocket and two hundred plus of beef and bone at his disposal. As a matter of fact, he rarely had more than one month's wages as a cowhand, along with whatever winnings bucking faro or beating poker put in his jeans. As for size, he was only a welterweight, with heavyweight ambitions. What there was of him was lean and hard and rather drawn out. His nose was short and his jaw was stubby. His eyebrows grew straight across and bushed out in the center, so that he always seemed between good nature and a frown, although he was a smiling fellow.

In his eyes was fire. Sometimes it smoldered, sometimes it danced and leaped, sometimes it raged with a green devil glinting through, but always the fire was in the eyes of Sammy Day.

The cow range was his home. He had worked it from Montana to Chihuahua. Occasionally little happenings forced Sammy Day to abandon the reaches of his native heath, broad as that was, and so he had had glimpses of far lands as well. He could talk a little Chinese for you in a pinch, and, when he was stripped, one could see the horrible, unmistakable scar that was made when a Malay kris dagger was driven home. The scar was under the left shoulder.

Now he was up in the white North, a stranger there but one who was accustomed to the role. Another little "accident" had accounted for his journey north. The accident occurred in a Montana mining camp. In it, there had been mixed-up poker chips, a pack of cards flying in the air, much noise of shooting guns and men, and the acrid, choking smell of gunpowder in the air. Sammy Day had escaped through a rear window and hit the long trail. They rode three days to overtake him. He hid in a wolf's burrow and soaked in ice-cold mud for hours while he watched the posse pass. Then he started out again, followed the pursuers, slipped past them, and here he was in Circle City.

Much of the world, it will be seen, had flowed through the eye and even through the blood of Sammy Day. But for only ten years had he been a free, independent, self-supporting man. He was now just twenty-two.

Most of this picture of Sam Day—he was called by another name in a more southerly land—is necessary to understand what went through his mind as he fumbled fifty cents in his pocket and looked at a seventy-five-cent drink. He was as one who is thirsty, who has been thirsty many times before, and who has generally gratified that thirst.

Nagle himself was behind the bar, and he understood the direction of his client's fixed stare and the reason of it. "Have this one on me," he said.

"I never take the first drink of the day off the bar," said Sammy. "It's bad luck."

There was no argument. "What's in the back room?" asked Sammy Day, hooking a thumb over his shoulder.

"Nothing but a little game of craps."

"Why, nobody but me knows just how to talk to a pair of dice," remarked Sammy. "Big Joe and Little Joe is a pair of cousins of mine, and there's been seven days in every week of my life."

He went straightway into the gaming room. As he went, he whistled sharp and shrill, but made a melody through his teeth.

He found eight men assembled around a blanket lying on the

floor and folded long and smooth. They were bouncing the dice against the wall to make sure of an honest fall.

"I've got fifty cents," said Sammy. "Do I fade into this game?"

A redheaded man looked at him with a grin. "Here's fifty dollars, kid," he said. "You can fade in with that."

"I don't borrow stakes," said Sammy Day. "There's no luck in that sort of a play."

"You're in with your fifty cents," said the redheaded man. The dicebox had come into his hands at this moment, and he grinned at Day again.

For half an hour, that game continued, uninterrupted. Then Sammy Day put five dollars into his pocket; he kept another twenty-five dollars in the game. Fortune had been kind to him.

One sourdough mumbled: "Them that come in with nothin', they can't lose."

Sammy overheard. "That's true," he said. "But turn and turn about is fair play. I've lost my stake, in my day, to a good many bums with a two-bit stake."

"You've lost your stake?" sneered the sourdough.

Sammy was holding the dicebox. He paused and looked considerately and steadily upon the sourdough. There was a green glint in his eyes.

"If you start starin' at me," said the sourdough, more ugly than ever, "I'll give you a good reason for lookin'. Go on with the game!"

For only an instant Sammy continued to watch the face of the other, and then he said cheerfully, "All right!" and cast the dice. He rolled an eleven and took in the bets. He had fifty dollars to play now. But his heart was not in the game. His heart was back there at the bar, thinking about the seventy-five cents that he could not afford to buy before. He could buy it now, and its twin brother to go down with it.

"I'll fade twenty of that," the sourdough was saying.

He drew aside that much of the money and covered it with his own. He had a hand that looked fit to throttle an ox. He was brown as old mahogany, and the bony ridges stood out along his cheek at jaw and forehead. He was about forty. He would, perhaps, have been a terrible antagonist in hand-to-hand conflict.

The side glance of Sammy Day was never far away from him. A fond look was in his eyes. He grew dreamy. If his mind was partly on the drink in the barroom, it still hovered about the formidable figure of the sourdough, nevertheless.

Then came an interruption. A door slammed, and shouting roared through the big barroom. Someone called out that Rush Mahan had just pulled in and that he had Klondike with him.

The gamblers scattered. Even the sourdough exclaimed. Money was scooped up and pocketed.

"Who's Rush Mahan?" asked Sammy Day.

As though he could not find a better interlocutor, he addressed the big sourdough. The latter looked at him with an evil eye.

"Keep your mouth shut and your eyes open and maybe you'll find out," he declared.

"I'd rather find out about you," Sammy Day said.

"About what?" snorted the other.

"About the insides of you … whether they're stuffed with man or feathers," said Sammy.

"Why, I gotta mind to break you in two," said the sourdough, amazed and contemptuous as he measured the smaller body of the man from the Southland.

Then the pressure of the other gamblers, as they made for the door, forced the two apart and swept the sourdough into the next room ahead of Sammy Day.

"Who's Rush Mahan and Klondike?" he asked of his nearest neighbor.

"You don't know?" came the breathless answer. "Rush is the finest musher that ever pushed a team to the North Pole, and Klondike is the best leader that ever smelled out a trail."

Then they were drawn into the barroom, and Sammy Day got

a corner position, the strategic place that he always desired. It put the wall at his back and allowed only half the world to get at him at once. Also, it enabled him to keep the whole scene under his eye.

He had been thinking that they were a lethargic lot, these men of the white North. Nothing mattered much to them, winning or losing, drunkenness or sobriety. But now the proper event had occurred to sweep them out of their indifference. A man and a dog had appeared on the scene.

To young Sammy Day, it seemed that neither the man nor the dog was worth such particular observation, magnificent as they were, both of them. For there was a girl in the room now who filled his eye and his mind. The clumsy swathing of her furs could not hide her, and her face shone like a mysterious sun into the very soul of the young man.

He had to repeat his question twice and again to the man at his shoulder before the head of the latter swung about impatiently.

"That?" said the man of the Northland. "Why, that's nothing but Rush Mahan's kid sister. There's Rush himself. That one there in the center. That one with Klondike standin' beside him. What a man!"

CHAPTER TWO

Sammy Day, connoisseur of men, had to admit that Rush Mahan was worthy of an exclamation point or two. He was one of those perfect men who begin as perfect boys and continue through their lives wise, noble, and strong. He must have filled a mother's heart as fully as, one day, he would fill the heart of a wife. His brow was open; his eye was calm. He looked into the faces of other men without either challenge or inquiry, but with a cheerful acceptance of all around him.

Big of heart, big of mind, he was big of body also. He was one of those rare creatures who can use upward of two hundred pounds of bone and brawn, rather than merely carry it. Now and then, one sees such a man stand out like a star in athletics—a football player, a sprinter on the track, the stroke in an eight-oared crew. It means that bulk is not furnished at the expense of an adequate nervous system, that mere size and rough-hewing are not the goal in the making of such a prodigy among men.

Now that this magnificent monster of a man was being made the hero of the hour, he accepted his honors gladly and modestly.

Young Sammy Day looked at him, with head slightly bowed, from under gathered brows, his jaw setting and his eyes glinting that green light that was familiar to certain of his former associates in sunnier regions to the south. For Sammy was one of those types that are not impressed or appalled by size. In this he resembled the Louisiana Negro who said: "Ah whittles 'em down to mah own size, suh." And when Sammy saw this prince among men, he could not help measuring the distance between himself and the other. *Well, a small blade with a wonderful edge might cut as deep as a great one that is dull*, he told himself. Whatever else he lacked, he had an edge.

Then, turning his eyes from the face of big Rush Mahan, he considered the girl again. He was rather amazed to see that her straight blue eyes were looking straight at him, reading him, judging him, not judging him kindly either. Her expression hardened as she glanced away from him.

Sammy Day merely laughed. *You look at me today, beautiful,* he said, *and you'll follow me tomorrow.* He said it inwardly, with a hot electric flush leaping all through his body. *You'll follow me tomorrow*, he said to himself again.

He forgot all about the center of the great demonstration. What was Rush Mahan to him? As he looked at the girl, he told himself that his life had reached a stopping point beyond which it would never flow. She was his goal and the end of his voyage, so far as women went. There would never be another for him.

There is a solemnity about final convictions, even the swift ones that are reached by one outward bound of the young spirit. He was rather grim than gay as he stared at her. He told himself that he would make her look back at him. There was such a thing as feeling the weight of an eye, and she would have to feel his. He would draw her glance back, through the crowd, in spite of all the men who were crowding, speaking to her and admiring her.

Presently, he had what he wanted. Through a gap among the many heads, he saw her face turning, and she looked full at him.

Insolently, triumphantly, he smiled and raised his hat. It mattered not to Sammy Day that her head jerked suddenly higher and turned hastily away. Even in the distance, through the smoke-dimmed air of the room, he could see the flare of her sudden color. She hated him now. But that was all right, he told himself. At least, she would never forget that mug of his. It would be printed in her mind to the end of her days.

He was something like a cowpuncher, who feels content and master of the situation if he gets his rope on any obstacle, even if it is the plunging head of a landslide, He had made his contact, and he felt competent to manage the rest.

Rush Mahan was wading through the crowd of his admirers to the bar. They still shouted and cheered him. He had won the Nome Sweepstakes—$10,000 and an inscription on the famous cup. He had beaten the finest dog teams and the finest dog mushers in the Northland. And that was hardly to be wondered at, for he was the sort of man who was bound to win at everything.

They cheered him without envy, as subjects willingly cheer their king when he passes. There was only one dark, keen, closed mind in the room—Sammy Day's.

Waiting and watching, he took note of the little open circle around Rush Mahan. Such distance would hardly be given to a prince, in the rough etiquette of the North. But it was given to Mahan, and to his dog.

With an unpracticed eye, Day looked at Klondike. Dogs were not his specialty. Horses were what he knew. He could read the points of a horse as another man reads the pages of a book. He had traveled thousands of miles with them. He had won and given them his confidence. He had watched over them, and, in the dangerous wilderness, they had watched over him like another man, a partner. Horses, therefore, were the open gateway to his heart, but dogs were a different matter. They were all right to tree a mountain lion or when hunting a grizzly; otherwise, they were sleepy beasts that clutter up a ranch house and scratch at their fleas in front of the stove in winter. He had no understanding of the species, but he did not need understanding to see that this Klondike was a lord of his kind.

He had the coat of a wolf and the kind, open face of a Newfoundland. He was bigger than any wolf that Day had seen, a hundred and twenty, a hundred and thirty pounds, even. Under the fluff of his long hair and the closely fitted coat of fur that lay next to his skin, one could sense the big muscles, made strong and hard with constant labor. But, as in the master, it was rather mind than matter that counted the most. He had the look of sapience; he had the bearing of the unbeaten.

"Yeah, that's a dog," Sammy Day found himself saying.

A glass of whiskey appeared at his hand. Everyone was preparing to drink. Nagle himself was beating on the bar for silence. Then he roared: "Here's to the kingpin dog musher and straight shooter, Rush Mahan!"

Sammy Day glanced across the crowd, and he saw Mahan's sister laughing with rosy joy. He forgot his whiskey. It stood untouched.

"This is mighty kind of you, Nagle," said Mahan. "But give honor where honor is due, you fellows. Here's to the dog that pulled the team through, and me along with it. Here's to the dog that smelled a trail a foot deep under the snow. Here's to what pulled us through a hurricane. Here's to old Klondike, bless him!"

"I'll drink that, too," said Nagle. "Goldie Mahan, won't you drink to that?"

They turned their heads, all the men, and smiled at her.

"I'll taste a drop in honor of old Klondike," she said. "Bless him."

They handed her a glass. When all the glasses rose and shone, all save that of Sammy Day, he saw her taste the liquor and try hard to keep from making a face. He laughed again, cheerfully. Then he tossed off his own glass. He would rather, for his part, drink in honor of the dog than the man.

There was a second round, of course, for Rush Mahan this time.

It was greeted with a whoop, such as a dog-puncher utters when he starts his team. Sam Day did not drink.

"Has Grant come in yet?" Mahan asked loudly. "Any of you boys seen Phil Grant?"

They had not. "You mind sitting here by the stove and waiting a while, Goldie?" asked her brother. "I want to play a couple of rounds of poker with the boys. I haven't handled a card for weeks. Boys, who'll give me a game?"

Goldie Mahan was willing enough to wait by the stove, it seemed. She took a chair in a corner, and it was plain that she would not lack for company while she waited. The crowd promptly split in two, half going with the gamblers into the adjoining room and half of them herding off toward the girl.

"This makes a dry business for me," remarked Nagle, grinning behind the bar.

Sammy Day chose the gambling room. There he found much dispute as to who would sit in at a table of six. "Here!" called the big sourdough with whom he had crossed swords before. "Here, boys! We'll draw. Four aces and the king of spades sits in with Rush!"

Sammy Day reached in his turn. He drew the king of spades. As he drew it, he heard the sourdough who was handling the draw snarl: "How does a damned cheechako horn in on this deal?"

"This way," said Sammy Day, and with a grin he turned up the king of spades.

The moment the draw was completed, they arranged the table. The sourdough, Digger Joe Williams, was nearest the window; Rush Mahan sat with his back to the door, a position which Day did not envy. The other three were introduced as Slade, Gravem, and Buck Chandler.

It was an odd thing, thought young Sam Day, that he was the only one who needed the introductions. All the rest seemed to know one another. In spite of the shifting population of Alaska, it seemed to be a closed corporation, all the members of which were acquainted.

But that hardly mattered. Poker was always poker. He had three things to watch outside the game: Rush Mahan and how he accepted fortune; Klondike, crouched behind his master's chair, watching with unflagging interest and affection every turn of Mahan's head; and finally Digger Joe Williams, whose face darkened every time he glanced at Sam Day.

The wind, which had been fairly quiet all morning, now suddenly swooped down, caught the house by the ears, as it were, and shook it to the foundations. The gust went screeching off down the street, the smoke puffing through every crevice of the big stove.

"This is something like," said Rush Mahan, shrugging his shoulders into the comfort of his coat. "Now we'll have a game, boys. Let it go fast and high. I can't keep Goldie waiting very long."

CHAPTER THREE

The wind, now that it had commenced, kept on, though always in gusts. Sometimes the roar leaped far away, and then it seemed to spring back with fury on Circle City, as though it were a cat playing with a mouse, and Circle City shuddered under the strokes, seeming to crouch closer and deeper in the snow. White smoke blew eddying around the corners of the houses, disappeared, and formed again.

It was in the midst of one of the strongest of these gusts that the door of Nagle's Saloon was opened, and a big fellow entered, jerked the door shut behind him, and stood for a moment, blinking the ice from his eyelashes, stamping the snow from his clothes, and clearing his throat to find his voice. Then he threw back the fur hood that covered his head and showed the face of a man in early middle life, now covered with two or three weeks' growth of beard.

He advanced toward the stove, his breath puffing white around him until he entered the warmer layers of air within the place. The bitter cold of the ice and snow on his shoulders turned into clouds of steaming vapor that trailed behind him as dust trails behind a galloping horse. He waved his hand toward the group that laughed and chattered around Goldie Mahan, then paused to warm himself at the stove.

"Hey!" called someone. "Are you just in from the outside?"

"I'm just in," said the stranger, "but I'm not carryin' any mail." He smiled and shook his head as he said this; apparently it was a question that he had been asked often enough before his arrival in Circle City. A groan of disappointment greeted the news.

Even so, his arrival was an event of interest. Men were not arriving every day from the outside world at that season of the year. So a group of them wandered with him toward the bar. Drinks were offered as iron-faced Nagle stood leaning an attentive ear to whatever news might be offered.

But the stranger said: "Boys, the only news I can bring you is that my name is Tuckahoe and that I come from the bare middle of Montana, jumpin' all the way from there to here as fast as railroads, ships, and dog teams could haul me. I haven't picked up enough news to fill the belly of a starved jackrabbit for five minutes ... unless some of you boys come from the middle of Montana. Devil Creek is mostly my hangout. Does that name mean anything to you?"

Heads were shaken. Dreary eyes looked at the stranger, as though he had just carried away their last red cent on a bet.

"I'm mighty sorry," he said, "but there's no soup in this tureen. I'm lookin' for news, instead of bringin' any," he said to Nagle.

"I ain't printed. There's some of me that wouldn't print, I reckon," said Nagle. "But I'm a newspaper, all right. You can turn back my file for eleven years, and, if there's anything that lies inside of that time and Circle City, I ought to be able to tell you about it."

"I don't need news eleven years old," said Tuckahoe, his lean face wrinkling with a smile. "What I'm after, if it's around this town, wouldn't be more than twenty-four hours old, I guess. I've been stepping on its heels for a couple of thousand miles, and more."

"A man?" asked Nagle.

"Yes, a man."

"Well," Nagle said, frowning, "it's a funny thing, but I disrecollect faces and names of men quicker'n almost anything in the world, especially when they been followed for two thousand miles."

The other sighed, and cast his eyes upward, as though hunting for another bent.

Nagle leaned a little forward. The room was still, and his lowered voice traveled to the farthest corner of it easily. "Unless," he said, "it's murder. Murder will out, even in Circle City, I guess."

The stranger scratched his chin before he answered. "It's kind of reverse English on murder," he said. "And that takes some explainin', I know. I'll describe this fellow that I'm after, and maybe you can talk then."

"Describing won't do any harm," said Nagle.

"Five feet ten," said Tuckahoe, "and made up of equal parts hickory whipstock and braided rawhide lash. Don't make no more noise than the sound of the lash in the air. There ain't any snapper on him, but he cuts deep. Does that fit anything you know?"

Nagle watched the other steadfastly. The others were silent, also. Goldie Mahan, her eyes calm, as one who has faced serious moments and many of them, leaned back in her chair, rested her chin on the palm of her left hand, and listened attentively. It was very apparent that something important was in the air.

"That don't exactly fit," Nagle surmised. "Maybe it might, when I know more. What sort of a moniker does your friend wear?"

"He ain't any friend of mine," said the other hastily. "But about names … why, it's kind of hard to locate him with a name. You wouldn't start describin' a man you want by sayin' the sort of hat he was wearin' two thousand miles back, would you?"

"He puts on names easy, does he?" asked Nagle.

"Much easier than a snake slips its skin … and takes 'em off again, too."

"Well," Nagle said, smiling, "I've met up with fellows like that in Circle City, too. What else can you say about him?"

"Why, he's got a cheerful way about him," said the stranger, "and he keeps smilin', but a smile don't mean any more to him than the hat on his head."

"Or the name inside the hat?" suggested Nagle.

"Exactly that way, old son!"

"What else?" Nagle asked. "I'm getting kind of interested."

"He's got a nose that looks like it had just been punched," continued Tuckahoe, "and a jaw that looks like it could stand a lot more punches. He's got brown hair and brown-black eyebrows that run clear across, kind of bushy in the middle."

Goldie Mahan sat up suddenly in her chair.

"He travels heeled," went on Tuckahoe, "but you don't see where the gun lies. He wears it under the pit of his arm. It's a single-action Colt, mostly, and the trigger ain't present to complicate things. Them that've seen him use that gun likely remember. They say that it's a picture to see him write his name with his thumb a hundred yards from his blackboard."

"You got me all fluttery and excited," Nagle said calmly. "Anything else?"

"Yeah. There's one thing more that I might mention. He's got a candlelight in each eye, and sometimes the candles burn yaller, and sometimes they burn green," ended Tuckahoe.

Nagle nodded. "That's all right," he said. "I guess we have the fellow you want. Age?"

"Twenty-two. Though how he's boiled down his life into that many years, nobody knows."

"Hey, Bud," Nagle said to one of the men present. "Just step in there and tell the gent that he's wanted, will you? I guess you heard the talk?"

"Yeah, I heard," said Bud.

He strolled into the next room, where the poker game was in

progress, a closely packed crowd about the players. "Hey, cheechako, you're wanted!" he called out.

"I'll raise you a hundred," young Sam Day said.

"That means you," said the sourdough, glowering at the young fellow.

"I'll see that hundred and raise you fifty," said Rush Mahan.

In the barroom, Tuckahoe was facing toward the door of the game room. He looked tense, eager, but not exactly apprehensive.

"About names," he was saying, "mostly on the parts of the range where I've been, they call this one the Joker."

"Joker?" Nagle repeated.

"Yeah, it's a happy card."

"Why that?"

"You noticed a joker in a pack of cards, I guess?"

"Sure."

"Kind of a happy card, ain't it?"

"Yeah, it's a happy card."

"Well, this kid is happy, all right. Noticed another thing about the joker?"

"What's that?"

"In most games it ain't much good."

"That's right," said the bartender, grinning with understanding.

"But," went on Tuckahoe, "wherever you drop the joker into a game, it sorter raises hell?"

"Yeah. I've noticed that."

"Well, down on the range where I've been, mostly they call this kid the Joker, as I was saying before," Tuckahoe said in conclusion.

Just then, through the doorway stepped the form of Sammy Day. He did not linger in the open frame of the door but glided catlike to the side, until the wall was behind his back. He had seen the form of the man at the bar, and a hand jerked up inside the loose flap of his coat.

He was smiling, and every person in that room remembered that smile, in after times, on many a cold midnight, awaking suddenly.

Tuckahoe had jerked up both his own hands until they were shoulder high.

"No guns, kid!" he called.

The hand of the other came reluctantly forth into view. He made a soft half step forward. "Gun, or knife, or hands," he said, "I'm ready for you, you snake, you Tuckahoe!"

The other faced him steadily enough. But the color was gone from his face, as though ashes had been dusted over his skin.

"I'm bringing you good news, Joker, not bad," he said. "And the only reason that I've brought it is because I lost a bet that I was fool enough to make."

"What bet?"

"I bet that the posse would catch you. And on account of losing that bet, I've had to go a coupla thousand miles and more on my own to tell you that Dan Bray didn't die after all. You split his wishbone, but he didn't die. And so I've got to admit that you ain't quite ready for a necktie party yet, Joker. But maybe your day ain't far off."

CHAPTER FOUR

When the Joker heard the last remarks, he made a little pause, with his head drooped down, looking up under his brows at Tuckahoe, after the manner that he had.

Finally, he said: "You're dead game, Tuckahoe, to come this far on a bet. But who made the bet with you? Who cared that much about me?"

"Lew Murphy."

The face of the Joker lit with a truly wonderful smile. "Lew is a partner worth having," he said. "But what made Lew so anxious to rush the news to me?"

"Because he said that you might figure that it was as easy to hang for ten dead men as for one. He was afraid that you'd run amuck one of these days."

The Joker shrugged his shoulders. "He was dead wrong," he said. "So long, Tuckahoe. I hope you have a good trip out." He turned and went back to the poker game.

Nagle and the others in the barroom stared after him. It was Goldie Mahan who spoke: "There's a bighearted man for you.

Here's a fellow who mushes two or three thousand miles to get a message to him, and he says … 'Thanks. I hope you have a good return trip.' He's a white man, this Joker, as you call him."

"He's hard," said Nagle, who knew men. "He's harder than ten-penny nails."

"Well, I'm no friend of his," said Tuckahoe. "That means that I'll never be any more than dirt under his feet to him. That's the way with him. If he's your friend, the sky's the limit. If he's against you, he'd walk ten miles and swim a river to do you a bad turn. I went against him once. There's nothing I can do to make up for that. Here's where I liquor again." He returned to the bar and drank.

Goldie Mahan stood up. "I'm going back to the hotel," she said. "Rush is in there for a long session, unless Phil Grant turns up. Which I suppose the piker won't. Good night, boys. But mark my word. That fang-toothed Joker will draw blood before the night's out, here in Nagle's Bar. You remember, Mr. Nagle, what I'm saying."

She went out the door. Two or three men hastily followed to escort her, but she laughed and waved them back. After all, she had trekked as many leagues as any of them through the difficult Northland. She was supple and strong, sure and patient of foot. She opened the door, and the white, dense flurry of the storm struck at her with its winged fury, then swallowed her up.

After she was gone, one of the men said to Nagle: "You know, Nagle, a woman's got intuition. You better watch out tonight."

Nagle nodded. "It don't take no woman's intuition," he said, "to figure out that the Joker is a serious deal, no matter what sort of a game he's dropped into."

This the players in the poker game had found out and they became increasingly aware of it as the night went on.

At 11:00 p.m., the Joker had $8,000 in chips before him. Then the deal came around to him.

"We'll have a new pack," said Rush Mahan.

The Joker looked up from under his brows at the speaker, but he said nothing.

At 11:30, he had a shade over $10,000 piled before him. The deal was his.

"We'll have a new pack," said Rush Mahan.

This time the Joker did not even glance at Mahan. He merely said: "That's a good dog you have, Mahan."

"Thanks," said Mahan coldly. "Yes, he's a good dog."

Then the game ran on. It was nearly 1:00 a.m. before they crossed swords once more. The table in front of young Sammy Day was weighted down by $20,000. Slade had been broke for the last hour. Gravem was hanging on by his eyelashes. The deal was coming up to the Joker again.

"We'll have a new pack," said Rush Mahan.

Then the Joker laid down the cards and looked long and steadily at Mahan. And Mahan looked long and steadily back. As they stared, with unwavering, hostile eyes, the others sat tensely, and wormed their chairs back a little from the table. They were ready to dive for the floor. Guns seemed imminent.

But the Joker said at last: "This is all right. Somebody call Nagle. He's not doing very much in there. Get Nagle to come in here and deal."

Nagle came to the door of the game room. "What is it?" he asked.

"You better come in here and deal," said the Joker. "One of the boys doesn't like the fall of the cards."

"Who doesn't?" Nagle asked.

"Somebody that's not used to good luck," said young Sammy Day.

Rush Mahan's lower jaw thrust out a trifle. Keenly, he fixed the other with his stare, and then, as though realizing his enormous advantages of weight and power, he leaned back a little in his chair. It was true that luck had favored him highly. It was the biggest game of his life, and he had $30,000 before him on the table. But he distrusted the dealing of the Joker. That was clear. So he nodded to Nagle.

"Come in and deal for us, Nagle," he said.

So Nagle took the sixth chair, vacated by Slade. Gravem was broke by 1:00 a.m. The game narrowed to four. Buck Chandler went out half an hour later.

That left three players. Chandler had been the big loser. He was one of the richest miners in the district, and he pulled out of the game not because he was broke, but because he said that $50,000 was enough to drop in one quiet evening. No one could deny that he was right.

The three played on. A crowd of a hundred remained, unwearying, to watch them. There was an assistant bartender continually busy. Chandler, the rich man, went behind the bar, also, and scrupulously helped to serve the whiskey. Smoke thickened in the rooms. Once and again, the stove in the game room was refilled with wood. But the unregarded fire in the bar died out. Instantly, the frost rose out of the ground and stole through the air and a damp, horrible cold, like the cold of underground, filled the room. It iced the whiskey in the glasses. It turned the hands of the bartenders blue. But they paid no heed to this, for their thoughts were turning constantly to the game that went on at the table.

Bigger games than this, even, had gone on at that very table in that very bar, but not many. On the table was $115,000.

Then Rush Mahan held a queen full on fives. He took $10,000 from Sammy Day before the latter turned down his hand. He took $14,000 from Digger Joe Williams, who called. The stakes, after this were about $55,000 for Mahan, $40,000 for Sammy Day, and $25,000 for Digger Williams. The betting had climbed till the sky was the limit.

Digger Williams, sour, intent, gloomy, watched the fall of the cards, scowling, and always his scowl rested on the face of young Sammy Day. And the ice-cold glance of Rush Mahan dwelt there, too.

The same feeling communicated itself to the crowd. If there

were crookedness in this game, the Joker was guilty of it. Mahan and Digger Williams were both very well known.

Then, in the dead hour, between two and three, another great hand came out of the dark, as it were.

Digger Williams opened for $5,000. He had $30,000 before him now, and before the draw he was forced to his limit. They drew. Digger took $20,000 from the pot and bet it. He was good for five times that much, everyone knew.

Even that was not enough. Rush Mahan raised $10,000. The Joker saw him and raised him five. It seemed a small bet, but the Digger, shaking his head, turned down his cards. Rush Mahan, after a moment of cold, calm thought, merely called.

The Joker laid down four kings neatly side by side in a perfect row.

And then, as Mahan exposed a beautiful ace full on jacks, the Joker dragged in the big bet of the evening. He had $115,000 before him. And the Digger owed the pot $20,000. A scant $5,000 remained before Mahan.

No one spoke. The air in the room suddenly hung dead and still. No one could have said why, but a frightful certainty was in every mind that there had been crookedness in that game, and that the Joker was the guilty man.

He himself, his eyes cast down toward the table, was smiling a faint smile, and the active, lean, hard fingers of his right hand were drumming noiselessly upon the table's edge. Nagle began to shuffle, mixing the cards with a fluid swiftness.

"Wait a minute," said Mahan. "Just keep that pack for a curiosity, Nagle. It might interest some of the boys. We'll break open some new cards now."

Then the eyes of the Joker raised at last to those of the big man. "Mahan, it's been a jolly little game. You see the pot I've got in front of me," he said. "Everybody's in this. We'll draw to double this pot, or nothing. The first ace, eh?"

A white smile appeared and disappeared upon the face of Mahan. Then he nodded. His neck seemed frozen stiff. Digger Joe started to speak, changed his mind, and sat back in his chair. He nodded, also.

It seemed that the game was apparent. The Joker had palmed an ace, of course. But he forgot that the pack might be counted over afterward. Well, there would be ways of catching him.

Nagle held out the pack and kept his hand lightly on the top of it. From under that hand, they drew, slowly, turning their cards up, one by one. Not a thing showed for two rounds. Then Digger Joe turned up an ace of clubs!

CHAPTER FIVE

Everyone knew long beforehand what it meant. All the money on the board, except the $5,000 before Rush Mahan, went to the lucky fellow who turned that ace. The great winner had previously been the cheechako, from the outside, Sammy Day. He had suggested the turn of the ace to decide everything. He, it was rather naturally taken for granted, was bound to win—on some crooked deal or other. Then hell would flow its brightest red in Nagle's Saloon.

But all expectations were disappointed. Digger Joe had won the entire pot. Rush Mahan remained with about what he had put into the game. And the cheechako, the supposedly crooked gambler, was flat broke!

What a new air this gave to everything. The cheechako emerged with clean hands, at the cost of a good many tens of thousands of dollars. The whole game was given an air of mystery.

They looked, of one accord, all of those hard-boiled miners and adventurers of the North, upon Sammy Day, and behold. He was laughing with an unaffected carelessness, though he appreciated a strange jest that no one else could understand.

"That ends the game for me," he said, "I have fifty cents left. That what I began today on."

Digger Joe, scowling, but in thought now, more than in criticism, began to rake in the enormous heap of his winnings. Mahan, as though bewildered, stacked up his own money for return to his poke.

Then Sammy Day said: "Mahan!" There was a cool, clean ring to his voice, almost as of one speaking a surprised, friendly greeting to a man from home.

Mahan, putting away the last of his stake, looked up in surprise. "Well?" he said.

"Four times," said the cheechako, "when I dealt, you asked for a new pack of cards. There were a lot of other people dealing, now and then, but you never thought about changing the pack at those times. What in hell did you mean by asking for the change when I handled 'em?" There was one word in this speech that made it not a request for information, but a challenge. Those who stood by and listened understood immediately. And then drew back softly, with glances at one another. Whereas there had been a closely packed circle all around the table the moment before, there was now a clear avenue in a straight line that crossed the chairs of the Joker and Rush Mahan. Bullets might fly at any moment. Bullets must fly, after such a speech.

Mahan, for a moment, regarded the stranger with the calm gaze of a man who is familiar with danger. Then he said: "You don't want talk."

"I've asked for talk," said the Joker.

"You don't want talk," persisted Rush Mahan.

"Hold on, boys," said Nagle, "I don't want any rough stuff in here. I won't have it, either."

The Joker turned to him with a strange look. "Nagle," he said, "you talk as though all of this were over your head. It's not over your head. You know that I've got some change coming back to me out of this game, and I'm going to get it."

"Change?" said Nagle.

Digger Joe Williams broke in. "Look here, kid," he said, "you've gone bust, but you're all right. I'll stake you. I'll stake you up to ten grand or so, and I'll do it with pleasure."

The cheechako sneered at him. "I was dirt under your feet up to a minute ago," he said. "I wasn't good enough for you to look at. I was a crook. I had crooked the cards. Admit that it's so … in your mind."

Digger Joe was a firm man. He said now, with his usual growl: "Yes, that's what I thought. What of it?"

"I'll tell you what of it," said Sammy Day. "I come from a part of the world where they call a man a man when he is one. They don't make up their minds the way you fellows do up here, on the look of his face. I don't claim to be a beauty, but I do claim to be straight, and before I get through with Circle City, I'm going to show you how to rule and measure me."

He was lost in his passion of fury, as a drunkard is lost in the grip of alcohol. He swayed just a little from side to side as he spoke. He had thrown the glove down before. Now he had followed it with a verbal blow to the face.

"You want me to fall on my knees to you," asked Rush Mahan, calm as ever, "or else you want me to fight you? Is that it?"

"Mr. Mahan," the Joker replied, sneering, "you talk as if you had a brain somewhere."

"I'm a good deal bigger than you are," said Mahan. "I suppose that you want to fight with guns?"

"Mr. Mahan," the Joker repeated in the same tone, "you're a regular prophet, is what you are."

"Well," said Mahan, "I won't do it."

It made a thrill leap through the heart of every man there. They had admired Rush Mahan many times before. They never had admired him more than they did now. Few men in the world have courage enough to refuse to fight.

"If you don't fight," said the Joker, his voice trembling, "I'll make the world laugh in your face."

"You may make the world laugh in my face," replied Mahan, "but we don't live in the century of dueling. I've never used a revolver in my life, because it's good for murder, and nothing else. I've used a rifle, now and then. I can shoot game, but I don't shoot men. I don't want your blood on my hands, nor do I want to soil my hands with your dirty blood. I won't fight you."

The Joker sat, still and stiff, in his chair. They could see his head tilting back a little as he filled his lungs each time. But those who faced him shuddered a little, at the green gleam of his eyes. He was smiling, too, stiffly, fixedly.

"You don't like guns, but you like to talk," said the Joker at last. "Just now you're a small king to these pennyworth men around here. You could talk down to me. And that's what you did. Well, I'm going to have your heart out here on the floor of Nagle's place. I'm going to show the boys that it's yellow, not red. You won't fight with guns, eh? Then what about knives?"

He leaned forward a little with a dreadful eagerness, as he spoke, and the lip of Mahan, unafraid but disgusted, curled.

"You ought to talk to wolves and dogs," he said. "I don't fight with my teeth, and I don't fight with knives, either."

A shudder went through the people who listened to Mahan. And those who watched his sneer shrank, as though inwardly.

"You don't fight with guns, and you don't fight with knives," said young Sammy Day. "That's right, isn't it?"

"That's right," Mahan said. And he pushed back his chair, about to leave the place.

"No, you wait a minute," said the Joker.

"I won't wait," said Mahan. "I've had enough of you and your kind. Murder is not what I want to rub elbows against."

The Joker smiled a little more broadly, if a smile it could be called. "You wait a little longer," he said, and he leaned a trifle farther forward. "If you move out of that chair before I say the word, I'll kill you."

Not a breath was drawn, except by Digger Joe Williams. He, for some moments, had been looking from one antagonist to the other. Now he drew out a long, blue-barreled Colt revolver and laid the muzzle of it on the edge of the table. "The first flash of a gun," he said, "and I shoot the hound that shows it."

Young Sammy Day paid no heed to him, beyond saying: "Don't be careless, Digger Joe. You're on the tightrope, too. When I'm through with this four-flusher, I'll shake the rope for you."

He was facing Rush Mahan as he said this, and Mahan, his hands still gripped about the edge of the table, had not stirred since the last warning. Neither had anyone in the room. Mahan seemed in doubt, rather than frightened. He was frowning, but only in thought.

"You won't fight with guns and you won't fight with knives," said the Joker. "Then what about hands?"

CHAPTER SIX

There is a true tale of a man who took his bull terrier to the zoo, and when they passed the cage in which the king of beasts was pacing to and fro behind its bars, he said, out of a gay spirit: "Take him, boy." At once the little terrier flashed for the bars, and the waiting claws of the lion would have opened his skull if the master had not snatched him out of the air.

Something like that was the challenge of the Joker to big Rush Mahan, except that there was no master to draw back the Joker after his challenge was delivered. The men in the room might exchange glances, but not one of them dared to speak. Only Nagle muttered: "The devil. And he's not drunk, either."

The calm of Mahan, however, was not disturbed. He did not measure the Joker with his glance, but merely said: "Day, I weigh about sixty pounds more than you do, and I know how to use my hands. You don't mean what you say."

"Don't I?" said the Joker, rising slowly to his feet.

"I can't touch you, and you know it," said Rush Mahan.

The Joker slid his hands up inside his coat and brought them back, each one holding a gun. He held them out behind him.

"Somebody take these and keep them," he said. "There's nothing this far north that's like 'em, I guess." Then he added: "Mahan, stand up."

Mahan merely smiled and said: "This fellow may not be drunk, but he's crazy. I haven't any desire to crack the head of the whelp for him. Keep him away, boys."

The Joker slid out from his coat. He stood, wonderfully frail and trembling, but not with cold. He was slender, as all men saw, but as Tuckahoe had said of him, he was all hickory whipstock and braided rawhide. There was not a waste ounce of flesh on him. He was made like a cat, to spring, to seize, to tear, to reach the life. Even though the weapons that were as hands to him were now removed, he hardly seemed the less formidable, except when he was compared with the magnificent body of Rush Mahan.

"Mahan!" called Sammy Day again. "Stand up, will you?"

"I'll stand up, and I'll leave, too," said Mahan.

He rose as he spoke and was turning away, when the Joker, in three lightning steps, rounded the table and swung the flat of his hand straight against the cheek of Mahan.

The latter, stung, wheeled and by instinct struck. Only by instinct, but straight and true shot out that powerful left, the shield and chief reliance of every boxer. One did not need to tell that he was a skilled man in sparring. Heel, shoulder, and fist were in a straight line as he flashed the punch. It should have gone home. It should have reached the face of the Joker, lifted him from his feet, and sent him crashing, senseless, against the wall.

By a hair's breadth only it missed the mark. The Joker had not ducked or sprung back. He merely swayed his head a little to the side, and as the arm of Mahan, ponderous and rigid as a walking beam, drove over his shoulder, everyone in the room heard the hard fists of the Joker go *spat, spat* into the face of the bigger man.

Then they saw little Sammy Day slip clear of the other, dancing lightly, his eyes as green as the eyes of a cat, when it crosses a road and crouches with turned head, when the flash of a light stops it.

Rush Mahan was still cool. He stepped back a little, smiling a trifle. "I told you boys he was crazy," he said, "and I wish that some of you would hold him. I don't want to kill him." Then he licked his lips and tasted his own blood, a thin trickle. At that, an oath burst from his lips. There is many a calm man, many a fighting man, who is aroused by the thought that he is bleeding. The brute in Mahan, generally so perfectly under control, now asserted its mastery in a single bound.

"I'll break your back," he said through his teeth, and leaped in.

There had been insult and injury enough to make any man forget differences in size. As he came in, he did not strike out blindly, but with a cunning, curving punch that rose in the air, and chopped suddenly down at the end. Men who stood there, watching, knowing, appraising, called it a perfect left hook.

The Joker glided inside that punch, and with both hands he hammered against the body of the big fellow. They were not casual or blind punches. They struck true and fair into the pit of the stomach, where a small tap will often unstring the strength of a giant and make him a gasping, puling, staggering, wind-broken hulk.

But the hands of the Joker now bounded away from a cushion of smoothest, deepest Indian rubber. A network of mighty muscles covered the whole vital part of the big man's midriff. And the Joker ducked out to safety, frowning seriously. As he went, a flashing uppercut grazed the side of his head and staggered him. But that was not what mattered to him.

He was asking himself, seriously, whether he had a chance to dent the iron strength and the bulk of this monster. Other men, bigger men than this one, he had met before and "whittled them down to his own size," but this was different. This was no slow-moving hulk, but a man of training, cool, keen, cunning, with muscles like the power of an engine, and a rapid wit to direct his movements. Every punch, every step was in perfect and rhythmic balance.

Now he came in, following up, perfectly under guard, ready to block or to strike, his long, mighty left carried well before him like a shield, or like a club to strike a short punch well capable of dazing. The right was back, poised. Once that right touched body or head of the Joker, solidly planted, the battle was over. This the Joker knew as well as any man in the room, but he was not appalled. He was frowning because he was seriously thoughtful, not because he was afraid.

Suddenly, as he felt the arms of a corner surrounding him, he leaped straight out at the giant. The latter paused, braced himself, and struck for the face with the rapid left. The Joker gave his face to the punch, but so rolled his head upon an apparently jointless neck, that the blow was hardly felt, and he, rushing on, ducking lower, drove his own left with all his might into the body of big Mahan again.

Under the very arm of Mahan, he slipped out to safety. As the latter turned, a howl of applause for the little man ringing in the room, the Joker smote him twice again, and each time on the left eye.

If he could act in no other way, perhaps he could blind the big machine, and then cut him to pieces at his will.

But there was no flinching on the part of Mahan. He knew pain, the incredible pain that the white North can deal out to those who dare adventure into its mysteries, and this twinge was nothing to him. The hot pain only made him more eager, cleared his mind, spurred him with shame.

He could see and hear them now—the whole crowd was yelling and cheering for the smaller man. They could not help it. No matter how great a favorite the giant might be with them, no matter how well tested and tried his virtues, they could not withhold their admiration from the apparent underdog. Besides, there was a touch of the mysterious about the Joker that appealed to all of them.

Tuckahoe stood in the doorway, scowling. One of the spectators, in a gasp, asked him: "How long will the Joker last?"

"Him? Till he dies," Tuckahoe answered rather bitterly.

As he spoke, in went the Joker again, a dipping flash like a snipe on the wing. He feinted for the body. He reached for the head, and suddenly the inevitable happened—inevitable, considering the speed and the force of Mahan's blows. He no longer was aiming for that elusive, bouncing, rubber-ball head of the smaller man. Instead, he took a punch off his hip and smashed it full at the body of Sammy Day.

It landed. It was not a squarely driven-home blow or the ribs of Sammy Day must have burst with the weight of it, but it ground a foot of flesh along those same ribs, and it picked Sammy up off his feet and hurled him backward through the air.

Backward he tumbled, with a feeling that a red-hot sword had been thrust through his body, from side to side. He struck the card table. It collapsed under the impact; head over heels he tumbled, but the table, for all the ruinous noise that it made, had helped break his fall, and its upturned legs served to break, for an instant, the furious onrush of Mahan. The giant wanted to kill now. He wanted to kill with his hands and, all the more, as he felt his left eye puffing, swelling, its vision blurring. Before long, that eye would be shut!

So he rushed to get at his man and finish him with one solid stroke. He found Sammy Day as the latter rose to his feet. The swinging punch landed on the side of the Joker's head and rolled him into a corner. He should have been finished by that, but again the blow had glanced. No man can hit accurately with the vision of one eye badly impaired. A man blind in one eye can hardly box at all.

In rushed the big man again, and Sammy Day, hastily gathering himself, rising to hands and knees, plunged like a swift-moving football tackler straight at the knees of the giant. Hardly fair tactics, but it brought Mahan down in a heap, and the Joker was the first to stand up.

He put one hand upon a leg of the overturned table and rested against it. He heard the yelling, the frantic cheering of the crowd.

He heard Nagle shouting: "I'll bet you at evens that the kid pulls through! I'll bet a hundred!"

"Don't be a fool," said somebody. "Mahan will eat him all right. But the fellow's as game as they come."

Fortune and football tactics had not helped Rush Mahan. In falling, he had struck his head heavily against the side of the wall. There was a great bump rising under his scalp; his head rang, and his left eye was dimming rapidly. Worse than that, as he got to his feet, he heard the mocking voice of the smaller man, calling: "This way, Mr. Mahan! This way, if you please!"

He charged like a bull, half-blindly, his skill forgotten in his rage—a sick rage, as he heard his own Northland people yelling for the southern invader. He came in and bumped his right eye against two pile-driver punches. He struck and hit the air. He whirled and rushed, and the right eye got it again. Beautiful marksmanship! The eyelashes seemed to be turned in, as though his eye had been thumbed. Both left and right eyes were terribly painful. Tears filled them. He was more than half-blinded.

And the Joker, watching with a cruel coolness, his eyes glittering, stepped in and struck again at an almost helpless victim. He could pick his mark securely now. He did not need to start punches flashing from the hip. He reached an arm's length behind him, and hammered them home overhand. *Thud, thud!* With right, with left, with right again, he found the very button of the other's jaw, the point from which the side shock is transferred to the base of the brain. No man could stand such punishment. Even the knees of Rush Mahan sagged.

A dreadful roar of horror, amazement, and savage, furious delight arose from the watchers.

Once more, teeth set, insane with conquest, but calm with the calmness of murder, the Joker smote, found the mark, and Rush Mahan fell like a house of cards.

CHAPTER SEVEN

The Joker did not wait to enjoy the fall of his rival or to see him revived. Instead, he slipped out of the cardroom into a little adjoining chamber, where he put three chairs together and threw himself down on them, coatless as he was, although the damp, icy air of the place began to eat at him like a wolf at once. There as he lay, eyes closed, every breath a faint groan, a big man came in and found him. He did not open his eyes, for all that.

"Hello, kid," said a growling, gruff voice. "How's things?"

"Go to the devil," said Sammy Day.

"Yeah. I been there, and I've come back to look for you."

"Well, here I am."

"Feeling pretty sick?"

"None of your business," said Sammy Day.

"All right. Here's your coat and here's a rug. You'll freeze stiff in ten minutes, if you don't wrap up in something." He swathed the fallen warrior. Then he began to chuckle. "I know how you feel," he went on. "Nobody else ever socked you as hard as that before."

"No," said Sammy Day, "but I've been kicked in the ribs by a mule before."

"About the same, eh?"

"He's worse than a mule," said Sammy Day. "Now shut up and leave me alone."

The big man chuckled again. "What you learned in the ring saved your bacon from a better man than you are, Joker."

The Joker opened one eye, and in the dim light he made out the hulking shape of Digger Joe Williams. "You've had your cut out of this party, Digger Joe," he said. "Now, you start in backing up and get out of here."

"I thought I'd bring you your guns. Here they are."

"Thanks. Now, get out."

"How long were you in the ring?" Digger Joe asked, persistent and calm.

"I wasn't in the ring."

"You lie."

"I was in for about six months, ten months. Oh, that was a long while back."

"You never forgot what you learned there, son."

"No," said the Joker. "I never had a chance to forget. There was always some big sap looking for trouble."

"I'm glad to know that you was in the ring," said Digger Joe. "It'll smooth things over for poor Rush Mahan a little. He'll be taking this pretty hard."

"I hope he does," replied Sammy. "He tried to high-hat me."

"He wouldn't high-hat anybody," said Digger Joe. "Only, you rubbed him the wrong way."

"He nearly rubbed out one side of my ribs," groaned the Joker. "He almost put his fist clean through me. I never saw one like him."

"I'll tell him that," Digger Joe said. "That'll surely comfort him a lot."

"I'll get you, as soon as I'm able, if you do," said the Joker.

"I don't care what you get," answered Digger Joe. "I wanna ask you this. Why did you crook that draw of the cards?"

"How could I crook the draw of the cards?" asked Sammy. "Wasn't the hand of Nagle resting right on the pack?"

"It was a good trick and a smart trick," said Digger Joe. "But it was a trick just the same. I thought that you were gonna fill your own hand that way. I was ready to shoot and just then I get the ace that you'd fixed."

"You lie," the Joker said feebly. "If I was strong enough to stand, I'd get up and sock you on the jaw. I aim to treat myself to that anyway, one of these days."

"You can try your hand at socking me when you see fit," replied Digger Joe. "I ain't one of the boys that don't pack a revolver. I'm telling you that just in case. And I wear the same kind of a pair that you wear, son. When you come to meet me, you want to be shooting fast and straight. If you ain't, I'll part you in the middle like a ripsaw."

"Thanks," said the Joker. "I'm beginning to feel more and more at home here in Circle City."

"Yes," said the other, "we've been needing and missing you for a long time, son." He added: "About that draw, why did you do it?"

"Do what?"

"Crook the cards so that I won?"

"I didn't crook the cards."

"You lie. I seen you do it, slick as you were."

"I didn't crook the cards," repeated the Joker.

"All right, then, you didn't crook the cards. But how did it happen that I won all that coin?"

The Joker lay perfectly still, breathing slowly, a faint groan in every breath. At last he said: "You make me sick. You won't let a fellow rest a little. But I'll tell you something. If I had made a clean-up in that game, everybody would have thought that I was a crook, and that Mahan was right about me. Well, before that game was over, I wanted no money … I just wanted Mahan's scalp first, and yours second. If any one of the other three had stayed in the game long enough, I would have thrown the win to him before the finish. As it was, I had to pass the coin to you. That left me free. My hands were washed clean. Then I could make some trouble for Rush Mahan, the picture-book boy."

"He's a lot more than that. You and me together, multiplied by ten," said Digger Joe Williams. "He's worth more than all of us."

"All right," said Sammy Day. "I hear you talking."

"Here's a cut for you," Digger Joe said. "You started that game with fifty cents. Here's fifty thousand dollars."

"I don't want fifty thousand dollars. I don't want fifty dollars even," said the Joker.

"All you want is love, eh?" asked Digger.

"I want the room that you're taking up," said the Joker.

"There's the fifty thousand lying on the floor beside you," said Digger Joe.

"Take that money and get out," replied the Joker. "I tell you, I won't let people say that I had a split out of your crooked game."

"You're a fool," Digger said, "to think that I want your split of the coin."

"I'll throw this stuff away," Sammy Day said, rising on one elbow, in spite of a swimming head.

"Throw it wherever you please," said Digger. "I've seen the last I want of it."

"I'm gonna carve your heart out, one of these days!" shouted the Joker.

"You spend a couple of weeks sharpening your knives before you start carving on me," Digger declared over his shoulder, and straightway he walked out of the room.

The Joker lay still, miserable and sick in body and mind. What would people say when they learned that Digger Joe had left a cut of the winnings with him? Why, they would naturally suspect that the draw was crooked and that Digger Joe was no more than his dummy partner.

The young man ground his teeth. He wanted to murder Digger Joe. He wanted to destroy the whole of Circle City. His pride was touchy upon that point. He had been accused of many crimes of violence, but of dishonesty never.

Nagle came into the room, carrying a lantern. "Hello, kid," he said. "You in here?"

"Yeah, I'm in here. Listen, Digger Joe is a fool."

"Sure. Everybody is anything you want to make 'em."

"I tell you, Digger Joe is a fool. He's blaming me for his winning so much."

"He's right," said Nagle. "You crooked the cards for him to win."

"You lie," the boy declared.

"I don't lie. I saw you work. Mighty slick, but it was under the master's hand, Joker."

"Why didn't you stop me then?

"Because I thought you were going to treat yourself to an ace. I nearly fainted when I saw the Digger turn it up. He looked a little dizzy himself."

The Joker swore.

"You done it," Nagle said, "to clear decks and get at Mahan, I guess?"

"Yes, that was it. And I don't want this dirty money."

"How much of it did you say there is?"

"Fifty thousand."

"That's a good cut," said Nagle. "You can use five or ten thousand to wash up the rest, if you think it's dirty."

"Oh, go to the devil," growled Sammy. "I'll tell you what. You take that fifty thousand and shove it behind your bar, you hear?"

"Well, what about it?"

"Do what I tell you. Then every time a poor loafer comes along, hand him out one hundred dollars, or that much in trade, will you?"

Nagle did not answer at once. In the pause that followed, Sammy noticed his frosted breath on the lantern.

"D'you mean that, kid?" Nagle asked at last.

"Yeah, I mean it."

"Well, get up, and I'll show you to a bed."

"Shut up and get out," growled the Joker in answer. "Here's my bed, and here's where I sleep!"

CHAPTER EIGHT

There, in fact, he slept. The next morning, he hung, bent and grim, over an edge of the bar. "How did you sleep?" Nagle asked.

"I got such a freeze that I'll be cold storage for a year," replied the Joker. "That big sucker, Rush Mahan," he went on after a minute, "is making a fool of himself up here. He ought to chuck this nonsense about dog-punching and go to the States. Man-punching is worth a million dollars a year down there after you get to the top."

"Would Mahan get to the top?"

"Sure, he would. I hit him hard enough to blast a way through a tool-proof wall. But he just grinned and took 'em and let 'em bounce. I never saw anything like that."

"You're a small fellow, though," said the other, shaking his head.

"Am I?" muttered the Joker. "Let me hit any of them … where I want to and when they're not looking … and see how long they stand up. You can kill the strongest man in the world with a tack hammer, if you know just where to tap him. Well, I tapped the button of Mahan three times in a row last night before I could get him loose and ready to drop. It was the fourth sock before I managed to cut the wires that were holding him together. I never saw anything like it. Imagine a man standing, after he's been shot three times through the brain."

Nagle narrowed his eyes. "You talk like you meant what you said," he declared. "And I remember how those three punches clicked like stone hammers on the end of his chin."

"I never would have got him," said the Joker, with a sigh and a shake of the head, "if I hadn't managed to get in a couple of lucky socks that landed on his left eye, early. That put him off. He was missing his mark by an inch or two all the way through. He couldn't afford to play for the head. He had to go after the body. Even that way, he almost knocked clean holes in me. I never saw such a punching fool. In six months of good training, he could take on the best heavyweight in the world."

Nagle grinned and flushed. "I'm glad to hear that," he said.

"Say," said the Joker, scowling, "he's not your twin brother, or anything like that, is he?"

Nagle shrugged his shoulders. "We're all pretty fond of Rush Mahan up around here," he explained.

"Because he's got such a sweet face, eh?" demanded the Joker.

"Shut up," said the other, "and have a drink."

"I don't like your liquor," the Joker answered, snapping his jaws after the words.

The bartender merely laughed. "You can't fight with me, kid," he said. "Not till you unbend some of the frost out of your arms and legs, anyway. I can see the frostbite working in your hands, right now. They're blue."

The Joker began to chafe them together, and at the same time he did a few halting, limping steps of a clog dance. "I'm all right," he assured Nagle.

"How long were you in the ring?"

"Who told you that I was in the ring?"

"I was there myself," said Nagle, "a good many years ago. Ask a tailor if he knows homemade from perfect, will you?"

The Joker grinned suddenly in answer. "What made you stop, Nagle?" he asked.

"King Whiskey. What put you out of the ring, kid?"

The other cleared his throat and looked steadily at Nagle.

"Excuse me," said Nagle. "I thought you asked me the first question."

"Oh, that's all right," replied Sammy. Still he hesitated. Then finally he said: "You know how it is ... a little trouble with a manager about a split in a purse."

"Yeah, I know," Nagle agreed.

"He seemed to think that I owed him the fight money and my cuff links, too. He had a bill to show for it."

"I know," Nagle said sympathetically. "I had the same thing happen to me, a coupla times. But it didn't stop me from going in and getting socked. How did it rule you out of the ring?"

"In those days," Sammy Day said carefully, "I was a little argumentative."

"How you've changed in between," Nagle joked.

Sammy Day rubbed his chin in thought. "Well," he said, "it was all right, until my manager got all excited and pulled a gun." He paused and cleared his throat.

"Pulled a gun on you, did he?" Nagle said, nodding. "That's always a play that I hate to see."

"So do I," remarked the Joker eagerly, "because it always gets me heated up. I sort of lose control of myself when there's a gunplay. He flashes a gun under my nose, and I duck a half-inch slug of lead by dropping for the floor, and start shooting as I fall."

"You had a gun yourself, eh?"

"Yeah," said the Joker. "Now, here I am, fifty cents in the pocket, no job, and nowhere to go."

"You stay here and be an entertainer," suggested the other.

"On my face?" queried the Joker, grinning again.

"Or a bouncer," Nagle opined.

The other shook his head. "I hate a fight," he said, "except when I get crowded a little."

"Well," said Nagle, "you've got $50,000 in hard cash waiting for you behind this bar. You should burst into tears about being broke when you've got that to tap."

"Not a penny of it," the Joker said firmly.

"You'll take this, though," declared the bartender. He reached under the bar and threw a fur suit across the rail. "There you are," he said. "Lynx paw mittens and the whole shebang, including mukluks, and the weight not more'n seven pounds. Yet it's warm enough to make you comfortable sitting on top of the North Pole in a gale. Believe me?"

"I'll believe you," said the other. "But how do I rate this handout?"

"There's a fund here," said the bartender, smiling, "that's held for boys that are down on their luck. You get this and breakfast, instead of a hundred dollars. Or d'you prefer the cash?"

Young Sammy Day looked carefully at the make of the suit and then weighed it in his hand. "All right," he said. "This is worth more than a hundred dollars, but who am I to look a gift horse in the mouth? I'll take it, and thanks a lot, Nagle. You're all right."

They looked in friendly fashion at one another. Nagle hooked his thumb toward another door.

"Go in there, and you'll find a bed," he said. "Turn in and have a sleep. You won't miss much. Hell is always waiting in Circle City. You can raise it any time you want."

"You're a good-natured fellow," said Sammy, then hesitated, swinging the clothes that hung on his arm. "I don't take handouts," he growled, staring up at the other from under his bushy eyebrows.

"You make me tired," said Nagle. "Jump in there and hit the hay. You're still only thawed out on the surface."

CHAPTER NINE

At that season of the year, the saloon of Nagle was generally full twenty-two hours out of twenty-four. This day was not an exception. By the time young Day had covered himself thoroughly with blankets and furs, he heard the noise of the first arrivals in the barroom. He heard the tinkling of glasses as he went to sleep.

His dreams were not pleasant. He imagined that he was standing before the diorite statue of an Egyptian king, which gave him a faint, prehistoric smile as the Joker hammered him solemnly, with all his might, upon the jaw. The result was broken hands and swollen wrists for the Joker.

At last he awoke, with pain in both his hands. He sat up in alarm and looked down at his appendages. The backs of them were slightly swollen, but he found that he could move the fingers easily. Therefore, he had no broken bones. He sighed with relief. He could not afford broken hands. A broken leg far sooner.

He dressed. Then he tried his two guns. There was more pain in wielding them, but he could manage them without real trouble. He sighed again. The world was safe for him, he felt.

Then he looked at his watch. Hours had slipped by quickly, like a smooth run of water downhill. It was late in the day already, and in the center of his being, there was a hungry wolf.

From the kitchen he got a pot of hot water, shaved the beard from his face, and then found a pair of scissors and clipped his hair. After that, he came into the barroom. Nagle spotted him first.

"Look!" he cried. "The kid's gone and made himself all beautiful. What's the matter, Joker?"

"I'm going courting," replied Sammy Day.

"He's going courting!" laughed Nagle. "Courting what?"

"Goldie Mahan is the lucky girl," answered the Joker.

There was a deep-throated roar of laughter from all who heard. There were oddly many points for mirth in this last remark of the cheechako. Then he was offered whiskey, but shook his head.

"I never drink before six o'clock," he said, grinning at them to indicate the lie.

"What are you waiting for?" asked someone.

"A job," said the Joker.

"Hey, Nagle, he wants a job!" cried out another.

"Who does? The kid?" Nagle shouted back. "I've offered him everything up to the roof, but he's too proud to work for me. One of you boys could take him on in the mines."

"I've got all the dynamite that I can use already," growled the deep voice of Digger Joe.

Men laughed again. Glasses rattled down the length of the bar. And the fumes of tobacco, liquor, and his own hunger swept up into the brain of the Joker and made him a little dizzy.

"He wants a job? Who wants a job?" said a harsh, loud voice. "I'm the only one around here that has a steady job to offer."

"Hey! That's an idea. Hey, you, Joker!" yelled Nagle. "Come here. Bill the Dogman is the only man in Circle City that always has a job to offer."

The Joker looked down the length of the bar, and he saw at the farther end a very tall man, four or five inches over six feet, with a face like a crag of rock, in which features have been broken by the iron hammer of time. He wore a rough gray beard, clipped raggedly short. He had a vast red nose and buried eyes, black as the eyes of an animal that hunts in the dark. His hair came low down in the center of his forehead, to a point, and his eyebrows were highly arched, so that his face had a half-inquisitive, half-demoniacal expression. His clothes were greasy rags. In appearance he was the most repulsive man the Joker ever had seen.

"Come along and meet Bill the Dogman," Nagle was repeating.

The Joker walked down the bar. He felt a battery of grinning eyes upon him. Then he was standing under the height of the leaning stranger. He took note of hands and feet of enormous size and great, pendulous arms. Despite his age, the man was still of unbroken, incredible strength, it was plain.

"This is Bill … this is the Joker," said Nagle. "Shake hands, you two."

Bill the Dogman, without a word, held out his great hand. It swallowed the fingers of Sammy Day and then crushed them in a terrible grip, while a faint, fiendish smile of content wrinkled upward to his buried eyes. And a yell of joy burst from the cruel throats of those who looked on.

Young Sammy Day could not strike a man of his age. Instead, he used the edge of his flattened left hand as a butcher uses a cleaver. With the bone-hard rim of his palm, he struck the outer muscles of Bill's arm, where the muscles are close to the bone. He almost broke his hand on the skinny arm of Bill, but the grip of the latter instantly relaxed. The nerves of that arm were paralyzed to the fingertips by the stroke.

"Glad to meet you," said the Joker.

The arm of Bill swung limply at his side. "Glad to meet you, kid," he said gravely.

The roaring wave of laughter had died out.

"What sort of a job do you offer?" asked Sammy Day.

"I offer a job for men only," said the other.

"Do you?" Sammy said, scanning the other up and down. "And do you find men that'll work for pigs in this part of the world?" Then he turned his back and walked slowly down the length of the bar.

Behind him, he heard a warning murmur: "Careful, Bill. That's the kid that beat up Rush Mahan. And he's a two-gun streak of lightning."

But the Joker mingled with the crowd until he found Digger Joe. "Why that?" asked the Joker. "Do the boys want to see me put down?"

"They want to get their laugh, that's all," said Digger Joe. "Whatcha wanna do, now? Kill the whole crowd?"

"I'd kind of like to," the Joker replied through his teeth. "He nearly broke my hand."

"He always does," said Digger Joe. "What did you do to him?"

"Little trick," said the young man briefly. "Who's this greasy pig, this Bill the Dogman? He looks like a dog … a wolf, rather, and a dirty one at that?"

"Bill raises dogs," Digger Joe answered. "Bill is kinder crazy, I guess. He breeds dogs. He's got all kinds out on his place. He spends his money and all his time breeding 'em. He says that he's going to breed the finest dogs that ever pulled a sled in the snow. He raises dogs, and he advertises for men to work for him. Five hundred dollars a month and found."

"Hold on!" said the boy.

Digger Joe laughed. "Aye, you'd like to try that, wouldn't you? But it's too much, even for you, you India rubber doll, you. No, you couldn't handle that job. Nobody could."

"Who's tried?"

"Oh, about a dozen. Picked men, too. They all come back."

"What happens to 'em?"

"Oh, I dunno. They never say, except Steve Rourke."

"What did he say?"

"Things it ain't good to repeat. He was out of his mind when he came in. Poor Steve ..."

"*Humph!*" said the young man, dropping his head a little and looking up under his brows, after his fashion.

"You think I'm joking, eh?" said Williams. "I tell you, Rourke was a 200 pounder, and all iron. He was a real man, and he took on that job, not because he didn't know that good men had failed at it, but because he figured that he could win through where the others fell down. Well, he knows better now."

"Go on," Sammy urged.

"There's no more to say. Pike Neil picked up Rourke wandering through the snow, blind and clean out of his head. Had to hit him over the head, lash him on a sled, and drag him into Circle City. He laid back there in that room for three weeks before he was really himself again, not his whole self, either, only a ghost. He babbled part of the time, and part of the time he yelled."

"What did he yell?"

"Crazy things. Nobody repeats them. They ain't good for the soul, not even the soul of a joker." Nagle shrugged his shoulders; his face was frozen with horror and something like fear at the memory. "Rourke got out of the country," he went on. "We never seen him again. We never want to. Well, here's your girl, kid. Let's see you begin your courting."

"Aw, shut up," said Sammy, for he saw Goldie Mahan enter the room.

She did not come far in, but stood at the door, closing it behind her. Her shoulders were covered with the powdered snow. "Has Phil Grant showed up yet?" she called.

"Not yet," said Nagle.

Digger Joe raised his big glass of whiskey and poured it down his brazen throat. "Here's somebody else for you, though," he said, and laid his hand on the shoulder of young Sammy Day who struck the hand fiercely away, but the gesture had been seen by all. "Here's the fellow that says he's going to court you, Goldie. Going to take him?" asked Digger Joe.

Her eyes, sweeping around the crowd, reached the face of Sammy Day and rested there calmly, coldly. For once in his life the heart of the Joker rose into his throat and fluttered there like a helpless bird. But many other eyes were upon him. He had to do something spectacular, according to his code. Otherwise, he would be shamed. He chose to step out before her and take off his hat with a flourish and a bow.

"You know, Goldie," he said, "now that we've found one another, we might as well make a long story short and get married. Why wait, except to kill time?"

The coldness of utter contempt made her eyes droop as she watched him. It was not hatred, but disgust that curled her lip a little. He thought her more beautiful than ever. Beautiful, in fact, as some fine poison that kills happily, with a breath, a touch. What would she say, if she spoke at all?

She chose to take an ironic vein. "We've waited a long time for one another," she said. "But hadn't we better wait till you have a steady job?"

"Such a job as I could give him," broke out the inhuman voice of Bill the Dogman.

She turned her head with a start and stared at the tall, bending figure of that self-exile. Then her smile deepened a little. "Yes, just such a job," she declared.

The younger man began to laugh. The older, instead of laughing, looked gravely toward him. And they saw him drop his head a little and look from under his brows, in a way that was already familiar to them, first at Bill the Dogman, and then at the girl.

"How long would I have to hold down such a job?" he asked her.

She paused, contempt and distaste in her wide open eyes. "A year and a day," she answered out of the book.

"And then we'll be married?" asked the Joker.

"Yes, I'll marry the Joker," she said, "after he's kept his place with Bill the Dogman for a year."

He turned his back upon her suddenly, and, staring at Bill, he said: "Will you hire me?"

The long lantern jaws of Bill opened wide in a silent laugh, like the laugh of a wolf. "I'll hire anybody," he said, "and I never fired a man yet. They fire themselves."

"Then I'm your man for a year and a day," said the Joker. He turned back toward Goldie Mahan.

"I have your word. These fellows are the witnesses," he said.

CHAPTER TEN

There had been odd bargains struck, many a one, in Circle City before this date. There never was one quite so odd as this, however. Goldie Mahan started for the door. Young Sam Day got there before her and pulled it open. They looked into each other's eyes—she coldly smiling, he fiercely contemptuous.

Apparently, they were bitter enemies. No one else was near. The men in that room had too much sense to approach the Joker at such a moment, and for a short while, the girl and the man spoke to each other.

The wind blew through the opened door and scattered the white powdery snow over the floor of the barroom. Their voices were lost in its gusty sounds.

"You mean this, Joker Sam Day?" she asked.

"D'you think that I talk to hear myself?" he replied.

"You want to make this a hard-and-fast bargain?" she asked.

"The bargain's made," he said, "whether you want it or not."

"I can step out now," she observed.

"You won't, though," answered the Joker.

"D'you read minds?" she asked him scornfully.

"You've given your word to the bargain before all these people," he told her, "and you're too proud to draw back from it now. You'd rather take poison. You'd even rather marry me."

She scanned him from head to foot. "You don't know Bill the Dogman," she remarked.

"I've heard what he's done to other men, plenty of 'em," he said.

At this, she opened her eyes a little. "You think that you can win where the rest fell down?" she asked him.

"I know I can," he said.

At this, her eyes opened still wider. She looked, suddenly, less mature, more like a very frightened child.

"That's right," remarked the Joker. "You have the chill in you now. You'll have it again before the year's out. Mind you, you play the game."

"I trust Bill the Dogman," she said. "You'll be either dead or a half-wit inside of three months."

"That's up to me. But you'll play the game."

"Tell me the rules, then?"

"Not even if Saint George came out of the stone and asked you to marry him, will you marry anyone else. And not even if they try with wild horses will they be able to keep you from Circle City a year and a day from this."

"No?" she said. "Are those the rules?"

"Those are the rules," he insisted.

She hesitated, and then he went on: "I know what's in your mind. But I tell you this, if you double-cross me, I'll do you harm … not to you, because you're a woman … but you have a family. I'll have their scalps, all of 'em, and when I take 'em, I'll send 'em to you by parcel post to remind you that you broke your word."

"What a cold, wicked devil you are!" burst out the girl, though she kept her voice down.

"What are you? You're asking me to go into torment for a year and a day," he responded. "You think that I'll be broken to bits. But you're wrong. You hate me because I broke Rush Mahan. You'll hate me worse, when you have to keep your promise. Right here in this barroom, a year from today, I'm going to marry you, my beauty. And then, I'm going to break you. I've broken wild colts before. I've caught 'em wild, and I've broke 'em wild."

She drew a trifle back from him. But then her assurance and her scorn returned. "You're talking ahead of time," she said. "A year from today, Circle City will have forgotten that you were here." Then she walked out into the street.

The Joker, after looking after her for a moment, with the icy wind beating across his face, closed the door, felt the latch click, and then went back to the bar. He walked up to the spot where Bill the Dogman stood. And it seemed to him that the black eyes of the tall man were bloodstained as he looked down into the face of his workman-to-be.

"What are the rules of your game?" asked the young man.

"Five hundred dollars a month," said Bill the Dogman.

"What do I do for that?"

"What you're told, and ask no questions."

"Not even now?"

"No. You keep your mouth shut."

"You don't fire?"

"No. I never fire."

"Well," said Sammy, "I'll make my own rule."

"What rule is that?"

"You can say what you want to me. You can give me any orders you please. But you can't curse me."

"I don't curse," said Bill the Dogman. He smiled, like the grin of a gargoyle, and showed yellow, ragged teeth.

"That's all, then," said the Joker. "I take the job."

Instantly, the claw of Bill the Dogman took a small pouch from a pocket and dropped it with a heavy thud upon the bar.

"Weigh that!" he commanded.

Nagle, in the dead silence that filled the room, poured the dust the little bag contained into one side of his scales. "Thirty ounces," he said.

"Five hundred dollars?" asked Bill the Dogman.

"Yes. A shade more, at seventeen dollars an ounce."

"That's your first month's pay in advance," said Bill the Dogman.

"Suppose that I don't finish the month?" asked Sammy Day.

"That's all right," said the tall grotesque. "I'll get five hundred dollars' worth out of you."

He began to laugh in a horrible, silent way, nodding to himself. That instant, Sammy Day made sure that his employer was insane.

"I've taken the job," was all that the Joker said. "Nagle, you keep that advance payment for me till I come back."

"You've taken the money?" asked Bill the Dogman.

"Yes."

"Then you're my man for the first month?" demanded Bill.

"That's the straight of it."

"You pack guns?"

"Yes. A pair."

"Lay 'em on the bar," said Bill. Only for an instant did the Joker pause. Then his gliding, cunning hands brought out the guns and laid them on the bar, the handles toward Nagle. The latter touched them almost reverently. "Will you keep them for me?" asked the Joker.

"I'll keep them," Nagle said with a faint smile. "Kid, you've made a fool of yourself today."

"Shut your mouth, Nagle," said Bill the Dogman. "The kid has some bone and blood in him. Your talkin' won't make him back down ... for a while."

He laughed again, silently. Never had young Day seen so much beast in a human face.

"That's all," said Bill. "That's all for half an hour. You can stay and drink your booze. I'll be back in half an hour with a team and a sled. Then we start. You take no guns with you. I don't care what else you take."

Then he left the room.

CHAPTER ELEVEN

The crowd poured about the shoulders of the Joker like sand around a stone. They made a few comments. They offered little advice. But each man looked upon Sammy Day as though he were already dead. He felt their looks as one feels the cold touches of dread and of inmost conscience.

Only Nagle said: "Get into your new outfit, son. You'll want a pair of good snowshoes. Hey, doc, get the kid that pair of snowshoes that Chief John gave me last month, will you? Kid, you mushed in from the outside, didn't you?"

"Yes."

"Then you know how to use snowshoes?"

"Yes, I know a little. I'm not the best in the world."

"Jeff!" barked Nagle.

A swarthy, deep-chested man answered: "All right, Nagle. What is it?"

"When the kid's dressed and got his shoes on, show him your tricks, will you?"

"Show him how to use snowshoes in ten minutes?" Jeff asked sullenly.

"You know what I mean," said the bartender. "You show him all that you can."

Sammy Day, in the cold of the corner room, stripped and dressed. Nagle went in to supervise. He looked at the lean, almost immature body of the Joker and shook his head.

"You oughta have some flesh on you," he said. "And you won't likely get fat with Bill the Dogman. Don't put on that underwear. I've got something better." He left the room.

By the time he came back, the body of Sammy Day was blue and pinched. But he nerved himself against this discomfort. He told himself that this was nothing, not even an introduction to the hell that he was to endure. *A year and a day!*

How easy it had been to make the contract when he stood in the warmth of the lit barroom and faced the beauty of Goldie Mahan. But now, it seemed to him as though he were facing an eternal damnation and without revolvers in his hands!

Nagle came back with a mere wisp of cloth in his hands. "Here's two suits. Put on one of 'em," he said. The young man looked at the underwear.

"I've my own suit of wool," he said. "You want me to put on open mesh linen?"

"Do what I say," said Nagle. "Put on one suit, and put the other in your pack. Those air spaces will beat wool. The mesh lets your sweat evaporate. It isn't dry cold that kills. It's the soggy wet steam from your own body that congeals and sends the ice through to the bone. And the core of the bone, at that. Do what I tell you. There's a good kid."

Sammy, without further argument, was stepping into the clothes. "Remember," said Nagle, lingering as the young man continued to dress, "when the bust comes, you can come back here and rest up with me. I dunno who you are, kid, but I know that you're game."

"There won't be any bust," replied Sammy, his teeth chattering.

"All right," said Nagle. "Perhaps there won't be any bust. Only, remember what I tell you. You can come back here any time."

Young Sammy Day paused in his dressing and stared at the man of the Northland. Then he said: "Nagle, I'll tell you something."

"Go ahead," said Nagle.

"If I come back here before a year and a day, I'll come back dead."

"Yeah," replied Nagle, nodding his head and half sneering. "That's all right, too. You go on talking that way as long as you can. When you bust, nobody'll blame you much, here in Circle City. A month is the most that anybody ever lasted before. And that was Rourke. He was proud. He held on till he went crazy. The rest ... well, two or three days was plenty for most of 'em. Take a drink before you start."

The young man finished his dressing. But he did not pause for a drink. Instead, he picked up Jeff in the barroom. The latter was already on snowshoes, and accompanied him out the front door into the street. He hooked his arm through Sammy's and led him to such a distance through the white smother of the storm that they could not be seen or heard by idlers in the saloon.

Then he said: "I can mush with anybody in Alaska, though I got short legs. Nobody knows how I do it. But Nagle, he's got a right to make me tell. So I'll tell you. Maybe you can learn something from it. Walk right behind me." He took twenty steps, with the boy behind, studying intently. Then he paused and asked: "Understand?"

"I see how you pick your foot up and put it down. But I don't see anything mysterious about it," Sammy said.

"Don't you?"

"No. What is it?"

"It's a figure eight. Not a big one. But it's a figure eight with each foot every time you take a step. Fast walkers do the same thing without knowing what they do, most of 'em. It's a little figure eight that gets your foot off the ground smooth and easy. Follow me?"

"I'm trying to," the Joker said, frowning with intense interest.

"Look!" commanded Jeff. And he showed, without moving the snowshoe from the ground, a slight fluctuation of his foot above the netting. "Here you are with it in motion," he said. With that, he dragged the snowshoe forward and indicated slowly, carefully, the movement that he had commenced before.

"It don't look like much," he explained. "It ain't much to see. And you got to study it until it ain't in the brain … it's just in the foot. Then you'll see the difference. Before ever I come North, I used to wish that I had an extra six inches on my short legs. So I studied heel and toe walking. I learned something from that. I could step by the long-legged boys, before I was through, like a hot knife through butter. Then I came up here. Well, you can't heel and toe with snowshoes the way you can without them. But you can make the middle movement the same. I tell you this. Snowshoeing is a kind of philosophy. The man that wins ain't the man that can make the fastest mile. It's the man that takes his pleasure out of making the snowshoes go over the snow so soft and slow, easy and smooth, that it's like ice skates going over ice."

They mushed along in silence for a while, then Jeff said: "Watch me, the way I show you. Put your brains in your eyes, and watch my feet."

He stepped out in front of the cheechako, and the Joker, watching with his brains literally in his eyes, was able finally to perceive the delicate weaving movement of his feet and the slightly curving lines along which the snowshoes moved. He strove to imitate this movement, feeling that Nagle would not have sent him out with a tyro. But it was hard slogging.

Then, it happened as though by miracle—his snowshoes seemed to leave the surface without effort. There was no drag, no delay. And they landed firmly, as though he were stepping on good, firm, turfy ground. In an instant, he was at the side of Jeff.

The latter stopped, scowled at him through the flying snow, and then laughed. "I've showed it to two others. I had to. Nagle made me. But it took them two days, and it's taken you about two minutes. You're gonna mush far and long through the North, if you want to ... if you got the heart to, kid."

They went back toward the saloon. As they moved, Sammy Day again felt that he was not moving upon the same sort of a surface that he had walked over coming up the street. There was a glide and a go to it. Snowshoeing had become a pleasure.

When they reached the saloon, they saw before it a sled with five dogs hitched. And such a mongrel collection the Joker never had seen.

Jeff laughed. "These are some of Bill the Dogman's prizes," he said. "Look at that overgrowed, long-legged rat with curly hair in the lead. That's pretty, ain't it? Look at that down-headed thing with the humped back behind it. That's what he gives his life to ... the worst teams that pull sleds into Circle City. But he goes on, year after year, breeding and praying, working and spending thousands of dollars. All that ever comes of it is when a team of these half-breeds pulls one of his sleds into town and pulls it out ag'in ... sometimes with a fool of a man like you walking behind."

So said Jeff, and Sammy Day, listening, in depression of spirit, could not but agree. They were not like any dogs that he ever had seen before, and he hoped with all his heart that he never would see such again.

A revulsion of feeling came over him. He could not place the breeds. Here was a short-haired, and there was a long-haired beast. Here was a short-bodied, there a long-bodied animal. Here was one standing high on stilty legs, and there one low to the ground, dragging itself verily in the snow. One had the tail of a wolf, bushy and big, carried straight out; one, the tail of a house dog, arching over the back; one a low-streaking tail that touched the ground, and bare as the tail of a rat. Their heads differed, also. One was like the head of a greyhound; one like a wolf's; one like a mastiff's.

Surely, it seemed, if a grown man devoted his life to the breeding of creatures like these, he was devoting it in vain. It was, in fact, a sort of madness. He remembered, then, what he had heard about Bill the Dogman, his ways, and how he broke the spirits of men. Now that he had seen the dog team, he felt that he was better prepared for whatever was to come.

He doubted himself. He doubted, above all, the clothes that Nagle had given to him, with so much assurance. His whole body was gloved and fitted as with icy water. He could not breathe an instant in comfort. This was what Nagle considered the ideal outfit, but who was Nagle to judge? Nagle, so far as he knew, lived in the stove-heated comfort of his bar, and could not judge of the necessities of the open range of blizzard-swept snows. He, the Joker, like a fool, had entrusted his equipment to a bartender. He cursed himself.

Bill the Dogman came out of the saloon and peered through the snow, flecks of it settling white against the shaggy, short beard that covered his face. "All right?" he asked.

"All right," replied the Joker.

"Learn everything from Jeff that you'll need to know?"

Jeff answered in the place of the Joker. "He'll walk your legs off … even your long legs," he interposed.

Bill laughed. The sound of the storm drowned out his laughter. Its cold fingers slid through the meager clothing of Sammy and pressed against his stomach, his ribs, and over his heart. Cold seemed to be gathering like a lump of ice in his very vitals.

"I ain't askin' you, I'm askin' the kid," said Bill. "You know everything that you need to know?"

The Joker, at that minute, was lashing his small pack of personal belongings upon the back of the sled. He looked up. "Somebody speak?" he said.

Jeff, loudly, boisterously broke into laughter that boomed with the very voice of the storm.

"Yeah," Bill the Dogman said savagely. "*I* spoke to you!"

"Well, then," said young Sammy Day, "shut your face till you get sense enough to talk to me, will you?"

CHAPTER TWELVE

He knew, of course, that he had said more than he needed to say, but, like one who had risked all, he cared not for details. His life, his reason, were to hang in the balance for a year and a day. Almost better for him if the crisis came at once.

Behind him, before him, and all around him, he could see the men of the saloon swarming through the white mist of the storm. They were shouting, laughing, and laying wagers.

"Two to one that the kid don't last ten days!" called out one man.

"I'll take that for a hundred at two to one," replied another.

"You're a fool to bet him as short as that. The kid has got nerve. He'll last like Rourke. A month, anyhow."

"He ain't got the fat and the beef to last as long as Rourke. Mind what I say."

"Here's five hundred to a hundred that the kid is back here before six weeks."

Then there followed a silence.

"Hey!" yelled a voice, and Sammy recognized it as Nagle's.

"I'll take that bet. Here's my hundred, you poor sucker. The kid will last more'n six weeks!"

"Here's another five hundred to a hundred that he don't do two months of time!"

"I'll take the short end of that!" boomed another.

And again Sammy recognized the voice. It was Digger Joe Williams.

He felt an odd sense of gratitude to these men who were betting on him. It was true that they might be trying to win easy money at short odds. But it was also true that they were betting on him. Suddenly, he began to laugh. The storm wind struck him in the face like a fist, blinding him and thrusting a cold, bony fist down his throat.

"A thousand to a hundred that the kid don't last six months!"

There was no answer to this challenge.

Again: "Listen, fellows, a thousand to a hundred that he don't last six months!"

Still there was no answer. All at once, Sammy Day saw that he was standing alone in the middle of the street, for the sled and the team had disappeared under the veil of the snowstorm. He hurried forward blindly. His feet slipped from under him. He was like one wading through thick mud. Then he remembered Jeff.

All at once, his way was smoothed. He was walking, trotting, running forward with a strange, effortless glide. Perhaps his hundreds of miles of mushing in from the outside had helped him. But certainly the brief lesson from Jeff had given a cutting edge to his knowledge and to his experience. Then he saw before him the dim silhouette of the dog team and the sled with its camel-backed load. As he caught up with it, he watched the gaunt, bending form of Bill the Dogman at the gee pole. And he felt that he saw his grotesque destiny before him.

They went on. In an hour, his legs began to ache. At the same time he became aware that he was no longer cold. The clothes he was wearing had scarcely a third of the stiff poundage that he had borne during his trip in from the outside, yet he was warm. The cold fingers were no longer clutching at his vitals. Nagle was right. He had spoken from the deeps of a real and long Arctic experience.

Furthermore, the way, he discovered, to cover the snow with the least pain was not to think about the pace or about the time he had been traveling, but about the manner in which he was making each step.

After that, he made better headway; the team seemed to be going more slowly.

At last, it halted. He was glad of that. But he was surprised to see the Dogman pulling out objects from beneath the tarpaulin that covered his sled and hurl them far. Suddenly, he realized that a great part of the weight of that sled was naked stones, and these Bill was throwing away. Did one need any greater proof that the man was insane?

The sled started again. Its pace was redoubled. He saw the Dogman running with great strides, and he began to run, also, but he was losing ground. As he ran, he strove to fathom the puzzle.

Why should the Dogman have placed a killing burden in worthless stones upon the top of his sled? What did it mean? A jockey may be bribed to slip an extra ten pounds of lead into his outfit. The horse runs as well, as gallantly as ever. It finishes hard under the whip. But it is beaten a length by the horse it once fairly beat. A slight upset in form.

And so was the Dogman performing. He was simply pulling the wool over the eyes of those scornful, laughing critics at the saloon of Nagle, those wise men who had mushed dogs all over the Arctic regions, to Nome, and beyond.

Then young Sammy Day said to himself: *Whatever else happens, I've got to stick to this. The Dogman isn't crazy, but he's deep.*

The thought led to others. Only a crazy man would wish to hire people at $500 a month, paid in advance, merely for the sake of driving them frantic and breaking their spirits. He told himself that the Dogman was not crazy. He was far from that. Very well, then, there was something behind his tormenting of his hired men. He was not merely throwing away money. He had a purpose to gain, and the young fellow swore that he would stay with the game until he had learned that purpose down to the ground.

Then the labor of travel became so great that he could not any longer think at all. He had to bend every energy of mind and body to the proper functioning of his feet and snowshoes. If only Jeff had had time to work with him not half an hour, but half a day.

The sled suddenly halted again, and he caught up with it in a few strides. The wind had fallen. It was hardly more than a whisper. They were among low hills, which no doubt helped to break the force of it, and now the raucous voice of the Dogman came crashing back to him: "Hey, you! Are you a tail to this kite?"

He forced himself up to Bill and stood before him, his legs spread a little, because he was afraid that he might reel from weariness. He said nothing at all. Then he saw the long left arm of Bill extend, pointing.

"You see that hollow, between them two low hills? You start on ahead of the dogs and break trail to that. Step short, break a good trail. When you get to the top of the rise, you'll see a long downslope. At the end of it, there's a single mound. You'll just be able to make it in this weather. When you round the side of that mound to the right, you'll see a long ways off what looks like a mist split in two. That's a lot of naked trees. You hit out for the place where that wood splits in two. All the time that you're travelin', you make it fast, and step short!"

Sammy answered nothing. He told himself that he had gone far past the point where words might avail anything. Nothing would serve now, except conservation of breath and of brains. He must think much and speak little.

So he swung out ahead of the team of dogs and began to break trail. He had done it before, and he had an idea of the right steps to beat down the snow. And these he made. But the leader of the team was always at his heels.

Then came the voice of Bill: "Hey, whatcha doin'? Goin' to sleep?"

I'm no good, Sammy thought to himself. *I'm not man enough to do the work.*

Still, he kept on. He forced himself to go faster, not blindly, but intelligently, using everything that he had learned from Jeff, the careful swinging of his legs, the delicate maneuvering of the snowshoes. They seemed to be growing bigger on his feet. The rims of them bumped constantly together. Then his brain fell into a swirl, and he saw and thought nothing clearly.

Suddenly, he felt alone. He looked back and perceived that the dogs were far behind him, almost lost behind the snow. That gave him heart. He was outdistancing the dogs! He pushed ahead. He swore that he would show the Dogman something. His confidence gave him a wild furious strength, and, full of that fury, he rushed on. For a long time, he struggled. Then he felt, rather than heard, something breathing just behind him.

It was the lead dog of the team, moving steadily, head close to the ground—the dog that looked like a great rat, its tail vastly lengthy, skinny as the lash of a whip.

No, he could not run away from the team. The Dogman was simply laughing at him, tricking him, keeping him well in hand.

The voice of the master came harshly through the rising wind: "Gonna stand there all day, you fool, when we just begun to line out on our trail?"

Just begun? Suddenly, he realized that it was true. They had hardly begun that day's march. Endless, terrible leagues were still before them before camp would be reached, and Bill the Dogman, so early in the game, already had made a fool of him and induced him, through pride, to burn up all the cream of his early strength!

CHAPTER THIRTEEN

It was a nightmare. It came like a mist of fire, and it remained in his brain and in his body. There was only one strength in him, and that was the rage of shame that burned in him, shame and hate, when he thought of the manner in which he had been tricked and beaten down by the cunning of Bill the Dogman.

Such trick insanity is fertile in, he told himself. But to be shaken off on the very first day—that was too much.

He heard Bill roaring behind him, urging him on to a pace, asking if he were a child, expecting later on a man's wages?

But he would not change his pace now. He told himself that he dared not make it faster, lest he should collapse. Even as it was, he dared not cast his imagination forward a single hour, but had to focus his mind upon each step as he walked along.

He could bless Jeff for that lesson in snowshoeing. He was moving with a minimum of effort. If only he had more power in those skinny legs of his to support him and to carry him forward.

Then a shrill yell went up behind him, and the lead dog came past, its ratty tail flicking the surface of the snow. The whole team and the sled with big Bill at the gee pole slid past him.

No word of greeting did Bill fling him, not even reviling, but his grim face showed for an instant through the snow mist, and then he was gone on. Sammy fell in behind.

The trail was infinitely better, where the sled, the man, and the dogs had all trodden before him. But now the pace of the dogs seemed to be redoubled. Bill himself was moving at a peculiar, shambling run, such as Sammy never had seen before, and he covered the ground with a mysterious ease.

The Joker had to run, also. After ten strides, he told himself that he could do no more. A jumping pain came into his side, bent him over, and twisted hard at him, as though with constricting arms. The snowshoes were always striking down into the ground, tripping him. He knew, now, that he had no hope, or so it seemed. There was nothing in his nature that could save him, except the power of a vast will. That will was in him. He would not consider the future. He would think of one thing only—to keep within sight of that sled until he dropped dead. Horses will run till they die. He told himself that a man could do the same thing.

Therefore, fiercely, he straightened his tormented body. He forced his lungs to breathe deep, in spite of the choking pain. He bent his eyes upon the surface of the snow just before him and considered fiercely, gravely the action of his feet on the shoes.

His body might be spent, but his mind could still pour itself into the exercise of snowshoeing. An hour before, he thought that he had thoroughly mastered the lessons taught by Jeff; now he saw that he was only beginning to learn. There were a thousand small, crafty things that could be done. The height that the foot was lifted, for instance, could be cut down to a fraction of his old stride. Furthermore, when the foot lifted so little, he was able to forget knee action almost altogether, and to make both the lift and the stride from the hips. Then, the agonized muscles along the front of his thigh were able to relax, and the pain smoothed gradually out of them. He was not resting, of course. But one part of him rested, while a bitterer effort was placed upon the rest of his being.

Meanwhile, the sled dwindled before him. He told himself that if it once disappeared, Bill the Dogman would dodge him, double back, hide out so that he could not be found, and sit in a secure place, rubbing his great mittened hands, rejoiced in the thought that another man was adrift in the white mist, lost, dying.

On the other hand, he had to keep down all sense of panic. A single panic-stricken burst would use up the last of his strength. No, he must save himself and make his efforts gradually. So he put forth just enough of himself to keep the obscure vision of the humpbacked sled wavering in the distance of the snow mist. Sometimes it quite disappeared, as a thicker cloud blew between. Sometimes it was a thing imagined, rather than seen, and others it was clear—sled, man, and dogs.

A calmness came upon the Joker. He was no longer struggling with his body. That had no existence. All that lived and moved in him was the mind, steel-cold, fixed upon its purpose to win or die. What filled him with a curious pleasure was that those dragging, weary limbs were forced to execute the commands of his mind. His will was still the absolute master.

The sled had not passed beyond his vision. It was there before him, unwavering now, a little closer. Suddenly, he was sure that he was gaining on it.

He came up close. Bill the Dogman, letting his team run freely ahead, confident in the wisdom of the leader, fell back a trifle behind the sled. Now he was moving with effortless, marvelous strides beside the shorter-legged man.

"Ain't tired, are you?" he shouted at him.

"Hell, no!" yelled Sammy.

"That's good," said the other. "We've only come about halfway, now."

The words fell like a club upon the brain of Sammy Day. No

matter what he did with his brain, he never could force his body to continue again for the number of miles that they already had covered. Still he did not give up, or fling himself down, or turn back. Instead, he set his jaw and faced into the wind, keeping his mind firmly fixed on the next instant, not the next hour, of existence.

He only dared to tell himself, at this moment, that when once he came out of this adventure—if out of it he could ever hope to come—he would never again in all his days complain of his lot, so long as he could sit at leisure for one short hour in a working day.

There were clerks, were there not, who merely had to sit on stools all day. Yet these fellows often considered themselves overtaxed and were exhausted by their toil. Toil? Mental labor? The mind cannot toil! Only on the body falls the curse of Adam.

Such were the thoughts of Sammy Day, when he stumbled and fell to the ground. He thrust himself up at arm's length. His legs gave way at the knees and refused to buoy up the burden of his slender body.

"My legs are trying to quit on me, but I'll show 'em!" exclaimed Sammy.

Again he struggled, and again he bent all his will upon the task. Gradually he rose, stood erect, but tottering. Just then, he saw the sled disappearing over the top of a small hummock, with the tall Dogman looking back, a horrible laughter on his horrible face. The sled and the driver sank out of view.

I'm a dead man, thought the Joker in his darkening heart, *but I'll die on my feet. I can do what any good horse will do, I guess.*

And he commanded his body with all the force of his will, and the body answered and strode up the slope. At the crest, he saw the sled wallowing down into a great, shallow hollow, covered with brush and trees. All were naked, and every branch and twig were outlined with white chalk strokes of the snow. In the midst of this hollow, there was a white mound, and above the top of the mound projected something that might be the top of a stone-built fireplace—a chimney! Suddenly, he knew. Hysterical joy and hysterical rage swept up in him.

The journey was almost finished. The Dogman had lied. Bill, having striven in vain to walk his hired man off his feet, had tried to break his spirit. Well, Sammy knew his man. There was that advantage. No subterfuge was too mean or too small for Bill. But what else could he expect? Mere lies must be the least part of it, after all. So thought the Joker.

In the meantime, he saw that his legs were acting very queerly for they bent like putty at the knees and would not straighten again. At length, he came to the easier walking at the bottom of the hollow, and there he discovered that he could go along well enough, though with pains of aching muscles that shot up to the roof of his brain and lifted it into the sky.

So he came up and found that Bill the Dogman was kicking snow away from before the door of his house.

"Unload the sled," said Bill. "And step lively, will you?"

CHAPTER FOURTEEN

He stepped lively; that is to say, he stepped as lively as he could. Bill the Dogman leaned against the door of his house and laughed loudly, his long arms folded across his breast.

"You been drinkin' along the way, I guess," he said. "You walk like you was drunk, cheechako!"

The Joker made no answer. He told himself, once he loosed his tongue, his hands would soon be loosed behind it. He wanted to murder Bill. Indeed, a cold, grim conviction was born in him that he would one day destroy that tall devil. That day, he vowed solemnly, would be a year and a day from this one. To marry Goldie Mahan and strangle Bill the Dogman in one and the same day—that would be perfection!

So he set his jaw hard, and, verily like a drunken man who is striving to conceal his dizziness, he staggered back and forth, carrying burdens into the house.

Then two big, wide-shouldered Indians or half-breeds appeared. Each one of them was fully as tall as the Dogman, and each was at least forty or fifty pounds heavier. One of them picked up in a single armful all of the load that remained upon the sled. Bearing this huge load past the boy, he laughed in his face.

Sammy Day, reeling back against the wall, watched the big, dark-faced man go by. He looked at him as at a map—the receding chin and the projecting forehead, the great, broad nose, the vast mouth, hooked up at the corners by its grin. It was the face of a gargoyle. It seemed impossible to attach this creature by any ties to the same sort of humanity to which Sammy Day belonged, yet he was neither soft nor new to hard adventures.

The lofty form of the Dogman appeared before him. He seemed like the white-skinned father of the red men. That is to say, there was the same inhuman malice, the same ghastly contempt for human woes in his face that appeared in the face of the Indians. He held in his hands a great axe that he thrust toward Sammy Day.

"Wood!" he said.

The Joker took the axe and went to the nearest brush. He was numb. When he had stopped walking, the blood seemed to congeal in his veins. There was no flow of life in him. Thought, also, was like stagnant water. He was only conscious of one thing—that he was in torment. He began to swing the axe. To use his arms instead of his legs was a luxury. However, even a woodsman must keep his balance and measure his swing from the feet, and the legs of the Joker were lifeless.

His work, furthermore, was almost futile. The wood was not wood. It was iron. It bent under the strokes and cast the axe bounding back. He had to hack and hew, and gradually wear through a branch only an inch thick.

Back there behind him must be contempt, if any eyes were watching. Then he was sure of it, because the gigantic form of one of the Indians strode past him, encased in blowing furs, and took the axe from his numbed fingers. Easily, without a glance for him, the red man took the axe and swung it. With every stroke, he made a half step forward. With every stroke, a bush fell, cut through near the roots, or else a stout branch was cleft. He watched those strokes. To be sure, there was weight in the shoulders of the chopper, but there was also a consummate skill.

The Joker understood guns, knives, horses, ropes. But sleds, dogs, snowshoes, axes were still mysteries. For all that, he did not lose heart. He had been struck in the face, before this, by fate, and now he would not go down. He would stand his ground.

He picked up the bushes that had been cast down by the sweeping strokes of the axe, and strove to pull them apart. But they seemed bound by the ice as if with iron. They would not yield. Suddenly, he heard the strokes of the axe no more. Then the bush, with which he was struggling, was torn from his surprised grasp. There stood the big Indian before him, and the man ripped the bush apart, broke the fragments of the branches in immense hands, and cast them back into the face of Sammy Day.

It was too much. The Joker stepped in, fury in his heart, and smashed his fist against the jaw of the big man. Then he paused, expecting the other to drop. He had hit the button. No man could stand straight after that. But to his sickened amazement, the red man merely laughed, loud and long, and then struck him down.

He lay there in the snow on one elbow, considering, trying to remember. It had not been an expert's punch. It had been slow and deliberate, the stroke of a bungler. He had reared his guard against it. Still, with irresistible weight, the blow had beaten through his guard and knocked him to the ground.

He got up, his knees shaking. He turned toward the back trail. The whole thing was obvious, now. The Dogman had two supermen working for him. He, the Joker, was a joke indeed in such a place. There was no need of him. He was a mere superfluity. Yet he did not step out upon the backward trail, and it was not the thought of his weariness that constrained him. It was rather the indomitable will to conquer.

He said to himself: *These fellows look big. Well, big men are always slow. They look clever. That's because I don't know their specialties. When I know them, they won't seem so hard.*

He became almost hysterical as he staggered toward the house, laughing as he went. Then, as he neared it, strength seemed to flow mysteriously back into him, and he grew steadier on his snowshoes. Deep, deep fatigue was drenching the whole being. He was still laughing to himself when he entered the house door.

The Dogman stood by it, and beside Bill was a great gray wolf, not a dog.

No, the dog was never born that had such a head, such eyes. This was a wild wolf. There was still the stain of red in its eyes, the stain that the wilderness puts there. This monster reached to the hip of even a tall man like Bill. It had a head like the head of a wild mustang. And it stared hostilely at the stranger.

The Joker looked at the master and then at the beast beside him. He understood, in a flash, why the Dogman had forbidden guns, but had not cared about such lesser things as clubs and knives. Why should he care for clubs and knives when he had under his thumb the terrible fangs of this beast to turn loose against who he would?

Fatigue dulled and numbed the nerves of the Joker. He walked straight up to the monster and put his hand on its head. Under his hand the wolfish creature winced. The eyes narrowed, but did not quite lose all of their fire. That fire was green as a splintered emerald ray of devilishness. The eyes of Sammy Day were green, also, as he looked down at the wolf.

"Good old boy," said Sammy Day. Then he walked straight ahead and pushed the wolf out of his way with a thrust of his hip in passing.

There was a stove in the center of the room. By this, he stood and turned his back to it, while its sunny warmth struck through his vitals. He was aware, at the same time, of a pain above his left eye. He thought about it and realized that it was where the fist of the Indian had clumsily struck him, after beating down his guard.

The Indian came in now. He carried in his arms a great load of the frozen wood and threw it down with a crash beside the stove. Then he said, with a hooking of his thumb,"Put that in the fire," and turned his back. Over his shoulder, he laughed at the Joker as he strode off, and his laughter filled the one room of the house with thunder.

Sammy looked around the place. He could tell, now, that there was the one room and no more. He could tell that, by the row of bunks, five in number, fitted against the walls, and by the clothes that stood by them, by the improvised kitchen in one far corner, by the guns, the fishing rods, and various other implements such as shovels and picks, that stood along the walls. He hardly knew why it was a relief to him to realize that he had seen and understood such a simple fact as this.

Then he walked after the big Indian and tapped him on the shoulder. The red man turned. "You speak English?" said the Joker.

"Yeah, pretty good," the Indian said, nodding his head in a queer, childish way, as though he were pleased to be able to answer the question in the affirmative.

"If you speak it pretty good," said Sammy, "you listen to me."

"Have you got something to say?" asked the red man. And he laughed.

The Joker looked away from him. He looked toward the Dogman, and he saw that Bill was laughing, too, though without sound. The great beast beside him was panting with open mouth and seemed to be laughing, also.

Even to save his very soul, the Joker could not tell which looked more the wolf—the beast or the man.

"Yes," he said, looking back to the Indian, "I have something to tell you."

"You talk, then," said the red man.

"You hit me out there," the Joker said, pointing through the half open door. "Because of that, I'm going to kill you one of these days."

For answer, the Indian laughed again, and then he struck Sammy Day senseless to the floor.

CHAPTER FIFTEEN

Sleep must have begun where unconsciousness left off. Later, when Sammy Day woke up, he found himself lying flat on the floor and was almost frozen. A lantern, hanging from the wall, burned with a dim flicker. He got up on one elbow and looked about him.

Bill the Dogman was sleeping in a bunk, one lengthy arm hanging down to the floor. Beside him the gray wolf was couched, and its eyes, staring fixedly at the stranger, gleamed like emeralds, with streaks of crimson. There was lust for blood, his blood, the Joker thought, in the eyes of the beast.

The Joker got to his feet and looked at the faces of the sleeping Indians. He was weak with cold, weak with fatigue, weak with the sense of what lay before him. He had endured one day, and 365 more such days lay before him. Worse days they would be, if the Dogman could so contrive.

The faint odor of food reached him, and he turned toward the corner of the room, which served as kitchen. There he found in pots and pans, frozen coffee, ice-hard in the pot, and beans with a white scurf of frozen grease on top of them. He could see where nine-tenths of the supply had been scraped out in portions. This was left for him. He had not eaten for more than twenty-four hours. Hunger gnawed at his vitals. and he considered eating the icy beans out of the pan. Instead, he took them to the stove, built up the fire, and heated his food and drink—beans and coffee, a fine feed for a man half-dying with starvation. However, it must suffice.

When he began to eat, he thought that nothing so delicious ever had passed down his throat. He relished every morsel of it. There was not enough of beans, or of coffee. But there was enough to turn the razor edge of his hunger.

Then he went to an empty bunk and found that there was not a particle of covering upon it. Inside its high, polished rims, it was empty. Therefore, this bunk was useless to him. He would freeze in it as quickly as on the floor.

So he went to the bunk of the first Indian. The top blanket on the man was of rabbit's fur, woven close, deep and soft. This the young fellow stole from him. It took him ten minutes of careful work, while his legs shook under him, not with fear, but with fatigue. As for fear, he told himself, if the Indian woke up, he would murder the man at once. The hands of the red man stole down and grasped the edge of the blanket as it was withdrawn, but from the sleeping, nerveless hands, the edge of the blanket could be withdrawn again. Finally, Sammy Day had it.

He went to the second man, who had floored him twice that day. Looking down upon the copper-skinned, ugly face, he wondered how he could keep his hands from the throat of the man. The throat itself was like a brazen pillar. The big muscles swelled and stood up, metal-hard, while the fellow breathed. But from him, also, though consuming more time and requiring greater care, Sammy took another rabbit's fur blanket. Armed with his two prizes, he went to the empty, bare, wooden bunk, wrapped himself up warm, and went to sleep.

He did not dream that night, to be sure. Fantasy was far from him. The realities of life and of fatigue were too great. The instant that he closed his eyes, he slept again. It seemed but a moment before a hand shook him roughly by the shoulder.

He opened his eyes and looked into the eyes of the Indian, who had knocked him down twice the day before. The man seemed to have lost his command of English, and this was not strange, considering the passion that consumed him. He said not a word, but first he pointed toward the bunk that he had been occupying, then he imitated the action of one stealthily withdrawing a covering from another. Finally, he showed with arms wrapped about his body how he had shivered and shuddered all through the night.

The Joker slipped from his bunk and stood up. His legs were not all that they should have been, but otherwise his iron constitution had fully recouped the losses that it had withstood. He flexed his knees. He found himself fit. He touched the bump over his left eye. Then he took a knife out of his clothes and waited.

He measured the Indian, and the Indian measured him, but he thought he could see a waning both of rage and of determination in the eyes of the latter. He could see also the rising of the cold light of hatred in the eyes of the other.

Then the big fellow turned about and strode past the blanketed, immobile form of his Indian companion to Bill the Dogman. To him he talked with many gestures, indicating the white man. Then, catching up a coat and flinging it about him, he rushed out into the cold.

Bill the Dogman hooked a finger, but Sammy Day sneered. Again, the finger was hooked, and he remembered his promise to obey all orders.

Therefore, he approached his employer, who said: "You make trouble with these Indians and they'll cut your throat. Understand that?"

"Yes, I understand that," said the Joker.

"You don't care, eh?"

The Joker shrugged his shoulders.

"You know," Bill continued to explain, "that no one man can stay awake as long as two?" The Joker merely smiled. "Me," said the Dogman, "I don't care what they do to you. I'd rather that they cut your throat. I don't fire nobody, but you're the worst, no-good hound that ever come inside of this house. Other men that I've had … and they've all been bad enough … could cut some wood, anyway, and they could work for their livin'. You can't do nothin'. You can't even walk straight. You're no use to nobody. Understand that?"

Sammy smiled. "Listen to me, Bill," he replied.

"I'm listenin'," said the Dogman, "but I don't expect to hear no sense."

"Listen to me, anyway. You hired me. I told you that I'd try to do what I'm ordered to do. I didn't say, though, that I'd take seriously anything that you have to say, and I don't. Everything that you feel, I feel the opposite. Everything that you think, I think the opposite. You're a beast, I believe. I've got to work for a beast for a year from today. All right, I'll do it. But don't give me any advice. As for your two Indians, you tell them that I was raised to kill their kind. I know how it's done. If I feel hungry, I'll start feeding on Indian steaks. Tell them that, or I'll tell them myself. This big copper-faced bohunk, I have nothing against except his color. That other one, I'm going to kill anyway, before I'm through, because I already owe him more killings than any one man is likely to be able to absorb."

Now that he had said this, he went to the kitchen corner and looked for food, but the Dogman said: "You eat what's cooked for you, not what you cook for yourself."

"I'll see about that," said the Joker. "You hired me for five hundred and keep. And your definition of keep may not chime in with mine. I expect plenty of chow."

"Chow?" Bill exclaimed, grinning. "I'll feed you till you bust, if you can stay awake long enough to eat at the end of each day. Wait a minute, I'll call back John, and then we'll have breakfast."

His lack of heat seemed strange to young Day. But more important, he felt, was the utter indifference in the voice of the big man. For indifference, after all, is more chilling than contempt, even open contempt.

So, first, Bill fell to work and heated a pan into which he dropped fat slices of bacon. When the bacon grease was rendered in a swimming mess, he opened the top of a half-filled sack of flour and poured the grease into a hole that he scooped out. With the grease he mingled salt and baking powder. Then, with his dirty hands, he worked and kneaded the lump of grease and flour until the bacon fat had soaked up all of the flour that it was capable of accommodating. After that, he went to the door, opened it, and bawled loudly: "John! Hey, John! You damn' fool, John, come here!" After he closed the door, he went back to his cooking. Four of these great lumps of bacon grease, flour, salt, and baking powder he made, and fired all four of them upon a great pan above the stove. He pronounced them done at the very moment when John, the Indian, opened the door and walked in. He carried a rifle in his hands.

Bill walked to him, took the rifle, and, holding it by the stock, smashed the muzzle against the floor. The weapon broke at the stock. He threw the gun into a corner. It exploded, and sent a bullet across the floor.

Then said Bill the Dogman: "You, John, and you, Pete, you wanna kill my new worker, the Joker. He wants to kill you. I don't care who kills anybody. You can kill him. He can kill you. I won't tell any secrets out of school. Only, I'll tell you this … if you start playin' with firearms, this white kid, he'll kill you both, like nothin' at all, because he can make guns talk. He makes gun medicine. I like you fellows a lot better than I like him. I need you, and I wish that he was in hell. You can kill him with knives or clubs or hands. But if you take to guns, he'll turn the bullets back in your faces. Amen!" Finishing on that strange word, he began to laugh in his silent, red-eyed, wolfish way.

The Joker lowered his head, observing the others from beneath his brows. He said nothing. Neither did the Indians. But he knew that they thought the more, though their faces were copper masks.

CHAPTER SIXTEEN

After the day had begun in this cheerful manner, the Joker went out with his employer. He had expected to find nothing but a howling wilderness. He had forgotten the reason for Bill's nickname, and now he found out.

For he found scores and scores of dogs penned in great runs around the place. The runs were fenced in with tangled brush piles and with intercrossed branches and saplings of a height that no dog or wolf could leap, and planted so firmly in the earth that no wind could blow them down.

There were small runs, only a hundred feet long. There were larger ones that covered acres, all fenced in the same secure fashion—a labor that astonished the Joker. He wondered what was the source of the Dogman's income. He had heard that the man did not sell dogs and here were scores and scores of them.

More bewildering than the number of the dogs was the variety of them. There were purebred wolves, distinguished only by their great size. They shrank from the approach of the men as though they were seeing the human kind for the first time and hating it.

"There's wild sense for you," said Bill the Dogman, pointing with his mittened hand. "They can live on hope and blowin' snow for half a year. They can run and fight hard when they're only a wreckage of bones covered with loose hide."

The young fellow, wisely, said nothing. He saw that he was speaking to a master concerning the one topic that enthralled him.

They went on past a smaller run, in which was what looked like an igloo. At the whistle of the man, a pair of white bull terriers came out of the entrance and stood humped up in the cold, their slant eyes drawn to little points of dark light by the continued pain of existence. Then, seeing that there was no food in sight, they turned and went back into the igloo, their tails between their legs.

"Bull terriers!" the young man exclaimed with an inevitable reaction of horror. "Bull terriers up here?"

"The last two that I have," said the Dogman. "They don't last long … none of that breed … in this cold. I've had twelve, fifteen of 'em, and they all die fast. Maybe six months, maybe six weeks, maybe a year or two. That's the last couple. They been with me for a year now. But they won't last out this winter."

"Short-haired, thin-haired dogs like that, how'd you expect 'em to last?" asked the Joker. "How d'you expect 'em to live up in this cold?"

"I ain't a fool," said Bill. "I don't expect 'em to. They won't live, and I know it."

"For knowing that and doing it," said the Joker, "you'd get yourself shot at some points I know farther south. The poor beasts," he added, looking at the small, snow-heaped house in which the unlucky dogs had to live.

"I ain't at one of those points farther south," said the Dogman. "I'm here. And here I'm the king. Don't forget it!"

The Joker said nothing, loathing grew in him. It turned to actual rage, a moment later, for out of another house, very like that of the bull terriers, a single male greyhound stepped with little, mincing steps. He was pulled into a bow by the terrible, piercing cold.

Bill the Dogman was saying: “You take a bull terrier, and he’s got the fightin’ heart. Other dogs’ll fight, but a bull terrier fights because he loves it. He ain’t the brightest dog in the world, but he kills the other dog.”

The young fellow hardly heard this last speech. He broke out: “Greyhounds! Up here!”

“Yeah, greyhounds.” The big man nodded. “They’re the worst of the lot. Got no more lungs than a knife blade. They go quick. They go mighty fast, I’m tellin’ you.”

“You like to see ’em die, is that it?” the Joker asked fiercely. “That’s why you raise the dogs, eh? You like to see ’em die?”

Bill the Dogman looked at him with eyes no larger than little bright beads. “I don’t mind seein’ ’em die,” he replied, “but that’s not why I got ’em here. You open your eyes and use your brains, if you got any. Here’s a kind of dog that don’t die in the cold … and here’s a dog with brains.”

They had left the smaller pen of the greyhound, and now they came to a larger yard in which half a dozen big, long-furred dogs were romping. They were solid black in color. Oddly they stood out like small black bears against the dazzling whiteness of the snow.

“What are they?” asked Sammy as the dogs sighted the men and rushed to the fence, barking, bounding with pleasure, standing up and striving to put their heads through the small apertures in the barrier.

“You don’t know what they are?” asked the Dogman.

“No, I don’t know much about dogs,” admitted the Joker.

Bill shook his head. “I’ll tell a man that you don’t know much about dogs!” he exclaimed. “Can’t you tell a Newfoundland when you see ’em? Can’t you tell ’em by the stop and the shape of the eyes? Look at the body and bone of ’em, too. Look at the brain room they got! Those are dogs that are dogs. Born to love men.”

“Yeah?” drawled Sammy. “I don’t know why.”

Bill was not offended by the implications behind this speech, it appeared. He merely said: "I dunno, neither. There ain't any explainin' of the way a dog is made up. There's some big souled with little bodies, like bull terriers. And there's some with big minds in little heads. But there ain't no more soul, there ain't no more mind in any breed of dogs than there is in Newfoundlands. They jump into the ocean to save the life of a tramp that they never seen before. They do it by instinct, too. Nobody needs to train 'em much. They take care of a master the way that a nurse takes care of a fool kid. Them there dogs, I'll tell you what ..." He leaned a mittened hand upon a stake of the fence and paused to consider his words. Then he said: "Them there dogs, you could teach 'em to read Greek, in about a month. You can teach 'em anything."

"What d'you teach 'em?" Sammy asked sharply.

"Me?" Bill said angrily. "What should I waste my time on dogs like that for? Why should I teach 'em, when they ain't fast enough to get out of their own way?"

He led the way on toward another run. In front of it he whistled, and instantly three or four short-haired black-and-white pointers came running out from their kennel. At the touch of the daggerlike cold, they stopped and shuddered. But, lowering their heads with a resolute obedience, they ran instantly toward Bill the Dogman. There they stood before the fence, shuddering, but wagging their tails and trying to squirm through the barrier to get to the hands of the men.

It was too much for the young fellow. Tears stung his eyes. He put his hand through and let the poor creatures lick it. In his heart, there was a bitter curse. Then he heard, through a red mist of hate and passion, the voice of the Dogman.

"They don't do very well. They don't last much longer than the greyhounds. They're a lot of trouble and bother to me, I can tell you. But still they're worth their salt. They can think, too, next to the Newfoundlands. They got the brain room, and they're nacheral slaves for men to kick around. Kind of makes me sick, the way they cringe and fawn. But what nature give 'em and man sharpened was the nose. They got the only hair-trigger nose in the world. A bear, a wolf, he ain't got a nose at all, compared to a first-rate bird dog. A bird dog like these, he can read a trail two feet under crusted snow. I mean what I say. A dog like that, he's got a nose that's better than a telegraph to tell him what's on the wind and on the ground and under it. Come along!"

He waved the dogs off. But Sammy Day did not follow instantly. He paused to say: "Lemme tell you something, Bill."

"Go on and tell me," said the Dogman. "But I ain't interested in anything that you can say."

"No?" said Sammy. "I only wanted to say, you ought to be in hell."

"That what you think?" asked the big man.

"That's what I think, and I'm right."

"Maybe you are," Bill said with a strange gentleness of voice. Then he paused and looked hard at the boy. "Listen, son," he said, "you think I oughta be in hell, but where d'you think I am?"

CHAPTER SEVENTEEN

There were in this speech implications of a conscience and of a self-knowledge that staggered the Joker. It arrested the flood of his condemnation.

They had come to a run of dogs very different from any that he had seen before on the place. In fact, whether they were dogs or wolves, he could hardly be sure, except that he never before had seen wolves with coats broadly slashed with white, brown, and black, as were the coats of these. They seemed much larger, also, than the average wolf. They were big enough to stand, say, with Newfoundlands or the heavy Saint Bernards. Their heads, too, were of varying shapes, some very wolfish indeed, but others with more pronounced stops, others with no more stop than a bull terrier.

Bill the Dogman looked over the great yard of these animals. There must have been fifty of them. "Look at 'em!" he said. "There's fifteen years of work."

"What are they?" asked Sammy.

"They ain't anything," said the other. "Fifteen hard, sloggin' years, and the cursed breed won't stay fixed. They can run. They can stay. They got noses. They can read a trail. They'll work faithful. They got affection in 'em. But they ain't fixed. Cross 'em together, and the get is no good. It's enough to make a man sick. You say I oughta be in hell. Well, I'm in hell, all right, and there's a part of it."

Sammy stared, transfixed. He understood, now, in part. Bill the Dogman was literally giving up his existence to create a breed of dogs that could endure Arctic weather, which would have the well-furred coat of a Husky and the nose of a bird dog, the brains of a Newfoundland, the wild, savage will to live of the wolf, the foot of a greyhound, and the indomitable grit, the great fighting heart of a bull terrier.

As the young fellow realized this, he was impressed, softened. He almost pitied the great, fierce, brutal man. In his way, Bill was an artist, and a great one. Yet he had nothing to show but failures. He had got a magnificent type of dog, but he could not make the breed stick, as he put it. The interbreedings of the type simply proved that it was a species.

Suddenly, he said: "You haven't had time, Bill, to melt all of those alloys into one bit of the right sort of metal. You need more time."

The tall man turned to him with a sigh. "Yeah, I know," he said. "I need more time, and I need more money, too, and one more year ain't … Here, come along, will you? I'll show you something pretty to the eye."

He led the way, and the young man followed, deeper in thought than ever. He concluded, from what had just been said, that the Dogman had used up nearly the last of his resources. There remained to him about a year. That was all. After that, he must call his magnificent experiment a failure. Yes, the time was short, and Bill was no longer young.

"You want a perfect dog, eh?" asked Sammy.

"I want a perfect dog," agreed Bill, "and the Nome Sweepstakes. A perfect dog, that'll breed true. That's all that I want."

They came, now, to the next run and, in it, Sammy saw two or three score of the oddest mongrels he had ever seen in his life. As a lot, they were as motley as the team that had pulled the sled into Circle City.

"You picked your team from this lot, eh?" asked Sammy.

"Maybe," answered Bill. "I ain't saying. Look at 'em. These are the failures. These are the rank failures. Most of 'em are the get of that lot of the right breed in the next pen. Cross those demons, and this is the result … anything. It's enough to make a man's heart break, I'm tellin' you."

"Yes," Sammy agreed with all his heart, "it's enough to break any man. I'm mighty sorry for you, Bill."

"I'm not askin' you to be sorry," replied the surly Bill. "But look at the mangy lot of 'em, will you? That bunch that I've bred to the right type … that bunch that I was gonna make a new breed out of and call 'em the Billdog … well, this is their get. They ain't no more fixed than nothing at all. They're just a ragged lot of useless tramps … except here and there is enough to pick out a team that's better than anything they have driftin' around Circle City. But they ain't what I want. They're mongrels. They ain't a type."

Sammy nodded. "You never could fix a breed, eh?" he asked.

"Yeah, I fixed a breed," replied the other. "You come, and I'll show you what's left of 'em."

They came to a small run, the fence of which was of a double thickness and a double height. It was all snow, within, without a sign of a shelter from the wind and the cutting cold. And on the snow lay a big dog, short-haired, insensible to the weather, as it appeared, for it lay flat on its belly, with its nose between its paws.

Then Sammy started with a new idea. "There's one of your dogs frozen to death," he said.

"That there dog?" said Bill. "Frozen to death? That's one of a breed that don't freeze. That limb of Satan. No, he ain't a limb. He's Satan himself."

"I should think that that wind would blow straight to the heart of him," said the boy.

"Look at his fur, you fool," Bill the Dogman said.

The Joker looked closely, and now he saw that the wind was parting this short hair, but never parting it deeply. In fact, it was what Bill had called it, not hair at all, but a silky, close-growing fur. A seal could not have been better protected against the freezing waters of the Arctic than was this animal by his coat.

"Short," went on Bill, as one thinking aloud. "And light, too. Ain't nothin' to pick up water and let it freeze to ice and clog him. Ain't no weight to that fur, but it's warmer than toast. He don't need no shelter from nothin'. If he did, he'd dig a hole right through the bottom of Alaska, and come out on the far side, around one of them South Sea Islands. That's the kind that little beauty is."

"Hey, you!" Bill called out. The dog did not stir.

"Deaf?" asked Sammy.

"Deaf?" echoed Bill. "That brute can hear them talking in China. He hears us thinking like you hear a watch tick. But he don't feel like payin' no attention."

Sammy yelled again: "Hey, Satan!"

The dog raised its head, turned it, and yawned in the direction of the men. The heart of the young fellow leaped. "That's the finest head I ever saw!" he declared.

"That's the finest dog that you ever saw," said the other. He paused, nodding, filled with thought. "That son of sin, he's the finest dog in the world."

"Is he?" Sammy asked, ready to be convinced. For there was something at once so wise and so wild in the appearance of this dog, that his whole being was stilled with admiration and with awe.

His employer went on: "There's about a hundred twenty pounds of him. He's as strong as a horse, as wise as a fiend, as brave as a devil, and as fast as a greyhound. He can scent a bird on the wing in the middle of the sky. He can jump up there among the clouds, catch that bird, and have him for dinner. He can lick ten times his weight in wild wolves."

"I thought," Sammy said, in the pause that followed, "I thought that no domestic dog could ever stand up for a moment against a real wild wolf. I thought they had biting powers that ..."

"Can you bite India rubber?" asked Bill. "No more can you bite Satan, there. The teeth of a lion, they'd slip off of him. The horns of a wild bull, they'd glance away from him. He's everything that I've said about him, and yet he ain't worth a damn!"

"Not worth ...?"

"Not worth a feather. Not worth anything cheap that's good for anything at all. Believe me when I tell you. I know. I've tried to train him and his kind. It ain't any use. I been ripped and chawed from head to foot. Pete brained one that had me down by the throat ..." He fumbled at his neck and sighed. Then he continued: "John, he shot one that had me down by the leg and was workin' his way up to my throat in his turn. No, they ain't a thing that can be done with them dogs. Satan is inside of them all, but this is the chief devil of the lot. Satan is his right name and his only name."

"Too bad," said Sammy. "You can't do anything with him?"

"Haven't I tried?" Bill the Dogman shouted, suddenly wild with fury. "You fool, would a man pick up a diamond that weighed a pound and let it go without putting it in his pocket and giving it a shine? Of course, I tried my best with him, and I know dogs. But there wasn't any use. He was always waitin'. And what he waited for was my throat. Finally, I give it up. That Satan, there, he learned even to wag his tail, to put me off guard. He used to whine, he was so glad to see me. It was all a lie. He even learned to lead a dog team, and didn't eat the other dogs because he was so busy waitin' for his chance at me. And when he led a team, that team traveled, I'm tellin' you. He can follow a trail that's a foot under the snow. He's got brains ... he's got everything ... but his name is Satan!"

Sammy gasped. "Useless, eh?" he asked.

"Useless and accursed," said Bill the Dogman. "Look at him laugh at me now."

"Couldn't beat him to it?" asked the boy.

"Beat him? I've beat him till I thought that he was dead. And when I come close enough, he opened the only eye he was able to see out of, and he sunk his teeth in my right foot. That's why I'm limpin' today."

CHAPTER EIGHTEEN

Still, in a silence, they considered the great dog. He stood up finally, and returned their stare with green-eyed interest. That glance was enough to convince Sammy.

"Yes," he said, "you've found the right name for him." Bill said nothing. "Speaking of the wolves," said Sammy, "did you ever see him fight one?"

"No," answered the other thoughtfully, "I can't hardly say that I exactly seen him fight with 'em, but I seen the results of the fight. Sometimes, along in the white starving time of the winter, the wolves, they come around here pretty frequent. There ain't anything that a wolf likes better than good, fat dog meat. They're like the Indians in that. But mostly always they find that the fences are too hard to break through, or else there's too many of the dogs inside.

"But one night I heard a ruction out here, and that ruction didn't stop for a long time. Finally, I come out to give a look and see what was happenin'. And there I found that three big timber wolves, fightin' thin, had started clawin' and chewin' and scrapin' their way through Satan's fence, and Satan, of course, he'd done his best at fightin' and chewin' and scrapin', to get out to them. That's the way that it looked. Anyway, the wolves got through. I guess they felt pretty lucky when they seen that there was only one dog all by himself. And so they got inside, and they must've pretty soon wished that they was outside."

"But," said Sammy, "if they got in, three in a pack … I thought that wolves knew how to hunt and fight together?"

"Yeah, they know that. But they don't know how to hunt Satan himself, I'm tellin' you. They don't anywheres near know enough for that."

"What happened?"

"How do I know? I told you before that I didn't see any of the fightin', except the last bite."

"What did you see then?"

"I seen two wolves lyin' dead on the snow, with their throats tore open, and I seen Satan lyin' on top of the third wolf and chawin' his neck, kind of calm and leisurely, like he wasn't much interested."

"Was he bleeding all over?"

"I didn't come close enough to see that. He was bloody all over, but I don't guess much of that blood was his. I raked out the bodies of those wolves and I patched up the fence. While I patched it up, Satan came down and stood there on the inside, and just hated me with his eyes."

Sammy shuddered. "You found the right name for him," he remarked. "Satan … I don't see how he could kill three wolves in one fight, though," he added.

"Because he was bigger, stronger, faster, trickier, and had had a pile more professional experience, if you want some reasons," replied the Dogman. "He knows all the tricks in the world. I seen him break into another yard out here and kill another dog … one of his own breed. That was something to do. What he done was to dive into the snow like a seal and come up like a snake, with all his teeth locked in the throat of that cousin of his. I ran as fast as I could, but that other dog was dead in five seconds. Then I stood there for an hour with a rifle at my shoulder, wantin' to shoot the brains out of his head, and him ravin' and ragin' at me, and darin' me to do my worst, though he knows damn' well just what a rifle means, and mostly he's as careful as can be when you got a gun in your hands."

The curiosity of the Joker was growing apace. "How did you start this breed?" he asked.

"I didn't start it," was the surprising answer. "It was a chance cross. A way-out cross that I never had planned. And the litter founded this worthless breed of fiends. Ever since, I've kept them to themselves, hopin' that one day I'd be able to get a tame one out of them. But I ain't never had luck. I've begged and prayed to let one of these dogs be right, but my prayers ain't been heard. Maybe I didn't pray right, so far as I know."

"Maybe not," said Sammy with a faint smile.

"Well," said Bill, "come on and see the rest."

He led the way, but the Joker lingered behind to have another look at the glorious head, the flawless body of Satan. One did not need to be told that he was a rare creature. His body had the hound lines that mean speed, and yet he was heavy and strong. His head had the stop that gives plenty of room for brains, and he looked as light and agile as a cat, even while standing still, with his 120 pounds.

They came to the next run. There, lying on the snow, was a dog so like Satan that Sammy cried out: "How did he get in here so quickly? I thought that there was a fence in between!"

"It ain't Satan," Bill said. "Here's a dog that weighs fifteen or twenty pounds more than Satan. There ain't so much poison in him … there ain't so much speed, brains, or plain devil. But he's worse than a tiger to try to handle. The whole breed is. I got ten now, and every one of 'em has to have a separate run. A million dollars' worth of dog flesh, if it was only right in the head and the heart … a billion dollars' worth of fame for me, too. But it's all wasted!"

"Can't you even turn the females and the males in together?" asked the boy.

"It's mighty risky," said the other. "They might be friendly for five minutes, and do murder afterward. There ain't any friendship. There ain't any trust. There ain't any faith in any of these brutes. They're wrong. They're all as wrong as fiends, and I mean what I say."

He turned suddenly about and strode toward the house. Sammy followed him, graver and more thoughtful than before, wondering much at what he had seen and what he had heard.

They had almost reached the house, when the big man turned and called sharply: "Get an axe out of that shed, there, and go cut some brush."

"How much?" asked Sammy. But Bill the Dogman had turned and walked on toward the house without making a reply.

It had seemed to the Joker that the barrier of hostility between them had been broken down somewhat. Now he saw that his trials were beginning all over again. Yet he felt that they could never be quite so maddening as he had found them before, for he understood the background of torment that was pinching the brain of Bill the Dogman, the peculiar despair that shrouded the existence of the older man, and he had a sympathy for it.

The ambition of Bill might not be the loftiest in the world, but he had come maddeningly close to achieving it. He had formed a type of sled dog that was probably a higher average than any other in the world. That type he had been unable to form into a fixed breed. He could produce it only for one generation, at the terrible expense of constantly breeding and interbreeding with other stocks. Worst of all, he had finally produced a breed, a true, new breed, worth more than all of the rest, but this breed was cursed with a temper like that of Bengal tigers. Yes, it was enough to drive a man mad. It was not strange that people thought that the brain of the Dogman was unsound.

So thought Sammy, as he forced open the ice-encrusted latch of the shed and, in the dimness and cold within, found the axes. One of these he selected, one of the lightest. Then he went out toward the trees to do as he was bidden.

Before him stalked Pete, the Indian, and from the door of the house came the voice of the Dogman, calling: "You do what Pete tells you to do! You keep stroke for stroke with him, or I'll know the reason why." Then he began to laugh.

Yes, the talk about Satan had put the same cruel spirit, it appeared, back in the heart of the Dogman. And Sammy went up the slope behind the Indian with drooping spirits and stumbling feet.

He prepared himself for the worst. But the worst was much worse than his imaginings. For Pete and his axe were tireless. He was an old and practiced woodsman. He knew exactly the science of the axe.

The skill of the woodsman is difficult to attain. The practiced hand swings the heavy head like a feather and makes it work with its own weight. The bungler laboriously strikes out small chips, misses the mark, takes a bite too big, or a bite too small. But most terrible of all to Sammy was to see the Indian striding before him, felling a tree with every stroke of the axe—while his own tool rebounded helplessly from the frozen surface of the wood. But he stuck to his task.

At midday, Pete put his axe on his shoulder and returned to the house. Sammy went with him and was stopped by Bill at the door.

"Go back!" roared Bill. "You ain't done a half day's work. You cut down what Pete done in his half day, before you get food or drink out of my house. Five hundred dollars a month? You ain't worth five hundred cents a year!"

The Joker considered the tall man, with a futile desire to brain him with the tool in his hand. Then he turned on his heel and went back to his task on the hill, laboring at the small-trunked, ironhard trees. All the rest of that day he worked, and all through the evening. Into the dark he still kept on with aching arms and staggering brain, until, at last, his swath through the woods was as deep as Pete's. Then he went reeling down the hill toward the house.

He found the door secured. The brutal voice of Bill the Dogman roared from the inside: "You're after hours! Nobody gets into the house at this time of night. You stay out and sleep with the dogs. I don't care if you have to eat snow!"

CHAPTER NINETEEN

Inside of that house there were three big men, well-armed in many ways. They were determined, all of them, to keep him out, and he knew it. The proof was the loud and exulting laughter of the two Indians. Inside was danger, but inside were warmth and food, also.

Sammy did not hesitate. He swung his axe with all his might and smashed the latch. The door creaked and sagged slowly inward.

As he stepped through, he saw the Indians prepared for him and in a manner that he had not imagined. They had taken the hint from their employer and were not using guns, but each of them had in his hand a long fish spear. Big Bill had half-stepped from his bunk, grasping a hand axe with a double-bitted head and a curved handle.

His other arm he extended toward Sammy, thundering: "You've broke your contract! You ain't obeyed orders. Get out of this house and get fast! John, Pete, run the skunk through with your fish spears. Ram 'em through his dirty heart!"

Sammy kicked the door shut behind him. He had broken the blade of the axe in shattering the latch; it now terminated in a jagged point, and he grinned as he looked down at it.

"You three," he said, "I'll split the head of one of you, no matter what the other two do to me. Ram a spear into me, and I'll push myself up the haft of it till I get a fair swat at the head of one of you. You, Bill, you're a liar, a sneak, and a hound. You hired me for cash and keep, and keep means food and shelter. Blankets, at least, to keep the cold out. You can't drive me out of here living, even if you can't throw me out dead. I'm going to eat, get warm, and have a sleep. I've done my day's work!"

"You've done a half day's work," said Bill the Dogman. "Pete, work around there and get behind him."

The Joker swayed the axe up in his sore hands and held it poised. The green devil was in his eyes. "I'm watching you, Pete, and you, John. I'd as soon split the skull of one of you as eat a beefsteak. Back up, or I'll brain you."

They did not back up, but neither did they advance.

"Well," Bill said sullenly, "I guess there's something in what you say, anyway. I said money and keep. Which I was a fool to say that last. Money and keep for what ain't more'n a kid, so far as usefulness goes. But if I've let myself in for something, I ain't through with you, Sam Day. Mark what I say … I ain't through with you!"

"I'm not through with you, either," answered Sammy. "Not for a year from today."

"Put the spears down," the master ordered.

He was obeyed, while Sammy, flinging his axe into a corner of the room, went looking for supplies.

Bill blew out the lantern, but enough light filtered through the cracks of the hot stove to show the Joker what he wanted.

It was cold beans and horrible coffee again. But the beans, half warmed, and the coffee, half heated, seemed delicious once more. Starvation had him by the throat, and his weary, sore hands shook so that he could hardly control the spoon that carried the food to his lips.

Yet he finished eating, and the snoring of three men was heard before he had finished filling his stomach as well as he could. Then he flung himself into his bunk and noticed, with grim amusement, that the twisted rabbit-skin blankets were still lying there. The Indians had not attempted to take back, it seemed, what he had stolen from them the night before.

He stretched himself on the hard boards of the bunk, felt his bones begin to grind through his soft flesh, and then was sound asleep before the sense of trouble grew into an actual ache.

When he awoke, it was because Bill the Dogman was shaking him.

"You don't work one day and sleep two around here," Bill said with a snarl so savage that it twisted his whole face. "Get up and come alive. You always got a talent for eating. Eat your breakfast now, and then we march."

"Where?" asked Sammy.

There was no answer. But, after breakfast, a five-dog team appeared, driven by Bill, and, at his command, Sammy, with the snowshoes strapped to his feet, started out across the white wilderness.

* * * * *

They marched for a week. Or was it for an eternity that the pain endured? For every day was as bitter to him, almost, as the horrors of the first march out from Circle City. Every day would have been worse, had it not been for two things. The first was that, after three marches, terrible as they were, his leg muscles grew more accustomed to the terrible labor to which they were subjected. They were still so sore that he hated to put pressure on them with his hands, anywhere from the hips down to the ankles. But underneath, the muscles were toughening to the new strain; at the same time, he was perfecting, carefully, his skill with the snowshoes. Jeff had been right in every particular. But Jeff was a strong man. Sammy applied to the same problem not only intelligence, but the additional intensity of a man weaker than his companions, striving to make up with craft for physical frailty. For frail he was, compared with such giants as the Dogman and the two Indians. So, after the third day, he was better able to keep up with his leader.

The second factor that eased those grim marches was that they had what appeared to be a comparatively young team of those fine animals that Bill wanted to fix as a breed and call the Billdogs. For their sake, Bill was breaking his heart.

However, this team being young, the leader repeatedly went wrong and had to be corrected. Then there were fights in the team, and the fights had to be untangled. All of these things gave Sammy breathing spells. They also gave him a chance to learn how a team is trained, to learn it from a master.

What surprised him most was that there was no petting, no coddling, no rewarding. The highest reward seemed to be merely that there was an absence of punishment. The second thing that amazed him was the patience of the Dogman when he was teaching a lesson. He was not tender, but he simply endured. With a hurricane blinding and freezing him, he would go out fifty times to show the leader the same fault and correct it. Before that week was out, it was plain that the dog was making vast strides in his advance.

A dumb, dull, speechless week it was for Sammy, days passing when he hardly exchanged a single word with his traveling mate. But on the seventh day, he ventured: "That dog is going to make a great leader, eh?"

"Great?" said the tall man, dropping his hands and staring at the boy in something like horror. "Great leader? And you've seen Klondike?"

"I never saw Klondike work," replied Sammy Day.

"Klondike's a great leader," the Dogman said. "I could name you four more. I only seen five great leaders in all the years of my life. But that thing out there, he ain't a great leader. He's hardly a leader at all. He's got nose, and wind, and strength, endurance, and speed, but he ain't a real leader. He'll just barely do. Leaders ain't made by men. They're born that way!"

He said this with a peculiar fervor, and Sammy Day did not answer. His respect for Bill the Dogman had increased a little during this trip. They had spoken very little together. But he had been forced to acknowledge the mastery of the older man in his craft. And mastery of any craft brings forth a warmth in the hearts of those who recognize it.

On the seventh day, they reached a shack that was a mere mound of snow. Bill the Dogman took out a shovel, pointed to the right spot, and Sammy trenched a way to a door, which was opened and showed, inside, a small interior walled with heavy, squared logs. There was a stove. Two bunks were built up off the floor. And there was brushwood to cut nearby. So they had heat, rest, and plenty of food for two days.

They were silent days.

As a horse will rest in a rich pasture, after the bitterness of a long winter of plowing, so Sammy rested now. He did not speak half a dozen words a day. He knew, now, just about what was expected of him, and he went about it grimly, telling himself that perhaps two or three percent of his year had been passed.

How slowly, how eternally slowly. Nevertheless, it had passed. He had made a beginning. He had snowshoe legs under him at last. He was beginning to learn something of the mysteries of training a dog team, of swinging an axe. He had learned to tolerate the food; he could assimilate it. He told himself that he was well on the way to victory.

Afterward, he could see that he had reasoned like a fool, but for the time being, he was clear enough in his hope. It gave him some little moments of comfort.

Two days they rested in the hut. Cold, damp days they were,

dark and miserable, but sunned by the fire that burned continually in the stove, devouring endless armfuls of wood.

Then they hitched the team and marched again. All of this time, Sammy had not asked once what their destination might be. So they marched out of the dim twilight of the day into the terrible blackness of the night. For five hours they marched before the Dogman made a halt.

Then he said to Sammy: "Wait here. I'll be back."

Leaving Sammy standing there, he disappeared instantly into the darkness, into the densely blowing snow, with the dog team. Sammy watched them go, glad of the chance to remain quietly, resting.

He waited half an hour and began to wonder. He waited for an hour. Then he had to stir about vigorously. For the wind increased, and there was nothing but movement to keep him warm. Doubt now, for the first time, entered his mind.

He waited another half hour, walking about, tormented by his own thoughts. At the end of that time, he knew perfectly the purpose in the mind of the Dogman—murder, without poison, knife, or gun. He intended to let the Joker perish of cold in the snow and win.

CHAPTER TWENTY

The thought literally struck him down, as though he had received a blow from a club. There, bowed in the snow, he told himself that he was no better than dead, and that the best way was simply to draw his knife and kill himself. He could fall on the point. That was one way. Or he could hold the point against a temple and hammer it into the brain with a stroke of the other hand. Then, like a bright picture illumined by the sun, he thought of Bill the Dogman and the two Indians, laughing brutally together, enjoying the end of him.

His body would probably never be found until the wolves had stripped it of clothes and flesh. There would be the skeleton, only, to blow to pieces in some Arctic gale.

He stood up. He had reached the rock bottom of despair in his fantasies. Now he rose and faced the bitter, cutting wind. He cleared his mind of panic by a great effort of the will. Then he told himself that there is a solution for every problem and that there was a solution for this one.

How could Bill the Dogman, for instance, find his way to the right trail through this smothering darkness?

No, Bill did not need to worry. He could simply get out of the way a sufficient distance and then camp. He had food with him, and the means of making a shelter. He could cook his food and the frozen fish for the dogs. They would burrow into the snow, and he would pull the warm sleeping pack about him. Yes, there was nothing for Bill the Dogman to worry about. Besides, he must have in his mind a fairly clear map of the country sketched out point by point. If it were a dark room, it was, at least, a dark room in his own house, and he could stumble toward the light.

But where could the Joker head? There was only one haven, and an empty one it would be, now. However, there was the means of warmth in it. As for food, that problem would have to be solved later on. His goal must be the little cabin where they had spent the two days. But he was a five-hour march away from it. He had not a compass to set his course, either.

Then he thought of the wind. Heavily or lightly, it had continued always from one quarter of the sky. It had beaten steadily under his right ear, all the way out. And if he could keep it steadily on his left temple all the way in, he might be able to reach the cabin. But then suppose that the wind shifted? Then, of course, he would be thrown out of all reckoning. But he had heard that for days and even for weeks the wind might blow steadily from one direction, in this frozen shoulder of the world. He must put his trust in that fact.

The thing was to note the hour on his watch, and then to abandon all thought save that of keeping the wind at the correct angle. For five hours of steady marching, he must keep hope and despair alike out of his mind. At the end of that time, he would have to begin to cut in circles to find the house. Unless he dropped from exhaustion, he would have to keep on marching until, when daylight came, he might have a sight of that low, unimportant mound of snow, so like ten thousand other wind-heaped bits of white.

He managed to light a match and look at his watch. He noted the hour in the very roots of his brain, and then he struck out.

Carefully, with every swinging stride that he made, he noted the direction from which the wind pressed against him. Now and then, he slipped a hand out of a mitten and held it up to judge the wind more accurately. Each time, he had to correct his course a little, sometimes to the right, sometimes to the left.

After a while, it seemed clear to him that the wind was pulling more into the north. Let that be as it might. For five hours he would not glance at his watch.

Five hours passed, and more, he could have sworn. He could tell by the steps he had taken, by the numb fatigue in his legs. Then he lit another match and saw that he had been a bare two hours on the way. He laughed a little. And the strong wind put its bony fists inside his mouth and puffed his cheeks like a balloon. Then he went on again. As for fatigue, he knew all about that. It was his neighbor, his familiar, now.

He passed the third, the fourth, the fifth hour, striking always into that howling storm, with the wind as his guard and guide. When he read the passing of the fifth hour on the face of the watch, he was about to commence cutting for sign. He remembered that he had had the wind behind him, coming out, and he had had to lean against it going in. His steps must, therefore, have been slower and smaller. Besides, there was the question of fatigue, like a bridle, pulling him back. So he decided that he would march on for another hour and a half to make up the difference.

It was a grim resolve, considering the wasted fountain of his strength, but, having made it, he grimly struck out again, and again he strove to banish the passage of time, all things, from his mind except the sense of the direction of the wind, alone.

At last he knew by the face of his watch that he had marched steadily for six hours and a half through the blind darkness. When he knew that, he paused and started cutting for sign of the cabin, moving around his halting point in small circles.

Before him suddenly a clamor of dogs began.

Sweeter than the sound of human singing voices was the noise of the howling, barking dogs. For where dogs were, men must be near.

Suddenly, he struck against a rock wall. No, it was wood, it was logs, and yonder was a thin ray of light that worked through a crevice. He fumbled. He found a latch—and blundered into the cabin that was his goal, to see Bill the Dogman sitting up in his bunk, with his favorite weapon, a hand axe, in his grasp.

The light that had shown through the crevice, the light by which he saw Bill, was from the worthless old junk heap of a stove that allowed the red beams to escape on all sides.

"Why, hello," said the Dogman. "Damn me, if it ain't the kid. Where you been keeping yourself?"

The young fellow went to the stove and spread his hands above its heat. It soaked into his flesh. It seemed to reach the bone. And the weight of death slipped away from his shoulders. Should he murder Bill the Dogman, as Bill had tried to murder him? He put the question to himself calmly, quietly.

Then he pulled out his knife and whetted its edge with his thumb. It was razor sharp. He held it flat on the palm of his hand and poised it. No, his nerves were too uncertain for a throw. He would have to come to close quarters with Bill, and a knife against an axe.

However, eventually he moved around the corner of the stove. A stool stood in his way. He kicked it to one side.

"'What's the matter, kid?" asked Bill. "Got the willies?"

The young fellow answered nothing. He was wondering whether he should try for the throat or trust to a thrust in the breast. He had made up his mind about one thing. He would throw up his left hand to catch the stroke of the axe, even if the blow cut through his arm and ruined it, even if he must bleed to death afterward. He would do that and the chance would come to work in close and strike for the heart.

That was the best way. An odd joy filled him. It made him smile. And, though he could not see it, it lit his eyes with green. But Bill the Dogman could see, even by that dim light.

"Murder, is it?" he asked. Suddenly he laughed and threw away the axe. "Don't be a damned fool, kid," he said.

Sammy reached the axe with a leap and picked it up. "This is a lot better," he said. "You think that you'll bluff me out by throwing away the hatchet? Why, you're no better than a fool. You meant the meanest kind of murder. Now you save yourself from me if you can."

"Murder!" exclaimed the Dogman. "You're here, ain't you?"

The young fellow laughed. "Yeah," he said. "I'm here, all right!" Then he laughed again. "Get out your knife, Bill," he ordered. "I know you sleep with it. Get it out, now, and make a fair fight of it for your rotten hide and carcass."

"Fair fight?" said Bill. "I'm fifty-five, and you're in your fightin' prime. Don't say fair fight to me."

"Murder, then," Sammy said. "Let it be murder. You deserve it. Or tell me what else was in your rotten heart when you abandoned me out there in the middle of hell?"

"Murder?" Bill echoed. "Why, you young fool, I was simply seein' if you had brains and endurance combined. That's all. How else was I to know if you had real sense in you, as well as the right kind of spunk?"

Sammy gripped the hand axe hard. But he did not strike.

Bill went on: "The wind would show you the way in, if you had any sense. If you didn't have any sense, you'd get rattled, and lie down and freeze to death."

"Well?" said Sammy.

"Well," the Dogman said, "what did I care? If you was fool enough to freeze, like that, the sooner out of the way, the better. I gotta pay you five hundred a month. Is any fool worth that much money?"

The Joker stepped back a little. "I almost think," he said half to himself, "that you mean what you say."

"Aw, shut up and feed your face and go to bed," said the Dogman. "We gotta make an early start, and I'm tired of all of this fool talk."

Only for ten seconds did Sammy stay poised, uncertain. Then, conquering temptation, he turned short away and did as Bill had commanded.

CHAPTER TWENTY-ONE

The beginning may, of course, be the most painful part of any task, but, though Sammy had gone through much, he did not find the days that followed much easier. For a demon possessed Bill the Dogman, a demon that led him on to torture Sammy with new and ingenious devices.

When he had nothing else to do, he sent him over the Grant Pass between Douglas Peak and Fern River Mountain. The pass was only six thousand feet up, but it was blocked with snow and slippery with ice. Moreover, at the time, a terrible storm was raging.

The passing of Douglas Peak was to remain forever among the nightmares in the life of the Joker. A dozen times on that expedition, he barely escaped death by falling from a dizzy height, and all through the long three hours when he was struggling down the summit, he nearly died from freezing. It was bitter cold and this, with the wind, made a torture such as he had never before experienced. Nothing pulled him through except the strength of body and leg that he had built up in the preceding weeks.

Then he made the journey around through the valleys, and there he found Bill the Dogman.

"Why did you do that, Bill?" he asked.

"I wanted to find out if the Pass would make a good shortcut," said Bill. "But from the looks of you, I don't think it will." He grinned at Sammy Day, indifferent to his sufferings.

"Why didn't you try me on this two weeks ago, when I had a touch of fever?" Sammy asked.

"I would have," the brutal Bill said, "if I'd known that you had any fever."

"You heard me chatter in my sleep all night long. That ought to have made you guess," suggested Sammy.

"No, I missed that," said Bill. "Harness up the dogs. We're startin' back for camp, and we're makin' forced marches."

"You're joking, Bill," said Sam Day. "You know that I've just come down from the Pass."

"I know that," said Bill the Dogman, "but we gotta start out. I got something on my mind."

"What's the good?" said the Joker. "You can't kill me by marching. I can keep up with you, now, and I can beat you, too, and you know it. You can't walk me to death, but you can make me hate you a little more. That's all the good it'll do you."

"Hate me?" the Dogman echoed, sneering. "D'you think that I care what a puppy like you thinks about me? Don't be a worse fool than you are by nature. Line out those dogs. We're startin' now."

So many blows had fallen upon the Joker by this time that he was not surprised, hardly resentful even, because of this command. And they made, by forced marches, the long, long trek back to the camp.

* * * * *

It was always like this. They were always, to him, insane, futile excursions. They took turns with him. It was either Pete, or John, or old Bill himself. He was never in camp more than a day or two at a time, then out he went on another agonizing march that taxed his strength to the uttermost.

He was worn as thin as a knife blade. No food seemed enough to nourish his wasting body. Finally, however, the flesh returned. It came back like strips of India rubber. It kept on increasing, until he was ten pounds over his weight of the years before. And all of this was power, ready to burn.

The cold could not kill him now. On the march, they could not pass out of his sight, leaving him hanging on the edge of the horizon. Instead, he was always alongside the sled.

But what was the purpose of these marches, except to torture him? They never carried any burden except clothes, tent, food, and stones. Yes, useless stones, the better to weight down the dogs!

And always there was a fresh team waiting for the Joker. He was working a half dozen teams of dogs in hard training, and always the pace was set by one of three fresh companions—three silent companions, at that. For both Pete and John had put the curse of speechlessness upon him. They responded to no remarks, and they made none. They communicated their ideas by gestures. As for the master, he spoke only to give commands, and one of his commands was this: "When you're on the trail with Pete or John, they're the straw bosses, and you're the gang. Don't forget that. You toe the mark for them just the same as though you were toein' it for me."

Sammy listened, nodded. Speech was not necessary, in fact, as he came to know the trail better and better.

As the months rolled by, he came to have a vast territory securely mapped in his mind. He had to have it there, regarding every possible landmark wherever they went, for he knew, by a sure instinct, that if ever he turned an ankle or struck any other bit of bad luck, his traveling mate would abandon him. Then he might have to crawl back to the camp of Bill the Dogman like a wounded beast.

He was running a thousand miles a month, he estimated. But every month, after the first one, the miles flowed more easily past him.

Yet the burden cast upon him was greater and greater. At first, the others used to take more than their share of trail breaking. Now almost all of this was left to him. He did the lion's share of the labor in pitching the camps, also. In his hands, entirely, was left the care of the dogs. When he remained in the camp, all the feeding was given to him. When he fed, on these occasions, he threw one extra fish to Satan, and smiled as the wicked monster snarled at him and snapped up the food.

But Satan pleased him. The emerald-green hate of man that gleamed in his eyes was a pleasant sight to the young fellow. He found in the dog something with which he sympathized.

Once, as he leaned on the fence of the run, staring at Satan, he found Bill himself beside him. "You like him, eh?" Bill asked.

Sammy glanced at old Bill, shrugged his shoulders, and walked away. For he attempted speech no longer with any of the three, except when it was absolutely necessary to ask Bill some question about work or about the handling of the dogs. The latter was a subject on which Bill was a great master, and it was the one theme on which he was willing to expatiate at length to the young fellow. In fact, he seemed willing to go out of his way to teach dog-punching to Sammy Day as thoroughly and as patiently as he taught his chosen dogs how to lead.

Two things kept the flame burning in the heart of Sammy. One was the sense of the passage of the months, faster and faster, and the knowledge that it brought him closer to that day when he could walk into the saloon in Circle City and call for Goldie Mahan. The other relief was to brood upon what he would do to Pete, to John, and to Bill the Dogman.

His hate was not evenly divided. Bill, of course, came in for the lion's share of it. Then followed John, the brute. Pete was a close third. As he detested them, so they detested him. And how he was to destroy them, one by one, was a problem that occupied him sweetly for hours and hours of almost every day. It shortened trails; it filled his soul with comfort. The end of the year and a day would come. When that moment arrived, he could fill his two hands with guns and start on the back trail toward his vengeance.

Sometimes he caught them casting furtive glances at him. Sometimes he heard the Indians murmuring secretly together, as they watched him. And he knew, with a warming of his whole being, that at such moments they were guessing what was in his innermost heart.

Then came the summer, brief, strangely full of flowers, and the clouds of flying birds, the scent of growth, the sudden green that covered the trees. It was not an easier time. Sleds went out, but packing came in, the building of packs on the backs of the dogs, and the running of them before him down the trail that he was beginning to know so well—running them with loads of wood or of stone. Sheer waste of labor, sheer deviltry on the part of Bill the Dogman to annoy him the more, so the Joker thought.

Always he had some companion to bully him; always there was the slipping of every possible task to him. And he had to grin and endure.

He was glad enough when the snows came again, and the white countryside called for the use of the sleds. Once more he was running before the team, breaking the trail or holding to the gee pole as the eager dogs whipped the long sleds over the snow.

There was a sort of joy in this, he found—joy in watching the dogs. He knew them very well. He knew the bluffers, who pretended to be pulling wholeheartedly, who even knew how to sham leaning into the collar, but who hardly kept their traces taut. There was the joy of reading the minds of the more willing.

He could delight himself with their splendid honesty and their splendid self-devotion to a blind cause. They seemed more and more noble. The Indians and Bill, and finally Sammy Day himself seemed, in his eyes, worthless beings, compared with the sublime devotion of those dumb beasts.

And still his time was slipping away, through the eighth month, and through the ninth month.

One day he said to Bill the Dogman: "It's no use, old-timer. You can't kill me by wearing me out on the trail. Look at me. I'm fatter than I ever was in my life. Why don't you give up this line and just take a club to my brains in the middle of the night?"

The Dogman merely grinned at him. "You're gettin' mighty tough, ain't you?"

"Yeah. I'm tough," Sammy said, sneering in return. "I'm the toughest man in Alaska, and you know it. But you don't know it as well as you're going to one of these days."

The tall man nodded. "You're kind of confident just now," he said. "But I'll take it out of you. You think you've been through hard times, but you ain't. You ain't even scratched the surface of hard times. Now I'm gonna put you right in the middle of the fire."

The young fellow waited. "When?" he asked.

"Now," said the other. "Go get Satan, and harness him up as lead dog in front of seven of his kind. You can pick the rest the way you please, but put Satan in the lead."

CHAPTER TWENTY-TWO

The dog, Satan, entertained in various ways, all of them enthralling. Sometimes he pretended calm indifference or actual friendliness, until he was close enough to use his teeth. At other times, he cast pretense to the winds and charged like a lion.

This day he was in the lion's mood. The instant that Sammy stepped inside the run, he charged. The Joker had prepared a weapon. It was a short club, the end of which was padded with several twistings of old fur. As the dog came his way, he struck hard for the head of the brute. He hit the air, and the teeth of Satan ripped open his leg above the knee.

He might have cut the tendons, had it not been that to keep his skull intact, he had swerved. As it was, he stung the Joker and made the hot blood flow. That was all. Then the penetrating finger of the cold pressed hard through the gashed flesh and began to freeze the blood, congealing and stopping the flow.

By that time, Satan was sitting down in the snow nearby, his red tongue hanging out, laughing to the very ears with delight as he watched the man and waited to see how much this first attack had crippled him. Sammy grunted, freshened his grip on the tough, rough haft of the club, and stepped forward. How vastly stronger was his grip, after these months of heavy work with the axe. How much stronger were his shoulders, too, how much surer his poise. He felt that he was twice the man he had been eight months before. And he knew that all his strength would be needed upon this day. So he measured his distance and watched the dog. When the brute got to his feet, the Joker was ready. As the dog charged, he feinted his first stroke and saw the monster swerve in and leap high—for the throat. He had not time to make a really stunning blow after his feint. He could only snap the head of the club around, quick and short, and he had the satisfaction of feeling the shock of the blow go home against the side of Satan's head.

It knocked the dog out of line. His great white fangs snapped on the empty air, but the weight of his shoulder, striking that of Sammy Day, knocked him down. To be down in front of that beast was, he knew, almost the equivalent of instant death. He twisted to his knees, therefore, with club raised, and was just in time to meet the furious onslaught of Satan, leaping through a cloud of snow dust.

He struck hard and straight, holding the blow until he was sure of the distance—holding it for the vital hundredth part of a second, as he would have done in a gunplay. And this time the blow went home. It caught the wolf dog fairly between the eyes and rolled him over and over.

The Joker started to his feet and ran forward, but Satan regained consciousness just in time. Like an eel he twisted out of the path of danger, and when the man turned, he saw the dog sitting a little distance off, his red tongue no longer lolling, but with his head tilted a little to one side in the very attitude of canine thought, while he considered his antagonist.

"That wasn't so good for you, my boy," said the Joker. And the beast, surprisingly, shook his head in agreement. That was merely to shake out the last cloud that the shock of the blow had left in the mind of the animal. But there had been a human signification in the gesture that almost paralyzed young Sammy Day. He shook his own head, in return, and set his jaw by way of reviving his own ferocious mood.

Somewhere, hidden by the brush, he knew that Bill the Dogman would be watching and enjoying this contest. But he felt, somehow, that the thing was more important than Bill knew. Bill was not in the picture. It was between himself and Satan.

As he stepped in, the sitting dog rose on all fours and swiftly circled his foe—circled, reversed direction, and then suddenly darted in. The eye could hardly follow the speed of this adroit movement. He worked on the loose surface of the snow as though it were solid. The big pads of his feet knew, somehow, the right manner of gripping that yielding surface. He bounded high. The Joker swung up the club to meet an attack upon his throat. But Satan had made only a feint, a short bound, and, descending from it, he shot in low at the man, then struck with his fangs as a snake strikes.

He aimed at neither the throat nor the legs, but right across the breast, and the fangs cut through the fur, cut through the underclothes, cut through to the skin, and opened a long gash in the flesh of the Joker. He thought he was killed. He would bleed to death before he could beat off this fiend and regain the house. But, turning, he saw Satan spring for his throat, and again, more by luck than by skill, he struck the dog fairly between the eyes. The bulk of the beast flew by him and landed heavily in the snow, plowing it up.

Turning, he forgot his wound. The pain of it was already diminishing, and he could guess that it was only a surface slash. But now he hesitated to strike again. There had been such a weight behind his stroke that he feared he might already have dashed out the brains of the beast. So he reached down and laid his grip upon the hind legs of the brute.

It was as though he had touched a snake. The dog twisted out of his feigned trance; he had been playing 'possum and he fastened his teeth in the left arm of the Joker. The man slugged him on the head with the club, and that grip loosened.

More than half-stunned, the dog lay, with terrible teeth showing beneath his grinning mouth. Then madness seized Sammy Day. He dropped the club and caught the dog by the throat with both hands, letting his grip sink in. He could feel the effort to breathe swelling beneath his hands. He could see the lolling tongue, flung out till the roots showed. But, still, the powerful, claw-shod feet of the great dog ripped away the clothes of the man. He was almost naked when that powerful body ceased struggling and lay limply in his hands. He was so naked that the cold thrust into him like knives of ice. He knew that he had only a minute of life left, unless he got to the house.

So he did not pause to learn whether or not the dog still lived. Instead, he caught the beast by the hind legs and rushed to the house, dragging the limp weight behind him. He reached the door, cast it open, and pulled his burden in with him. Then he saw that the three men were still there. Had he not heard the echo of their laughter as he approached?

Yes, there they stood before him, their laughter gradually ceasing. He could even guess why they were laughing—because he had gone out to harness Satan for a dog team. So he dropped the limp burden to the floor, and the dog lay where he flopped. He, the Joker, was bleeding from the arm, the leg, the breast.

He gave his wounds one glance. They were surface affairs, save for the two deep incisions of the fangs in his arm. Perhaps there might be blood poisoning as a result of them, but he could not bother about such a matter now. Chance would have to be trusted.

"Give me some clothes to wear," he said to the Dogman. "Your damn dog has spoiled these."

Bill went to a corner of the room and began picking old garments off pegs on the wall. Over his shoulder, he said: "You brought me in a dead dog, eh?"

The young fellow said nothing except: "Give me those clothes!"

He took them. The Indians stood in a corner, looking at one another and then at the beast that lay still, near the stove.

The Joker cast off the tattered fragments of his other suit and put on the new outfit. It was old, it was malodorous. Here and there, chiefly about the breast, the clothes were encrusted with grease. But that did not matter. They were twice or three times as heavy as the clothes that Nagle had given to him. But they were at least warm. Now that he was an iron man in body as well as soul, the weight of clothes did not trouble him. Silence reigned for a few minutes.

He had hardly finished his dressing, when the dog coughed and rose shakily to its feet.

Pete took a rifle from pegs on the wall. John grasped a fish spear. Bill the Dogman gathered up one of his favorite hatchets.

But Sammy walked straight up to the monster. He had beaten him once with his bare hands. He would beat him again.

The dog grinned horribly and showed his shining teeth. But he was still staggering.

The Joker took him by the scruff of the neck. "Show me the harness that goes on this brute," he said.

"Where's the other dogs of his kind that go with him?" Bill the Dogman asked suddenly.

"If you want a whole team like him, you can go harness them yourself," said the Joker. "I've done a day's work!"

CHAPTER TWENTY-THREE

The Dogman did not argue. He gave Sammy Day a harness and muzzle for the killer, and the Joker put them on. After the muzzle was in place, the eyes of the dog ceased looking red and dazzled, and began to appear their natural, fiendish green.

"How did you do that?" asked Bill.

The young fellow laughed. He was feeling the pain of his three wounds, and when he laughed, he particularly felt the newly formed scab cracking and breaking along the gash across his breast.

"With these," he said. He held out his hands, and specifically watched the two Indians gape and stare at him. They regarded his hands as though they had been pointed guns.

The young fellow laughed again. He felt both bitter and proud.

Bill the Dogman appeared satisfied with what he had seen. Now he turned sharply around and muttered in Indian dialect to his two servants. They grunted in reply and immediately left the house. Then Bill began to pull on a parka. When he had done this, he yawned and sat down on a stool, regarding the young fellow.

"You've got everything beat, ain't you?" he said.

The young man grinned in reply. "I've got you beat," he said, "you murdering four-flusher. I've got you lashed to the mast."

"Have you?" the Dogman asked in as weary a voice as a parent receiving a thousand-times-told answer from a child.

"Yes. You may finish me off some night when I'm asleep," said the Joker, "but that's the only way you'll beat me. Understand? Otherwise, I've got you stopped."

Bill grinned, his long chin resting in the hollow of his palm. "All right," he said. "I hope you're right."

"Yeah, I'll bet you hope I'm right," said Sammy.

"You done enough for glory already," said Bill the Dogman. "Look at Rourke. Even the little while that he lasted, it made him sort of famous. They still talk respectful about him. You done enough for glory. Now you got four months of misery left before you. You've got five hundred a month for the time you've worked, too. That's four thousand dollars. I'll pay you off in gold dust. Why don't you take the four thousand and quit and walk into Circle City? Nobody'll mock you. They'll all admire you, walking into town in my clothes. Nobody'll laugh at the clothes, and nobody'll laugh at you. They'll want to know how you did it."

For the first time, the young fellow stared in total bewilderment. He felt that he could understand and interpret every other thing the Dogman had said to him, but not this. At last he found a clue. "You'd rather pay the cash and get rid of me," he said, "than have me beat you on the bet? Is that it? But I'll see you in Hades first. I'm going to fill out my year with you.

"And then come back and do three murders, eh?" said Bill.

Again Sammy was stopped. For those very words were on the tip of his tongue. "Well," he said, "this isn't the last year of my life. But it may be next to the last of yours."

"Sure," Bill the Dogman said. "I might die tomorrow, for all I know. It'd grieve me a lot to die, if you wanna know the truth." He grinned a wide, inhuman grin.

Just then one of the Indians shouted outside the house. The Dogman rose and led the way out, beckoning to the Joker. And there they found seven dogs hitched in front of a single long toboggan.

They were all of the breed that the recluse wanted to make famous as the Billdog. They were all of the breed that couldn't be fixed. And magnificent fellows they were. Every one of them, at one time or another, had acted as leader in the teams that Sammy constantly drove for this strange master.

Bill looked them over, his eyes narrowed, his head far back. "How's that," he said, "for a team to win the Nome Sweepstakes? They'd feel kinder funny, wouldn't they, if I went out and won that race with them dogs? Answer me! It'd tickle them right in the middle of the funny bone, wouldn't it?"

Sammy Day could not help answering: "Yeah. It'd tickle 'em right there, I guess. But you won't win."

"Won't I?" the Dogman asked with an odd humility in his voice.

"No, you won't win," said Sammy. "Nothing good will ever happen to you, you rattlesnake. There's too much poison in you already."

"Yeah, there's poison in me," Bill replied, nodding his head almost absently. Then he turned and spoke sharply. "Where's that Satan?" he demanded.

"Lying in a corner inside the house," was Sammy's answer.

"Go get him and bring him out."

Then Bill strode away toward the shed, while Sammy Day went back into the house and put the lead on the big dog. He did not try to resist. He seemed to know perfectly the meaning of the muzzle. He whined a little and swept the floor with his tail when the man approached. There was not the slightest token that murder was still in his heart. But Sammy could see the green in the eyes, and he understood.

The young fellow brought him outside in time to see old Bill striding along on his snowshoes and carrying to the loaded sled two heavy bands of iron, together with a powerful chain, shining with the grease that had been rubbed on it to keep away rust. He dropped the chain with a loud rattle upon the sled and lashed it in place.

"Put the Satan dog in the lead," he said.

Sammy obeyed. As he led the gray beauty to the first place, past the other dogs, he saw them shrink, one by one, wincing away from the menace as it drew near. Sammy harnessed Satan and then went back. He found Bill the Dogman in the act of putting two heavy hammers in the luggage.

"Mush away!" called Bill.

"Will Satan mush?" asked the young man.

"Try and see."

"What's the trail?"

"The Tree."

The young fellow nodded with satisfaction. He knew that trail perfectly. It was distant only half a day of steady marching, and there were no particular difficulties to master. As a matter of fact, it was the easiest trail that he could imagine.

The Tree had its name from the fact that it was a freak of nature and grew by itself in the midst of the Arctic plain. Besides being lonely, it was a comparative giant, for it had a trunk at least six inches in diameter and grew to ten or twelve feet in height. Within sight of it was no vestige of vegetation whatsoever.

That was why Sammy nodded and smiled a little with relief. He could not guess that all his difficulties, compared with what lay before him, had been as nothing.

"Start off! Mush!" called Bill the Dogman.

Long and high-pitched rang the cry of the young man, and as he yelled, he looked at Satan, wondering. Pearl gray, gray as creeping mist, statue-like, the dog stood in his soft, perfect coat, but at the call of command, he leaned into his harness.

The other dogs were slower on the start, well-trained as they were. They were so much slower that Satan took up all the slack between him and the sled, and still he leaned and lengthened, while the eyes started in the head of the boy. The big dog apparently did not have to paw and scrape for a footing. It was as though his broad pads found good ground firmly under him where he stood. All of his strength came to bear, and slowly, surely, the sled began to move from the single effort of this Hercules among dogs before the rest of the team jumped into their work, and off went the load at a trotting pace, then at a running pace.

"*Hai!*" cried the two Indians.

The Joker, as he flashed past them, could see that there was a leer on both of their faces—a leer, mingled with real wonder and curiosity, and something, he could not help feeling, like pity, also. What did they know?

He was running fast on his snowshoes, running, now, with all the skill that he had learned in one brief lesson. Running, also, with the months of experience behind him—eight thousand miles of highly condensed experience.

They went for half an hour like this. He was hardly aware of the effort he was making to keep up. He was too concentrated on the work of the gray marvel in the lead. The whole team was transfigured. Every dog surpassed itself. After a few commands, he was amazed to see that Satan seemed to know the trail perfectly. It was not necessary to give directions after that.

Then, as the team fell to a hard-pulling walk, going up a steep slope, he was aware that he was alone. He looked back and saw the Dogman far behind, almost lost. Bill waved frantically, but the young fellow pretended not to understand. At the top of the rise, he sent the dogs on again at full pace, himself running with a long, free stride.

When he looked back again, Bill was lost to view. It was not a half day's march to the Tree, going at such a pace. It was a scant two and a half hours. He could hardly believe it when they arrived.

Reaching the Tree, Satan halted and lay down in the snow under its naked branches. The other dogs dropped, too, and no wonder. For the run had been hard. Past them and their heaving sides, their red, lolling tongues, he went with little interest.

It was the leader that he wanted to examine, for it seemed to him that the big dog had pulled at least half the load during the entire distance.

When he reached the dog, he paused in amazement, for Satan was not panting fast. His red tongue lolled, rather, in luxurious ease.

The man leaned and placed his hand over the heart of the gray beauty, the misty gray side of Satan. Under his hand he felt the soft fur, deep and warm, and the body shrinking in instinctive horror from his touch. The heart of the dog beat steadily, with a great, powerful, slow thumping.

No, Satan was not troubled by this day's mushing. Sammy was still marveling when Bill the Dogman at last came up. He was badly spent, his head more bowed than usual, and he was breathing hard. He said not a word, but slumped on the sled and sat there with his head fallen for half an hour, at least.

A sort of pity welled up in the young man, thinking of what the Dogman must have been in his youth—tireless, long-striding, his will indomitable. Even now he could beat most men on the trail, beat them with consummate ease. But he had trained a tireless automaton in the young man.

Finally, Bill rose and took the two iron bands and the chain attaching them from the sled. He took the hammers, also, and, with Sammy's aid, he riveted the first band of iron strongly about the bottom of the Tree. Then he went to Satan and unharnessed him and riveted the second band as securely around his neck. When he finished, he threw the discarded harness upon the sled and turned the team.

He stood beside the load for a time, scowling at Satan, then, shifting his glance, he scowled at the young man. “You’ve got so you can run a little,” he commented.

The young fellow said nothing.

“Well,” went on the Dogman, “you won’t have to do much running for a while. Stay here and keep Satan company till I come back.”

CHAPTER TWENTY-FOUR

Then he drove out of sight along the back trail. The young fellow sat down on a high-arching root of the Tree to wait. He sat there until he grew very cold, and still the Dogman did not return.

Satan had not stirred. Now he got up and suddenly began to dig in the snow. He dug down until he had made a good hollow for himself, and there he lay. Presently, the lips of the hole caved in. The dog was buried, but the Joker knew that he would be safe. Enough air filtered through to enable him to breathe.

Five minutes later he learned why the dog had buried himself in the snow, for a blizzard suddenly split the air and shrieked like a white-armed fiend through the branches of the tree, while its trunk trembled like a violin string under the bow with the vibration of the blast. It blew continuously for two days.

He dug himself into the snow like the dog. And there he lay. But he froze there. He had to dig down to where the dog lay curled, its tail over its nose. Sometimes, while he was digging down, the Joker felt that the wind would blow him off his feet. But he got down to Satan at last, and then he lay down beside the dog.

As the snow blew over them, increasing in thickness, he thought that he would stifle. He had to control his breathing, taking small drafts of the rank air. But gradually, he became accustomed to this. It was the cold on one side of his body that threatened to find his heart and stop it. He embraced the furry body of Satan and found half-warmth in that way, but his back was ice.

Again and again he worked out of the deepening hole in the snow and tried to face the wind. Again and again the cold fury of it snatched the breath from his lips and hurried him back to the shelter. During all that time, Satan did not stir.

Forty-eight hours is a long time to remain with a tree and a dog and a hurricane for company. There was only one problem to occupy his mind, and that was how he could remain alive. But a fascinating problem it proved.

He had to guard against frostbite. He had to guard against freezing. For the forty-eight hours, he did not sleep. In the meantime, famine began to grip him, working like an acid in his stomach. But that was as nothing to him. In those moments when the mere thought of existence did not enthrall him, he could ponder the question of Bill the Dogman.

He could see plainly that it was not a question, in the mind of Bill, of literally stripping him of the possibilities of life. It was simply a challenge to the Joker's pride. He was only half a day's march from the house. He was less than that if he got to his feet and allowed the hurricane to blow behind his back, hurling him along. But the man had told him to stay and keep Satan company. Why?

Perhaps it was merely the force of the blizzard that kept Bill from returning for him. He hugged that thought to his breast. Bill would come back when the wind fell. But Bill did not come.

The storm ceased. Sammy Day, cramped, numb, weak from hunger and sleeplessness, staggered about in the open, fresh air, and felt that the air itself, to him, was almost food.

But that day passed, and it did not bring the Dogman. Then he understood perfectly. It was a challenge to his pride. For he could very well walk to the house and say that the bargain was not being fulfilled, as he had said once before. He had bargained for food and keep, and he was getting neither now. No, it was not strictly within the letter of the law, but it was a challenge to his pride. Bill wanted to make him admit that he was beaten.

Well, why not admit it, for that matter? But at this possibility, he almost choked with wrathful determination. The Dogman had not been able to walk him or work him into submission and despair. Even with this new problem, he should not conquer.

Suddenly, Sammy heard his own voice ringing loudly in the still, white waste: "I'll be damned before I'll give up! I'll see the chain rust in two before I leave Satan!"

He was startled to hear his own voice. There is a saying, current among all dwellers in the wilderness, that when a man begins to talk to himself, his brain is losing its balance. He heard a soft sound of crunching snow, and, turning, he saw Satan's head and shoulders appearing above the brim of the hole in the snow. Steadily, head high, the dog gazed at him. It was as though he had understood the vow that had just been spoken.

The young fellow went to him, his heart suddenly warmed, and took the muzzle from his great head. The dog sank his teeth in the nearest arm! It might have been the end, but there was a weapon at hand. He picked up a short loop of the iron chain and smote the dog over the head. Stunned, but not dead, he dropped to the snow. Through the dirty furs that clad his arm, the man felt the bite. The teeth had grated against the bone. The pain was exquisite, and did not cease for hours.

But suddenly, through the fierce anger that he felt, came a new idea. It robbed him of his hatred of the beast. What he was, man must have made him. Or was it true that the entire breed was tainted with a peculiar madness? In either case, the dog was not to blame. So the man nodded and sighed.

He went back again to where Satan stood, his head high, but marked with blood where the heavy iron links of the chain had broken the skin across his skull. He did not flinch. Upon his head the man put his mittened hand, and there was no attempt to bite. Only the still, green fire burned in the eyes with a ceaseless horror of hatred.

"Look," said the man through his teeth, "I'm going to beat you, too, Satan."

And the beast, beautiful as a misty gray statue, stood motionlessly, regarding the man with that undying green light in his eyes. And, looking up, the dog saw the same color in the glittering eyes of the man.

The third day had ended. The fourth day began. The hunger pangs were worse than before, worse than the man ever had known, though he was not unfamiliar with them. But the terrible cold of the Arctic was eating into his vitality. Already his head swam. His feet tottered as he walked. He would have to give up.

But something kept him from walking toward the house, no matter how many times he turned toward it. The thought of its warmth, its comfort, its food was an agony that drew his face a thousand times in that direction. But always his pride welled up and stifled such an impulse. He told himself that he had taken his oath. A sort of madness came over him. He was willing to die for his determination.

Meanwhile, he must live if he could. He must fight for that. He must live, and the dog must live, also. He went to Satan and felt his belly. The beast was frightfully wasted. There was no snarling, no complaint. In the eyes of the dog, there was only one yearning—to be at the throat of the man. But he had learned his lesson several times over—it was dangerous to put teeth in the body of this man. The aftereffects were bad. So he was waiting with consummate patience for a better opportunity. When it came, one side rip of the fangs would be enough. And the man knew the mind of the beast with a perfect knowledge.

Then Sammy made up his mind to the proper idea. Somewhere

there were probably rabbits, lean and thin, at this time of the year, but if there was a bare spark of life in them, it was life that he could transfer to his own veins and the veins of the dog. So with his knife he cut some twigs from the branches of the Tree and made little snares, as he had made them in a more southerly land in his boyhood. He made them and voyaged out into the snow to find rabbit tracks.

The day was still. The sky was the color of Satan, pearl gray, and presently, a mile from the Tree, he found what he wanted—the unmistakable signs of a rabbit run. Then he set the traps, five of them.

He looked at the last one with a sigh. They had been made and set. Now he would have to wait. He waited the rest of the fourth day, grinning at the pains of famine. Then he went out and looked at his traps.

They had not been set in vain. By two of them were bits of fur stuck to the snow with blood, and the broad tracks of a wolf were around them! He turned, marched across country for an hour, found more and thicker signs of rabbits, and set the five traps again.

He waited through the fifth day, and on the sixth day of the agony, he walked slowly, feebly forth to see the results.

There were four spots of blood by the traps and the baits of tender lichens that he had collected. There were four spots of blood where four rabbits had been. And the tracks of the wolf were there, also.

A wolf! A whole month of food, if only he could put a bullet through it. But he had no gun. No, Bill the Dogman had seen to that. He had included the oath against guns in the first contract.

Sammy, gathering up the traps, knew that death was looking him in the face. Then he turned and went back toward the Tree. As he went, he heard a strange music that wailed through the buzzing in his ears, and, lifting his head, he saw not a hundred yards away, the form of a gray wolf, a monster, howling as if in mockery.

CHAPTER TWENTY-FIVE

The seventh day passed in a stupor. He tried to think, but thought was impossible. The springs of his imagination had dried up in him. He could only remember that a fat wolf was the best of diets to a hungry Indian. He could only think of gristle and meat and bone under his teeth—a whole wolf, a whole mountain of meat!

Slowly, he trod over the miles that he had walked in this desperate land, taking the steps one by one in his imagination.

Then the eighth day came, and he knew that he was near the end. It might be that he could still drag himself over the white waste to the house of Bill the Dogman. But he could not be sure. Besides, he had barred the thought with a resolution too great.

So on the eighth day, the long and terrible eighth day of his misery, he went forth to try the rabbit traps again, his mittened hands full of bait. He tried a fourth direction, set the traps, and then started back toward the Tree. Twice his snowshoes dug into the snow and he fell on his knees. Each time he rose slowly, pushing himself up on his hands with trembling arms.

The white universe was spinning about him as he came to the

Tree, and there he saw, with utter amazement, that Satan was licking his breast and his paws with an air of well-fed content.

He came closer, bewildered. It was the red stain of blood that he saw! Blood from what?

There was a cut on the back of the dog's neck and another on his shoulder. Amazed, he stared at the dog, and Satan, his tongue lolling, seemed to grin sympathetically in response. He looked off in his bewilderment, and then he saw the cause—a great gray wolf limping far away, on the horizon, looking by that dim light as large as a horse.

The wolf, then, had come in to dine more liberally than on rabbit meat, and he was going away on three legs! Three legs? Yes, and there were probably other wounds as well. The man, drawing in a great breath, began to laugh. He reeled with weakness as he laughed. Far spent was he.

Then he took the trail of the wolf and walked steadily along after it. He was weak. His knees sagged, but a terrible fire of hope was burning in him. He remembered how he had completed those first trails behind Bill the Dogman, how he had thought out his work step by step. So he did now. He possessed the skill. It was only weakness that made him blunder with the snowshoes. But weakness may be supplemented by skill. With careful pondering he walked along the trail until he almost stumbled over the body of the gray wolf.

The beast sat on its rear legs, huge head and shoulders raised, and snarled at him. Then it rose and went skulking ahead on three legs, wavering, but out of sight before it ended its run.

The man, dizzy with weakness, continued along that trail. Now and then he looked for blood, but there was no blood. And sometimes he told himself that he was a fool. If the wolf was losing no blood, it was losing no strength. He tried to remember how it had looked as it had sat on the snow before him, but he could not be sure. Had it been worried about the throat? Was there blood there?

Into the ninth day walked the Joker. Then he found the gray

wolf at the death. It lay prone, head outstretched on the snow, but when he came near, it got laboriously to its haunches. It bared its great fangs and waited silently. Death must be close to it, but death was close to the man, also.

He started around the great beast. Bigger than a lion it seemed as it hitched itself around painfully to meet him. Its hindquarters seemed paralyzed, but there was no lack of fire in the eyes, and there was danger in the fangs. He took out his knife and gripped it. His hand was trembling. He stripped off the mitten. In twenty seconds that hand would freeze, but now his grip, for the instant, was surer. Then, making three quick steps around the struggling brute, he flung himself in.

It was all in that first stroke. Either he would find the life of the wolf or the wolf would find his. Driving his knife down with the weight of his fall behind it, he struck in. The shock of the fall knocked the breath and the wits out of him. Then, rising slowly, pushing himself up on his shaking hands, he saw the wolf lying still, its long red tongue protruding. The knife point had found the heart!

He dragged the mitten back over his numb fingers. Then he began to work with the knife again. It bent back, as though the razor edge were dull. Such was his weakness, he could barely get on with the work, worrying the knife through the joint as he quartered the carcass.

The lightest quarter, when he had finished, made his load. It could not have been more than twenty pounds, but the weight seemed to drag him down to the ground. Then, with dizzy head, he started on the back trail.

He had little memory of that homeward trail, if the Tree could be called home, with Satan for company and host.

Once, he remembered, the icy numbness, the dreadful fatigue, overcame him, and he recovered his senses, lying face down in the bitter cold of the snow. But he got to his feet and went on. Once he paused, standing stock-still, and wondered why he did not eat some of the meat raw.

But the madness drenched and darkened his brain. It seemed to him that there was only one escape for him, and that was to reach the big dog and share this prize with him. Greater follies have obsessed the brains of men near to death.

So he continued on that dreadful trail, the worst that he had ever known. To make each step required forethought and unending labor. And when he saw the Tree at last, wavering against the horizon, it did not seem close, but a whole infinity of labor distant. A hundred yards from his goal, it seemed more impossible than ever. Then he stumbled to his knees and went forward, crawling, dragging the precious burden with him. He saw the tall, famine-arched form of Satan before him. And he laughed again. For Satan was the hunter. He laughed horribly, choking himself. Yonder wolf had been a great fool to come hunting for Satan himself.

Suddenly, there was the pearl-gray body of the dog himself within reach. He thrust the wolf's quarter before him, under the nose of the waiting monster, and then dropped prostrate in a faint, falling upon his side.

He should have died there, his face frozen, except that in falling, his outstretched arm came under his head, which rested upon it. When he wakened, with the deadly cold eating into him from below, he felt a crushing weight upon him and a mysterious warmth on his face.

He opened his eyes and looked up into the terrible face of Satan. The dog was licking him. As he opened his eyes, he saw a stranger thing than comes within the vision of most men, for the man-killer, feeling the human glance upon it, snarled terribly. The whole body of the man quivered with the vibrations of that sound. And he saw the lips furl back from the great white fangs. Yet, still snarling terribly, Satan licked his face.

Sammy moved with a groan. The dog leaped from his body

and stood at a little distance, the chain clanking as it stirred, its head high, its legs stiff, as though prepared for combat. The Joker pushed himself to a sitting posture on his shuddering arms, then he saw the greatest miracle of all. Yonder, a foot from him, was the wolf meat that he had brought in.

He tried to understand. He beat his half-frozen hands against his head to knock the cobwebs from his brain, and now he told himself over and over again that the thing was impossible. He thrust the wolf meat toward the dog, and he snarled terribly. What was the meaning of this? Why had the starving dog refused the necessary food, the food for which his whole being must crave? Then a possible explanation came to him. He touched the meat. It was frozen as hard as a stone. Still, that was not explanation enough, for the mighty jaws of the wolf dog could splinter bone. Why had he not eaten? That problem drowned all else in the mind of the man.

Then he went to the Tree and cut off twigs, small branches. He scraped the snow from the face of a flat rock that he had noted before. On this he managed to kindle a fire, and there he roasted the meat in small portions. When the first chunk was half done, he placed it in his mouth and ate. Looking at the dog, he saw the saliva of starvation hunger drooling from his mouth. That next morsel he held out upon the palm of one hand. Behold! Satan sniffed, trembled as with dread, then closed his eyes and licked the bit of food delicately from the mittened hand of the man.

Still uncomprehending, the Joker stared. Then the total realization came over him, and his spirit was lifted up.

"God Almighty himself wouldn't believe it," he said. And instinctively he raised his head and looked up through the branches of the Tree at the gray, desolate face of the Arctic sky.

CHAPTER TWENTY-SIX

Neither then nor later could he make Satan understand the meaning of a caress. From the touch of man's hand, the wolf dog instinctively shrank away, the green light flickered in his eyes, and his teeth glanced in the dull Arctic light. To the voice of the man, however, he listened with an unflagging interest.

According to the manner in which the voice of the Joker went up and down the scale, now softly, now loudly, now low, now high, the ears of Satan, sharp and short, quivered, sometimes twitched back, flattening angrily, and sometimes pricked more intently. Sometimes he lay laughing, as it were, sunning himself in the presence of his first master, and sweeping the snow with his tail.

Since it was to talk that Satan responded, the man chatted with him constantly. He had an almost irresistible desire to stroke the great head, or take the proudly arched neck inside his arm, but he managed to check these impulses. The dog and his green eyes were enough to discourage familiarity.

In spite of his triumph and a meal of strong meat, the man knew that the whole problem was not ended. His strength was returning with that single meal. And on the tenth day, he marched lightly forth, found the carcass and brought home, though with a good deal of difficulty, the remaining three quarters of it.

Satan came to meet him as far as the chain permitted, and then stood up and growled at him with great ferocity. But he knew that the growl was a welcome. He could tell that by the wagging of the tail. The growl was there simply because in the vocabulary of the dog, there was nothing except oaths with which to express whatever tender emotions filled him.

There was now a supply of meat. The dog guarded it, while the man marched far away to find fuel. He found it, at last, some ten miles off—a quantity of naked brush, growing low, looking like a patch of rolling smoke from a short distance. He pulled up or broke down the driest and the deadest of these shrubs, and brought them back in a huge heap to the Tree. And Satan howled wildly out of the far distance when first he saw his master coming.

He had not laid a tooth on the tempting meat. Neither would he touch a morsel of it at any time except when the man gave it to him out of his hand. Always he ate as though there were poison on the hand that presented the roasted meat.

Before the twelfth day, there was no need of wolf's meat for the Joker. He was catching enough lean, stringy rabbits to supply him while Satan ate the rest of the wolf, filling in the interstices, so to speak, with rabbit bones. Both the man and the dog felt that they were living rather high.

Slowly, slowly, their lean, hard bodies grew full and soft again, and the flesh that had melted from them in the fire of torment returned.

There was a great deal of hard work for the man, because he was continually moving. In order to maintain comfort, he made at least one trip a day to the brush and returned with a great, back-breaking heap of it.

By the end of the fifteenth day, he had woven for them a good, almost impenetrable windbreak, which he could prop in place against the Tree. Behind this he lived with the dog. The wind blew and the snow fell, but left them unperturbed. They had no need of any greater shelter above their heads than the thin branches of the Tree. They had one another, and every day they walked deeper and deeper into the mysterious knowledge of their own souls.

There was another occupation that amused the man. Whenever he built a fire, he made the flame as small and as intense as he could contrive it, always letting it play and lick around one link of the big iron chain. In odd moments, when he sat resting on his brushwood bed, after eating, he would pound that same selected link of iron with a heavy stone, a hard, flinty stone, black as ink, which he had found near where the brush grew, and which he had carried from that distance.

Eventually, he hoped, with continually heating and cooling, the iron would change its temper and become brittle. Then the hammering with the stone might one day break it. But how stubborn was that good Swedish iron. No wonder that the introduction of iron marked a new step forward, a new age in the developing civilization of man. For three weeks, in every spare moment, the man was heating or pounding that iron chain. But it was not until the twenty-second day that it snapped suddenly across and showed him its gray, clean, inside face.

He tied the remnant of the chain into the collar of the dog, and Satan was free at last!

That began a new life for them. The possibilities of it were such that the man could hardly believe in them at the first. There was no more solitary trudging through the snow, for the gray, soft-footed ghost of a dog blew soundless here and there across the face of the wilderness, running with head and tail stretched out, traveling with a lope like a wolf's, but longer striding, with almost the spring of a greyhound in it.

He was hunting—hunting the wind with his keen nose, hunting the ground, picking up scents that might be inches deep and months old under the snow. And, as it appeared, he was not hunting purely for his own sake. He was able to understand, as the man saw with delight, that there is such a thing as fair exchange in this existence of ours. Toward the end of his first day of freedom, he came up to the feet of his master and laid down a big rabbit, fatter than any that the man had caught in his traps.

The Joker split that rabbit in two on the spot and offered a half to the dog, but the strange fellow refused to take it, and then trotted back up the trail toward the Tree with his head turned a little, studying the man, wagging his tail, laughing with red-mouthed joy. He was like a proud little boy, swollen with delight because of some virtuous exploit, showing off before the eyes of the world.

From then on they hunted every day. They kept in good physical condition, and the man began to save rabbit pelts, tying them high in the branches of the Tree in a bundle. He could not tell, after all, how long he would have to exist out here. Perhaps that fiend, the Dogman, would not come for the whole period of the remaining three months and a fraction. In the meantime, clothes would have to be made or repaired. He made thread of untangled sinew. He made needles out of bone, burning little eyeholes in them.

He had constructed a sort of roof for his windbreak. He had dug through the snow to the ground, cleared a floor, and then, with a hoe-shaped root, he trenched around the outside edge of this ground space, so he could be sure of drainage. He had woven wings for the windbreak. Now, when he lashed the roof in place with stout sinews, he had a fairly secure retreat. Sometimes he was all alone in it, while the wolf dog went out scouting through the countryside with his untiring lope. Sometimes he was alone with the jingling of the chain links sounding somewhere near the shelter, for as the big dog moved, the iron was bound to clink like small, dull bells. Unless he stalked, for this he could always accomplish without making a sound.

Now, at just about the time when the Joker began to feel that he could wrest a living from the wilderness, even with his bare hands, so long as he had the teeth and companionship of the dog, he saw a spectacle that set him tingling with pleasure and with awe. One day, while he was marching toward his traps, a streak of low-running black far away flashed across the snows, and behind it glided the much taller bulk of the dog, that familiar, almost discernible puff of gray smoke.

Very swiftly that pair glided across the landscape and disappeared. The man walked on, and five minutes later he saw the black streak coming toward him. It had doubled, and now it was running with its last strength, dodging every little while to right and to left, for the great gray form was close upon it.

It was one of those rare creatures, a silver fox. There are few hounds so fleet that they can run down a fox in a fair match. Ordinary dogs and wolves are quickly distanced by the neat little heels of a reynard. But here was a fine specimen of a young fox fairly and squarely run down by the dog. It would never be given credence in a town like Circle City, where all the possibilities of sled dogs are known and well-canvassed. But now he could understand why Bill the Dogman had said, with such savage pride, that Satan was the finest dog in the world.

It was true. There was the strength of a steel trap in him, and there was the lightness of steel springs, also. He broke the neck of that fox at the very feet of the man, and the Joker stripped off the beautiful fluff of fur and gave the carcass to Satan.

It was another proud day for the dog. And it was the day that opened the eyes of the man to the full possibilities of the gray beauty. He no longer wondered how the big fellow caught so many rabbits. Craft, plus such speed and endurance, told the story.

As for the intelligence of Satan, it was not to be believed. There was hardly a thing the man wished to teach him that he did not pick up at once. Such matters as coming, sitting, lying on guard over a possession, even guarding raw meat without mouthing it—all of these things were mastered almost at a stroke. But there were far more complicated matters, far more necessary in the life that they were leading, for the great dog was usually ranging far, far beyond the reach of the man's voice. By gestures, then, he quickly learned to understand the most complicated orders. For instance, he could be sent to the right or the left, and told to move at speed or cautiously, or to stalk the district downright. So wonderfully did the dog understand these signals that finally the man used to have what he thought of as "silent conversations" with the gray beauty when they were on the trail or alone in the camp. Those bright, wide eyes of Satan would peer intently into the face of his master, straining his whole animal heart and soul to pass the bounds between man and beast and understand the human soul as well. Every flicker of the eyes had for him a meaning. An intense look cast into a corner was sure to make Satan rise and glide to it. He actually regarded a scowling expression with a silent, snarling mask of hatred, and a smiling look made him wag his tail slightly. The most casual bending of a finger would convey a message to him.

And these things were all mastered in the course of a few days, for on the thirtieth day, Bill the Dogman came back.

The dog knew, naturally, long before the man. Either he heard, or else he caught the scent upon a favorable wind. For minutes before the man was aware of anything, the fur was bristling along the back of Satan's neck. He stood up at last and laid his head on the knee of his master. The man, occupied busily in sewing rabbit skins together, looked up.

"What is it, Satan?" he asked.

Satan may not have understood the words, yet he knew perfectly well the rising inflection of a question, and now he turned straight about and faced toward the home trail. He looked back at the master and growled in his deepest key.

"It's man, eh?" asked his master, for he knew that note in the scale of Satan's expressions. "Man, is it?" repeated the Joker. "Bill the Dogman coming to pay us a little call, maybe?"

The dog glanced back, trotted away a few steps, and paused again, as though begging permission to be gone. But the Joker laughed, and threw upon the snow the rabbit skins on which he had been working.

"Guard that, Satan," he said. And then he watched the big dog lie down beside the skins with the air of one resolved to do his duty or to die.

CHAPTER TWENTY-SEVEN

Through the haze loomed the five-dog team of Bill the Dogman, who himself marched beside a sled, his tall, leaning form recognizable from a great distance. The dogs, as though recognizing a friend in the Joker, began to strain forward. He heard their short, sharp, eager barking, and he smiled. He could spot them all while they were still at a little distance—one by a peculiar swaying of the shoulders, another by a limping foreleg, the tendon of which had been a trifle shortened by some old cut. And there was the bald face of one, blazed with a great white stripe, and the peculiar cant of the head of the sled dog at the rear. Yes, he knew them all, and they knew him. Every one of them had known him for several hundred miles of trail, at the least. No wonder that they strained to come to his hand, away from the brutal treatment which the Dogman always meted out to his teams.

Sammy Day went forward a few steps, and Bill came striding to meet him. When he was close, he called out: "Hello, Sammy! How's things been?"

"Fine," said the Joker.

"Livin' on the fat of the land, eh?" Bill asked, coming straight up to his victim.

"Well, look at me," said the Joker. "Do I seem half-starved?"

Bill looked him over with a vicious sneer, and then he nodded. "I thought that you'd do pretty well out here," he said. "It ain't hard to boil plenty of lichen soup out here."

"Sure it isn't," said the Joker, "if you've got anything at all to boil it in."

"But, then, what's the use of boilin' the lichens and the moss when they make a pretty good green salad if you eat 'em raw?"

"That's what I thought, too," said the Joker.

Old Bill went on: "Look at the caribou, the way that they fatten up on greens."

"Yes, I've thought of caribou," admitted the Joker. And he smiled almost genially upon Bill the Dogman.

Nothing can be more perfect than perfection, and such was his detestation of Bill the Dogman. To look on him no longer made his blood hot and his brain misty; instead, a cold tremor of electric emotion, which was almost pleasure, leaped through him headlong.

"Well," went on Bill, rubbing his mittened hands together, "I knew that you'd get along all right. And if there was a little pinch in provisions, I remembered that you was only a little skinny runt of a man."

"That's right," Sammy Day said. "Just a smell of bacon smoke in the air, or a glimpse of wild goose on the wing now and then, is enough to keep the fat on my ribs."

The Dogman grinned broadly. Perhaps there was some relief in his expression. It might not have been too easy, after this guilty month, to march out to find the young fellow.

"Too bad," said Sammy Day, "that the hurricane came along and kept you from hurrying back to me here."

"Yeah. That's right," Bill affirmed. "It blew for two whole days, and I couldn't possibly buck my way through it."

"Must have blown all thought of me out of your head, finally."

"Sure," said Bill. "Matter of fact, after those first two days, I clean forgot all about you. I was kind of busy with the Indians and the dogs. There was a whole stack of work to do around the place."

"I thought it must have been that way," said the Joker. "I could read your kind heart all the way out here, Bill. I knew it couldn't be meanness that made you leave me in the lurch with the dog."

"Of course, it wasn't anything like that," declared the other. "The fact is that it was only this mornin' that I woke up and hollers to John … 'Hey, John, I've forgot something.' 'Yeah?' says John. You know how talkative he is, that John. 'By thunder,' says I, 'all at once I remember. I've forgot about the kid.' 'Yeah?' says John. So you see, the minute that I remembered, I rushed right out here to find you, son. And here we are. How's Satan been for company?"

He pointed toward the gray, still statue of the dog. And Satan, holding his eyes straight before him like a royal prince in a crowd of commoners, regarded neither the newcomer nor his team. Only by the light in his eyes could something within him be guessed at.

"Satan is all right," replied Sammy. "He's been good company."

"I thought you'd get on all right," said the Dogman. "You took the muzzle off him, eh?"

"You can see for yourself," said Sammy.

"Well, tie the brute down and get the muzzle on him again, if you can," said Bill. "We're starting back."

"Get your muzzle, boy," Sammy Day said.

The dog rose, glided into the shelter, and came out again, carrying his muzzle in his teeth. He dropped it at the feet of his master, and then looked up into his face expectantly, his tail wagging a little. Sammy Day did not look at the Dogman. He did not have to, for the astonishment of the big man was like a tingle of electricity in the air. The Joker tied the muzzle securely on the head of Satan.

"Want him in the lead?" he asked of Bill the Dogman. Then

he turned and saw that Bill stood frozen in his place, his hands awkwardly poised in the midst of an interrupted gesture, his mouth agape, his white breath blowing out and freezing upon his raggedly cropped beard.

He actually rubbed his eyes, shook his head, and stared again. "It's true," muttered Bill. "It's happened."

"What?" Sammy Day asked carelessly.

Bill wheeled slowly on him. "How did you do it?" he asked fiercely. As he spoke he raised his clenched fist and shook it at the young man.

Instantly, a gray bolt shot up from the ground. The muzzle effectually sheathed the teeth of the wolf dog, but his heavily muscled shoulder smote Bill to the snow like the stroke of a club.

"Here," Sammy Day said, calmly rejoicing, "you go back and guard those rabbit skins, old fellow."

The fallen man received one glance from the dog, which then turned, glided to the rabbit skins, and sat down beside them.

"I should have told you," Sammy Day said as Bill regained his feet in silence. "Satan doesn't trust strangers entirely, and he keeps a close eye on me. He knows that I'm pretty delicate, and he doesn't want to see me hurt."

Bill the Dogman shook himself, and the powdered snow fell away from him in a cloud. "You've gone and done it," he said huskily. "You've gone and made him. But look here … no leader can work free in a muzzle. Can you handle him without a muzzle?"

"Certainly," Sammy Day.

"And keep him from murderin' all the other dogs one by one?"

"Yes, of course," answered Sammy, "unless he kills 'em with the first bite."

"You lie," said the Dogman. "You can't do it. But go on, you liar! Take the muzzle off of him, and put him out there in the lead."

Sammy Day took the muzzle from his champion. "Heel, boy," he said, and walked to the head of the team with the gray ghost close beside him. There he harnessed Satan. "Come and pat him, Bill," he said. "You see how gentle and kindly he is?"

The Dogman grinned a horrible and twisted grin. "I know how gentle he is," he said. "He'll be dead before he's gentle. I'll give you ten dollars if you'll bend over so's he's got a free chance at your throat."

"Ten dollars is a cheapskate's bet," said the Joker.

"I knew that I'd get to the bottom of your bluff!" cried the Dogman. "I'll bet you a hundred dollars cash!"

"All right," answered Sammy Day.

So he leaned accordingly. And Satan licked his master's face.

CHAPTER TWENTY-EIGHT

They ran a mile. Then, in making a turn through a shallow gully, number two and three dogs got entangled and instantly were rolling on the snow, fighting furiously.

Satan turned, laid number four on the snow with a slash along the shoulders and a heavy blow, then sprang into the fighting pair that twisted on the ground.

"Hey, Satan!" shouted Sammy.

Slowly, the great dog raised his already crimsoned mask from the fight and looked at his master. Then, his head and tail down, he slunk back to his post in the lead.

As for numbers two and three, they already had more than enough. Dripping blood, but not deeply hurt, they returned to their posts.

"You ought to keep your teams in order, Bill," the Joker said in sham reproach. "Satan hates a fight unless he has a chance to get into it."

Bill the Dogman began to laugh hilariously. "Say, fellow," he cried, "you've gone and done it! You've made him a perfect dog, the finest dog in the world. Look at him, Sammy!" He dropped his great hand upon the shoulder of the young man, but Sammy struck the hand away.

"If you ever touch me again, Bill," he said angrily, "if you put even the weight of a finger on me, I'll cut your throat and give your rotten heart to the crows."

Bill the Dogman rubbed his forearm where the sudden blow had fallen, hurting him to the bone. But all he said was: "You don't find crows this far north, kid. And if you take my heart south to 'em, won't it be kind of spoiled meat before you arrive?"

There was no more talk, however, between them, and they went home the straightest way, the leader finding the trail always and with an inevitable skill, as though he had traveled over it a thousand times. Only once or twice did he pause and thrust his head down into the snow to sniff at the failing scent. Then he went on. Always he went right.

* * * * *

When they reached the house, they saw John outside of it. When he made sure that the gray Satan was in the lead, and that the second man must be the Joker, he threw his arms up over his head with a wild yell and rushed through the front door. Pete came plunging behind him and stood there, gripping at the door to steady himself.

So the team arrived. And Bill the Dogman said: "Here, you, Pete, stir around, will you? Unharness these dogs and feed 'em."

Pete shook his head. "I gone and told you a long time ago," he said, "that I wouldn't never try to lay hands on Satan again. I said it then, and I mean it now."

"You don't need to lay hands on him," said the Dogman. "The kid will handle him. Sammy, take Satan out."

The young fellow walked straight to Satan and leaned over the traces.

"Hold on, you poison-faced fool!" yelled Pete, stirred even for an enemy by this sight. "He'll tear your throat out."

But Sammy calmly unharnessed the leader. "Go take a little run, old fellow," he said, and instantly the gray monster shot off across the snow, gamboling, playing, now diving through the snow like an otter, now leaping high into the air.

Bill looked after him with the expression of one who is drinking nectar of the gods. "This little jaunt ain't been work to Satan," he said. "Look-it here, son. What kind of meat have you been feedin' him?"

"Wolf," said the young fellow. "Rabbits for dessert and silver foxes for variety." As he spoke he unrolled the small pack that he had put on the top of the sled load. He held up the priceless, white-frosted fur.

Bill shook his head. "It's all right," he said. "I know that I been beat again. But don't rub it in. A little later on, I got something to say to you."

Sammy Day merely nodded his head. They went in. From the door of the house the young fellow waved his arm. Instantly, the far-off form of the wolf dog turned and shot toward them.

"Don't even need your voice?" Bill asked.

Sammy Day said nothing. But a foolish glory and pride filled him. The gloomy, envious silence of the two Indians, while the four men were eating, did not trouble him. It was simply another kind of flattery, more poignant, however. Above all, he enjoyed their odd, frightened glances, one at the other. Something had happened that they could not understand. It was, in fact, so far beyond their comprehension that they plainly felt some sort of magic was in the air. It was medicine. It was strong medicine, and they perhaps had been foolish in helping their master to plague this slender white man.

It was not only the attitude of the Indians that was new; there was also the matter of the food that appeared upon the table. For once beans and coffee were not ample fare. Bacon appeared, fried in thick slabs, but all the more delicious for that reason to the starved stomach of the young man. A frozen side of venison yielded great steaks, which were consumed like bread. Yes, bread itself was baked with odd skill by the Dogman, a rich pone, and to eat with it, there appeared a great tin of plum and apple jam.

The Joker ate until his eyes were starting from his head. Finally, he leaned back against the wall and sipped at his fourth big steaming cup of coffee, and then he rolled a cigarette with fingers that felt thick and stiff, so unaccustomed had they become to that delicate and luxurious employment.

While he smoked, the master said to the Indians: "Rustle around, you two, and get the tins cleaned up. I gotta talk business to Sammy Day."

They rose and went about their work, but in their course about the room, never did they come within yards of the corner where Satan lay, carefully guarding a mitten dropped by the Joker.

Now, as they were employed in this fashion, Bill the Dogman rested the greasy, worn elbows of his fur sleeves upon the table and leaned a little toward the Joker. "There's one other little thing that we might talk about," he said.

"Go on and talk," said the young fellow.

"About Satan."

"Well?" Sammy sat up, no longer unconcerned, but cautious and suspicious again.

"You've done a grand job with him," went on the Dogman. "Considerin' what he was when you found him, you've done the finest job of trainin' that I ever seen. You got a genius for dogs. There ain't any question about that. And I kinder reckon that maybe you've growed to be fond of Satan."

The young fellow shrugged his shoulders.

Admissions of any kind to a fellow like Bill the Dogman were likely to be dangerous. He knew it, and acted upon that basis.

"Anyway," said Bill the Dogman, "we could look at it like this. You like Satan. You wanna have him for your own. Am I right?"

"I don't know," replied Sammy. "Look at it this way. What good will Satan be to you if I'm not here to handle him?"

The Dogman merely smiled. "I ain't gonna take that up," he replied, "because it ain't worth takin' up. But I'll tell you this … I'll make a little bargain with you about the dog. I'll sell him to you."

"I'll pay you a couple of hundred for him," said Sammy.

The Dogman sat and laughed. "Now, that's damn funny," he said. "You'll pay me a couple of hundred for him?"

The Joker considered. Perhaps at another time he would have delayed and tried to think up better ways of bargaining. He would not have revealed his hand so soon. But now he was very tired. The warmth of the room and the closeness of the air drugged him. His head was rather dizzy.

"You owe me five hundred dollars for every month that I've been with you. In a year that's six thousand dollars. It's the only money I've got. You take the whole wad and give me Satan."

Bill the Dogman writhed on the stool. He thrust out his head on the end of the long, sloping neck, and his grin was more hideous than the grin of a dead catfish.

"Have I gone and bred a six-thousand-dollar dog?" he said. The young fellow said nothing, for he felt that already he had talked too much. "Six thousand dollars," repeated the Dogman, rubbing his great, dirty hands together. "That's a pile of money. A man could step out and blow himself to a racehorse for that, and a damn good race horse, at that. Well, sir, the trouble is that money ain't something that means much to me. Dogs is what has the meanin'. Dogs is the things that's mattered to me more'n men or coin all my life. I've throwed away my years on dogs. And all I've collected is misery. But now I'm gonna collect something more. I'm gonna collect fame, and the finest dog team that ever pulled at a sled. You hear me?"

His voice rose. He was shouting. The two Indians stood enchanted with fear and expectation in the corner of the room.

And the Joker bowed his head and looked up at him from beneath his brows.

"Go on," Sammy said. "Stop your fooling around and tell me what you want."

"I'll tell you!" shouted the Dogman, pointing a long arm. "Out yonder there's about ten more of Satan's own breed. They ain't up to him. They're as much under him as they're over other dogs. Now you know what I want?"

"You know what can't be done," Sammy said, growing cold of heart. For suddenly he knew that he would have to own Satan, even if it meant murder for him. "You want me to break in those dogs, and it can't be done."

"Then if you can't do it," yelled the Dogman, "Satan stays with me, and you be damned!"

CHAPTER TWENTY-NINE

To break in ten more dogs like Satan was impossible. The young fellow was sure of it. When he stretched himself in his bunk, he was telling himself calmly that there was only one thing for him to do—wait until his year was out, marry the girl, and then complete the plan that he had formed so long before. There would be this difference—when he had shot the life out of the Indians and the Dogman, he would take Satan with him. That was all.

He had closed his eyes. He was almost asleep when Satan, on the floor beneath his bunk, snarled softly.

"Speak to your dog," said the voice of the Dogman.

"Steady, boy," said the young man. He reached down over the edge of the bunk and rested his hand upon the softly furred head of the dog. He could feel the tremor of anger in that great body; he could feel the coiling of the springs.

Then the Dogman stepped nearer through the thick darkness. When he was very close, he said: "You think that it can't be done, but give yourself a chance at it. You lie here, hatin' me. Instead of plannin' to cut my throat, why don't you make a try at the dogs?

Something tells me you can do it. If you murder me, you'll hang for it, sonny. Before I left Circle City, I wrote a note and left it in good hands. I guessed what might come to me from you, young man."

With that he stepped away through the darkness and left Sammy Day in a quandary.

He began to look at this matter not from his own viewpoint, but, for the first time, from that of the Dogman. He seemed to feel now that there was a mystery behind the actions of that strange and grim fellow. Perhaps, after all, he did not tempt men to work for him, merely for the inhuman pleasure of torturing them to madness. There might be another reason. In his own case, why had the Dogman chosen to hire him if, as it appeared, he realized from the first that he might well be murdered by his newly hired man? Well, that remained to be seen, also.

If he took the life of the Dogman, no matter how many thousand times that brute deserved to die, he would certainly be apprehended sooner or later. He would hang for it, exactly as the Dogman had said. How, then, was he to get his proper vengeance?

Even nearer and dearer than vengeance was the thought of the great dog who lay by his bunk, breathing softly. In all the world, he never had been so near to anything. Never before had he so completely possessed a living will and soul as he possessed this wild animal's.

Well, the bargain had been made. And there might be, after all, something in the suggestion that Bill had made. Better to try the impossible before admitting defeat. With that thought he fell asleep, and for twelve hours he lay like a stone.

When he awoke, he did not eat. His head was too dizzy with the foul air of the room, accustomed as he had been for a month to the cleanest oxygen of the outdoors.

Satan accompanied him to the run of the first of that gray, short-furred breed. It was the biggest of the lot, a good percentage more massive than Satan himself, and of a disposition only less fiendish than the leader's. He came raving to the fence and howled his fury into the face of the Joker. Satan sat down just outside the fence and looked up once wistfully at his master, then concentrated all of his alert attention upon the fury inside the barrier. Now and then he licked his lips, and Sammy carefully noted that, too.

He had with him a rope, the club that he had used on Satan in their first memorable encounter, and a harness. But clubbing and brute force had not managed to subdue Satan. Chance, the nearness of death, and an apparent sacrifice, had combined to change the heart of the big fellow. They could not combine again, ten times more, for the rest of the fiendish lot.

So, gloomily he stared through the fence at the other dog. It was a magnificent specimen, not put together in the matchless style of Satan, perhaps, but a thoroughly glorious dog—a sled dog, perhaps, for that team that Bill the Dogman desired. And a good sled dog is second only to the leader in importance—more important in many and many a crisis. And here was plenty of that power that can swerve the sled at the last second of hope.

Satan looked up again to his master and whined very softly.

"Yes," said the young fellow, "you'd like to eat him, wouldn't you? And why not?" he added fiercely to himself.

Suddenly, he stepped to the gate, untied the chains that bound it, and flung it wide. The monster inside came with the rush of a lion, but between him and the man sprang the gray thunderbolt, Satan. He shot in low and hard. The blow of his shoulder caught the big fellow by surprise and toppled him over in midair, flinging him heavily upon his back. Then Satan turned with wonderful speed and sprang in for the throat. One shout from his master stopped him. Then the wide noose of the rope fled from the hand of the Joker and whipped over the head of the fallen dog.

It was up the next instant, but this time the two-legged enemy was not in its thought. Straight at Satan it flew, but the slack of the rope was flung with a spinning twist toward his body as he sprang, and the coil settled around his front legs. He went heavily down into the snow just before the high head of Satan, who stood with stiff pride, trembling with eagerness, but enchained by the command of his master.

So, in a moment, running in, working the rope busily, Sammy entangled his prize. Furiously the big creature struggled, but he was securely held. The Joker, looking down at him, was bewildered to see the ease with which the capture had been effected. Satan had done the lion's share of the difficult work, of course. But still, there lay the gray monster, helpless and unscathed.

The Joker dragged him out of the run and tied his head close against a post. His teeth were helpless then. He could shake the post to its foundation, but his efforts served only to strangle him. At last he stood still, shuddering, while the man fitted the harness upon him. All this time Satan stood by and watched with an air of curious abstraction and interest combined.

The Joker brought a sled. In the lead he fastened Satan. Then he muzzled his new captive and fought him through half an hour of snarling madness, but at last he was fixed in his place. But how could he be made to pull?

For half of that day, the Joker worked until he was quivering with exhaustion. Then rage and despair filled him.

"Have it and be damned," he said, and tore the muzzle from the head of the new dog.

If he were weary, the gray fiend was weary, also, but he did not hesitate. As if from released springs, he hurled himself at the throat of the man. The full weight of the club knocked him to the snow.

"Take him, boy," the Joker said to Satan, and the leader shot in at his teammate as the latter rose.

It was not a long fight. The larger dog had strength, but he could not match the smoothly sliding speed of Satan. That worthy slid down and under and up and straightway put his kinsman down with a firm stranglehold on his throat.

The Joker, standing calmly by, waited until the eyes of the underdog turned glassy. Then he spoke, and Satan reluctantly stepped back. There was not a scratch on him. The throat of his victim was streaming with blood. He lay still. He would die, perhaps. Well, better dead than alive and worthless.

He got from the house what he needed—salve and a crude bandage—and he was back in time to see the wounded beast on its feet, but swaying, gasping for breath. He dressed the wound with one hand, holding the club ready in the other. Then he took the big fellow back to his run and turned him loose. He lay down a single step inside his gate and waited there, panting. Well, he would not bleed to death now. That much was certain. But what had been gained? Tomorrow would have to show that.

* * * * *

On the morrow, back he went, prepared for the same struggle. He was amazed when he entered the run behind Satan to see the other dog back into a corner. Satan drew nearer. His kinsman turned tail and fled along the barrier to find safety from this murdering fiend!

CHAPTER THIRTY

Fear is a shrewd teacher. The new dog learned in ten minutes, this second morning, that if he attacked the man, his leader attacked him. And he had found out that death was in the teeth of Satan. So he had nothing to do but submit.

Moreover, he had before him an example of what a dog must do in a sled team. Perhaps, in some mysterious way, Satan was conveying to his larger companion little messages of warning and little lessons in behavior.

At any rate, before that day ended, the sled dog was pulling and halting on command from the man. And he no longer bared his teeth or attempted to snap when Sammy Day came near him.

He was put back in his run. It was not the end. The dog might still go bad, but a vast victory had been won in this beginning.

For five days the Joker worked incessantly over his task. He made no attempt to win the affection of his big wheeler. Obedience was the first lesson, he thought. But he began to observe that the hate and dread that the new dog felt for his leader were so great that by contrast his aversion for the human master seemed much less.

It was Satan that he eyed with awe. He would even shrink a little toward the man to avoid that other tigerish monster.

The Joker encouraged him. He even patted the broad, powerful head, and was surprised to find that his new dog seemed to relish this reassuring touch. So five days passed, and the dog was made. That much of his training was absolute. He feared his leader like the fiend, and his affection for the protecting driver became increasingly great. The Joker called him Pat.

Next he picked out a powerful two-year-old dog of the same breed, and used Satan to knock him into submission. This second one was a more active fighter than Pat. He drew Satan's blood and got his own body pretty well ripped up. But he learned his lesson just as Pat had. Then he was put in the swing, to work between the other two.

There now appeared an amazing and most important factor. Satan knew perfectly, by this time, what was expected of him. He was the disciplinarian. He was at once a club and a sword in the hands of his master, but the blunt blow was more desired than the cutting edge. It was even more amazing to see Pat take up his new duties—teacher as well as pupil. He had hardly mastered his own work, but he delighted in bullying the new dog and putting him in his place. The breaking of Grab, as Sammy called the new dog from his habit of catching hold and freezing to his grip like a bulldog, was very quick.

Sometimes the work was harder. Sometimes it was easier. Poison and Crazy were the worst of the lot, and they were never trustworthy dogs. But the other dogs of the team broke and trained them, as in all of the other cases. It seemed a delightful peculiarity of the breed. Once they had learned a lesson, they took very great delight in teaching it to others with their teeth and claws.

From the day on which Sammy began work on Pat to the day when he pronounced the ninth dog a success, four weeks and two days intervened. He had now been working exactly ten months and a day for the Dogman when he drove up the team to the front of the house and shouted.

Bill came out and, shading his eyes with one hand, though the light was not great, looked over the team.

"There you are," said Sammy. He went forward and unhooked Satan. "There's your nine-dog team in exchange for Satan."

"Who's the leader?" asked Bill sourly.

"Toothwork, here."

"He's the smallest of the lot," said the Dogman.

"He weighs ninety pounds if he weighs an ounce. He can run all day. And he's got brains. You could make him love you if you half tried."

"What the devil do I care about his love?" Bill asked. "It's enough for me that he'll work. How long you been handlin' him?"

"Three weeks."

"You can't make a leader in three weeks."

"I know that. But he knows enough to fill a book already."

"You've made him in three weeks, have you?"

"Satan has made him," answered the young man. "Satan's a better and a faster teacher than I am. He's taught Toothwork all that he knows. Toothwork will lick any one of the rest of that team. He'll even give Satan a run for his money. He made that cut on Satan's shoulder. He'll pull almost as much, he'll run faster, and he'll never stop working. He has a nose like a bird dog, and the brains of a Newfoundland, plus sense of his own. He'll run down a wild wolf and eat the wolf at the end of the run. He'll smell a trail under the snow … he'll obey twenty signals without a word spoken. What more do you want?"

"Lemme see the team work," commanded Bill.

"All right."

"No, with Satan in it."

"There you are." He hooked Satan into place. Then he stepped back to the side of the tall man.

"Whatcha waitin' for?" demanded Bill.

"I'm not waiting. Use your eyes, now." He made a signal that Bill hardly followed, and instantly Satan threw up his head, uttered a short, high-pitched snarl, and then flung himself ahead. The whole team obeyed that order, and off shot the sled. Straight off it ran, for several hundred yards, and Sammy remained standing calmly at the side of Bill the Dogman.

"Gonna wait till they run in the Arctic Ocean?" Bill asked fiercely, his voice shaken with excitement.

The young man laughed, stepped out half a pace, and waved. Then it was seen that the team was slowly changing direction. In a great curve it altered its course, and at last was moving back toward the pair of watchers.

Pete and John came up, carrying wood, and they watched, amazed, while Satan led his companions through various evolutions—that is to say, he halted the team, then he started them. He turned right and left in rapid zigzags. He swept the whole line about in a quick revolution. Then on he brought them and stopped them before his master. His red-tongued laughter he turned toward the Joker, as though asking for appreciation. But the Joker, in turn, was looking toward Bill.

For a long time, Bill stared. Then he said: "Name 'em."

"Begin at the sled dog. He's Pat. Then comes Grab, Terror, Boxer, Cain, Crazy, Hurry-up, Poison, and Toothwork."

"Nice lot of pet names, ain't they?" growled the Dogman. "Do they know those names as well as you do?"

"Half of 'em do ... the other half will soon learn. Satan knows 'em all by heart, and he teaches 'em."

"How does he do that?"

"I'll show you." He turned the team loose, in harness still. They did not run about, but waited for a new command. "Pat!" called the young fellow.

The biggest and darkest-colored of the lot turned and came

running in, and stood stock-still before the master, wagging his tail.

"Likes you, don't he?" asked Bill.

"He likes me better than he likes Satan," replied Sammy. He called again: "Grab!" And Grab came swiftly, though when he paused there was no wagging of the tail.

"Don't like you so well, eh?" asked the Dogman.

"He doesn't like anything very well," observed Sammy, "except to pull like a fool every minute he's in the team." He called once more: "Boxer! Hey, Boxer!"

The dog did not move. "All right," said the Dogman. "You've missed there."

"I won't have to hunt him, though," answered Sammy. "Satan, go bring in Boxer."

At once Satan whirled about and, running on ahead, swept through the dogs, and each one flinched a little away from him.

"They know the king, eh …" Bill started to say, but paused with an oath of amazement, for Satan had caught the Boxer by a dangling bit of harness and was drawing him forward. The Boxer came along readily, not as though he wished to, but plainly because he was afraid to hold back. Hurry-Up and Crazy needed the same persuasion, but in a few seconds, the whole team was gathered around the feet of the Joker.

"What's next?" he asked of Bill.

"I reckon that's enough," Bill answered. He turned slowly toward the young man. "We start today."

"Where?"

"For Circle City."

A thousand hopeful questions were on the tip of the Joker's tongue, but he suppressed them. He merely harnessed the team in place once more. And when he finished, Pete and John were already carrying out the load to heap it upon the sled. Another sled was brought. The voice of the Dogman issued high and hoarse from the interior of the house, shouting commands. Rapidly, the two loads were built up, wrapped snugly in tarpaulin, and lashed into place.

Then the Dogman appeared, prepared and dressed for travel. Pete and John stood about in uneasy attitudes, with expressions of dismay on their faces.

The Dogman said to them: "I'll be gone two, three months. Take care of the dogs. You get double pay, remember, while I'm gone. But when I come back, you get scalped if anything has gone wrong. That's all."

This, with a wave of his hand, was his farewell. Then, looking toward the young man, he gestured toward the Circle City trail.

"Circle City?" asked the Joker.

The other shrugged his lean shoulders. "Where else?" he said. "Circle City and the world in general. I dunno that I give a damn who sees these here dogs."

CHAPTER THIRTY-ONE

It was not a good wind that raged through Circle City, for it blew Red into Nagle's Saloon. He got his name from the color of his face, his hands, and his hair. He was a hobo. He was worse than that, for he was one of those whose vices are so well known that he takes his infamy for fame. He was proud of his reputation, simply because his reputation was widespread. In person he was a wizened wisp. He was strong enough to stab a man in the back or shoot from behind, but he was too small to be threatened with physical violence. And he knew his privilege better than any king's jester. This worthless rag of humanity opened the doors of Nagle's place, and the wind hurled him into the room.

"Ain't got the strength to close it," he whined, hurrying toward the stove and letting the white pennants of the storm stream in behind him.

No one complained. Someone swore, but at fortune rather than at Red. He was beneath personal notice. A big miner stood up and slammed the door heavily.

Red, while he sunned himself at the stove and began to steam, waved his hand first toward one man, then toward another. He seemed to know the names of twenty who were present. But only one man deigned to answer him. That was Rush Mahan, gentleman extraordinary. He nodded and spoke the man's nickname quietly in response.

Instantly, Red left the stove and sauntered confidently toward the table where Rush sat with Goldie beside him. The brother and sister were in from a long trail; they had a longer trail before them. This was a moment of rest.

Placing a hand on the edge of the table, the hobo said: "Hello again, Rush. I see you ain't one to forget an old friend. The rest, they don't know a man when he's down on his luck. But you're different. You're the real quill. The rest … they're just a lot of damn pikers. A lot of tramps is all they are. They got some money in their pockets today, but they won't have none tomorrow. Oh, I know all about the kind that they are." He laughed sharply, unpleasantly as he spoke. Then, lowering his voice: "Ain't got a twenty about you, have you, Rush? I'm flat."

Mahan hesitated a little. Then, with an almost imperceptible shrug of his shoulders, he drew out a twenty-dollar bill and pushed it across the table. "There you are, Red," he said. "Go have a drink."

Red grinned, his yellow teeth showing, pointed like the teeth of a beast. "Sure, I'll have a drink. In your honor, Rush. Damn it all. You're a gentleman."

He went over to the bar and drank. The assistant bartender served him the whiskey, because Nagle was leaning over the bar at the farther end, pushing across a heap of supplies to a bearded sourdough.

Red heard the man saying: "This here fellow … this here Sam Day … he's the salt of the earth. I ain't the only one that says so. There's plenty more that have been down and out and thanked God and Sammy Day for a handout."

"I wish that the Joker could hear you say it," said the bartender, "but he'll never know what you think."

"I reckon he's dead," said the sourdough. "God help him. Something oughta be done about Bill the Dogman."

"The next time that he comes into this here town," said Nagle, "something will be done about him, right enough."

"Who's that?" Red demanded. "Who's this Sammy Day that gives handouts to them that are busted? I'm busted, Nagle. I'm flat busted, Nagle, except for a coupla dollars that Rush Mahan just loaned to me. I need a handout, if there's handouts goin' around."

The bartender sneered. "You can live on your face, you red rat," he said. "Don't bother me."

"That's the way I'm talked to, is it?" said Red. "I ain't one to forget, Nagle. Remember that. I ain't one to forget what you say. I'll remember and check it all up one of these days that ain't so far away."

"Go to the devil," said Nagle. "Drink your stuff while you can buy it, because this here is a public bar. Otherwise, I'd take you by the heel and throw you out into the snow."

Red, absorbing his second whiskey, appeared to pay no attention to this remark, and with the glass in his hand, sipping delicately, he turned toward a big blackboard on the side wall of the room. There appeared a number of names with figures chalked after them. Thus they read:

Rush Mahan 2–1½
Pike Sullivan 3–1
Denver Lew 5–1
Little John 7–1

There were several other entries upon the list, but Red regarded them no further. "That's right and proper," he said. "Rush had oughta be the favorite for the Nome Sweepstakes. He'd oughta be, because he's won 'em before … and he's the best dog-puncher, and he's got the best dogs. I know! But them odds are pretty short, even so. And down below, a dollar on Little John wins seven. Why, I know that breed. And he wouldn't be entered if he didn't have a bang-up chance of winnin'. He don't play nothin' but sure things."

"I seen his dogs," said the sourdough who had just received the impersonal alms of the Joker from Nagle. He spoke now, because his interest in the sweepstakes was greater than his detestation of this professional loafer. "I seen Little John's dogs. They're all right, but I wouldn't cry about 'em. They ain't the finest in the world."

"Lean and ragged-lookin', ain't they?" Red said, his voice sharp.

"Yeah. They don't look like nothin' at all."

"They are something, though," insisted Red. "Little John, he ain't much to look at, neither, but he can mush a team, and he can break a trail. He's another Bill the Dogman, that's what he is, and his ragged rats, they'll snake that sled of his in pretty close to the first place."

"Put up your money on him then," said the sourdough. "Money talks louder than all your yappin', Red."

"Yeah, and I'll have my money up before the race starts," said Red. "But Nome is where I'm gonna be before I do any layin'. I'll be on the spot before I put my money down, and I'll rake in some juicy odds, too."

"Where'll you pick up the money to bet, Red?" asked the miner.

"Out of somebody's pockets," said Nagle. "That's where he mostly makes his strikes. That and crooked cards."

Red looked at him with a silent snarl, like a fox eying a wolf. "If you're gonna be there, Nagle," he said at last, "I'll bet that I see you, and that I'll be bettin' more hundreds than you lay tens."

"I don't know how many pockets you'll be able to pick between here and there," answered Nagle. "But I'll be in Nome, if that's what you want to know. So will most of the rest of this crowd."

"Well," said Red, "I ain't tippin' you everything that I know, but I'm tellin' you boys that Little John could stand some backin'. That's just a little inside dope to pay you back for the heat of your stove."

Nagle yawned, like a lion at a rat. A rattle of voices stirred in the gaming room. Loud laughter, then, in a pause when the wind was quiet for a moment, a voice was heard dimly shouting a command in the street. The door opened, and the enormous form of Bill the Dogman stalked into the room, slamming the door shut behind him with a force that made the glasses on the tables clink softly.

He strode to the bar without a glance around him. But he was aware, certainly, that all talk stopped when he came in, that all heads turned toward him, and that one or two men slowly began to rise from their chairs. He regarded them not, but, planting his right elbow on the edge of the bar, he said: "Whiskey, Nagle, and make it a big glass." He pointed. "Make it the seventy-five-cent kind of poison, will you?" he added.

Astonishment overwhelmed Nagle. Never before had the Dogman tasted in that bar anything other than the cheapest alcohol. The hand of the bartender moved to execute the order. Then he paused and gathered himself. "Bill," he said, "you don't drink in this bar."

The Dogman did not start. But he thrust out his long jaw. He eyed Nagle steadily through a long moment. "There's blood in what you say, Nagle," he answered grimly.

The voice of Nagle was equally grim and quiet from behind the bar. "I've got my gun in my hand," he said. "Fill your hand whenever you want to."

"I'll know something first," said the Dogman, "and then I'll fill my hand fast enough. What's the meanin' of this, you rat?"

"Murder's my meaning, Bill," said Nagle. "You've done in the kid. You've murdered the Joker. And you ain't going to walk alive out of Circle City."

At this the lower, twisted jaw of the Dogman dropped, and a grin set his greasy whiskers bristling. "You guys, you love that kid, eh?" he said.

"You murdered the poor kid," said the bartender. "You've always wanted to do murder. What you done to Rourke was almost worse, but we stood for that. You was still kind of inside the law. But you're outside of it now. I'm telling you, and I mean it."

Goldie Mahan rose up from her chair. Her voice, in that dead silence that precedes a sudden and terribly important action, was audible throughout the room. In the cardroom, also, the sense of impending disaster had spread like a chill through the air. The card players sat as though stupefied in their places. "Rush," said the girl to her brother, "you've got to do something. You've got to stop it."

Mahan was already rising. "I'll stop it," he said. He went to the bar, where the pair eyed one another with a gathering fury, cold and deadly. Mahan edged between them. He faced Nagle.

"Nagle," he said, "I know what you mean and why you want to do it. Everyone does. I'm sorry for the Joker, too, though you won't believe' me when I say it. He proved himself a better man than I was that evening. At the same time, I hope that I'm good enough to stop this fight. If the Dogman has murdered the Joker, we'll attend to him … the men of Circle City … in the best sort of a court that we can rig up to try the case. But don't do justice with your own gun, Nagle. It isn't the best way. It would only put a rope around your neck."

Nagle, in spite of himself, could not help listening. Besides, other voices broke in from varying parts of the room, calling on him to hold his hand.

Then said the Dogman: "All cut up about the death of the kid, ain't you, Mahan? You, too, Goldie. Pretty near broken-hearted, ain't you, about him? Well, I'll break your hearts for you for certain, you hypocrites. You, there, Jackson open the door and call him in."

Big Jackson opened the door, then shouted with amazement—shouted a name.

They could not believe it. It could not be. The ways of the Dogman were too well known. If even Rourke could not endure, how could a slender young fellow …?

Cutting short all of their conjectures, into the doorway stepped the Joker, wearing a loosely sagging suit of furs far too big for him, and weather-browned as a berry. Behind him stalked a pearl-gray dog that made every dog-knowing heart in that room leap into the throat.

CHAPTER THIRTY-TWO

As he shut the door behind him, the young man looked around and waved his hand to the little crowd. Then he went toward the bar. There was a gradual swelling of voices, an uproar, all about him, extending into the cardroom, and a rush of many feet from that direction, as though they were swarming in to get sight of him.

Through that tumult he saw the stricken face of Goldie Mahan. He had been thinking of her these months as a shining moon in the heaven of fair women. He found her now as a pale statue. The Joker pushed the furred hood back from his rudely cropped head and stood before her.

"Hello, Goldie," he said, and held out his hand.

She did not stir.

There was a dark-faced, handsome fellow in his early thirties standing close by. He stepped to her shoulder now.

"Not even a handshake, Goldie," said the Joker, "with our wedding only a couple of months away? Less than that, even."

She drew in her breath, then she put both hands over her eyes. "Is it really true, Phil?" she murmured.

The dark-faced man, looking steadily at the Joker with such

eyes as he never had faced before, answered: "It's true. I suppose this is the one they call the Joker."

"Thanks, partner," the Joker said in reply. "Have you been calling yourself a lucky man ... till today?" He saw the other man's expression harden. Then he turned away and went on, smiling, toward the bar.

On the way he found that the crowd had recovered from its stupefaction. It swarmed about him. It beat him across the shoulders and wrung his tough hands. It laughed and shouted and cheered him. He was a hero in their eyes.

Above their heads he saw the solemn, sardonic face of Bill the Dogman. Seeing him, he could remember that he still had almost two months to work for his master before the bet was won.

Then Nagle grabbed him by both hands as the Dogman said in a loud voice: "You oughta like that fellow, kid. He was gonna kill me because I'd murdered you."

"I wish that he had," Sammy said calmly. "Nagle, I'm drinking with you!"

They filled their glasses. They looked with grim, smiling eyes at one another, into one another's souls. Then they drank. After that, glasses were filled up and down the length of the bar, and those hardy Northerners shouted before they drank, and shouted afterward, and their toast was for the Joker. Sometimes they called for Sammy Day; sometimes they yelled for the kid. He had come in a cheechako. He was now an "insider" of the "inside."

In that swirling, smoky air, in that dimly lighted room, warmth and happiness spread through the soul of the young fellow. There is no greater truth than that to be loved makes man desire to be virtuous. Hatred makes sin. Affection makes for goodness. In the hard life of the Joker, there had been respect, esteem, admiration, fear of him, at varying times and in varying ways, but more of fear than any other one element. Now there was an honest kindliness in the atmosphere around him. He rejoiced in it, and he looked around and suddenly stretched out his hands toward these grinning, shaggy-faced men, and said: "Fellows, I feel as though I'd come home. God bless you all."

He heard them growl answers out of the bottom of their hearts. It was home for him, they said. He was the right stuff, the true steel. He was what makes Alaska. They wanted him now, and all the time—they wanted him and his kind, if any more of that kind remained. Then they wanted to know what had happened to him while he was with Bill.

He patted the bar. The dog, a glimmering gray bolt, shot up and landed on the polished wood. He slipped a little, but braced himself quickly on pads that had long been aware of all the ways of managing slippery ice surfaces.

"There's the chief thing that happened to me," said the young man.

The crowd waited through a moment of wise silence as they considered. They knew dogs, all of them.

Then the sharply barking voice of Red called: "Kind of loaded in the shoulders, but he's a pretty good dog!"

"Bring that thing here," Sammy said, and pointed through the crowd.

The great dog left the bar with a long, arching bound. He landed at the feet of Red and caught him by the left arm. Red, screaming with fear, snatched out a gun. It was instantly struck from his hand by a bystander. Meanwhile, Satan drew steadily, gently back. If Red resisted, needles pricked the skin of his wrist. So he yielded and advanced. Pandemonium broke loose, thunders of wild applause shaking the air, until he was close to the Joker.

"That's all right, boy," said the Joker. The dog instantly released the imprisoned arm. "Here," said Sammy Day. Satan leaped again onto the bar. "Now you're a lot nearer," said the Joker. "Look at his shoulders again, will you? Do they look so loaded?"

Red was caressing his slightly bleeding wrist. Fury convulsed his face. That alone was not red. The eyes were bloodstained, too. He shook, wavering a little, as his weight shifted from one foot to the other. "You're bright, ain't you?" he cried out, snarling at the Joker. "You're a smart beauty, ain't you? But I'm gonna sink you one of these days, and what d'you know about that?" As he spoke he snapped his fingers in the face of the Joker.

A gray monster leaped from the bar. The Joker caught him out of the air and was flung to the floor by the weight. Even so, the teeth of Satan had missed the exposed throat of Red by inches only, and the creature shrank away into the crowd with his hands closed about his neck, shrieking.

The Joker got up and drew a breath. Once more he made the big dog leap onto the bar. "His name is Satan," he explained. "And it looks as though he wanted to show you why he's called that. Look him over, boys, and don't shake fists at me again while he's around, because he's unreasonable on the subject. He doesn't like to be touched himself, even by me. And he doesn't see why other people should touch me, either. It's his point of view, and all I can say is that he has his teeth behind it. I'd leave him strictly alone, if I were you fellows."

They agreed. "What can he do besides tricks?" asked Nagle. "Can he pull his weight?"

"Get Mahan's Klondike, and he'll pull a hundred pounds more than that dog," answered the young man.

They flashed glances at one another. Klondike was a famous Hercules among dogs, but when they looked at this specimen again they were unwilling to make hostile bets. It was true that he looked light, somewhat, for his height and ranginess. But his fur was only a third of the usual length among Huskies. No, it was safer not to venture money against Satan, they decided. No one offered to get Klondike for the trial.

"He might be a leader, eh?" ventured Nagle.

"Yeah. He's a leader."

"He might even," Nagle ventured further, "be a loose leader?"

Now, a loose leader is the valuable sort of dog that any dog-puncher can desire. He is that freak animal that is allowed to run ahead of the freighting team and pick out the trail. He comes to know, if he is a true prodigy worthy of the name, how broad a trail the sled needs, and how much thickness of ice there should be to support its weight. If there is a trail problem, he scratches through loose snow to find the buried stakes or the scent. He has a nose of the hair-trigger variety. He knows the peril of water on the ice, if a river trail is being followed. He is in all ways insurance for the rest of the team and the master. He can even shorten his step, to break trail before his laboring mates.

Yet when the question was asked, Sammy Day was able to answer without a moment of hesitation: "That's what he is, a loose leader."

They murmured and nodded, all of these men. Then a voice asked: "Is he yours, son?"

A loud voice answered: "He's mine, and nobody but me owns him!"

That was the snarling voice of Bill the Dogman, so hated in the ear of Sammy Day.

"He belongs to the Dogman," he retorted. "But if I'm alive two months from now, he'll belong to me."

"Yes," Bill the Dogman said, and then he laughed.

"What's the sweet laughter all about, Dogman?" asked Jackson angrily.

"If that little rat don't put his poison teeth into the Joker," replied the Dogman, pointing to Red, "then somebody else will. Because if they don't, he's gonna go up north and win the sweep-stakes at Nome for me. Because Satan ain't alone. There's nine more like him, standing outside the door, and if you don't believe it, go out and take a look!"

They went out with a rush to examine those pearl- or smoke-gray beauties. As for the opinion that they reached in that survey, it was expressed better by a notation that shortly afterward appeared on the big blackboard in Nagle's place, at the top of all of the rest:

Bill the Dogman Sammy Day driving 3–1

Three to win one on the Dogman's team.

But Sammy did not see this, for his eye was taken by Rush Mahan, who suddenly entered the room from the outside and walked straight up to him.

CHAPTER THIRTY-THREE

They were unnoticed. All eyes were fastened on the dog team. As Mahan stepped up, the Joker noticed that there was neither fear nor hate or any malice in his voice.

"Day," he said, "my sister wants to see you. Will you come along with me?"

"Of course," replied the Joker, nodding his head. "I've got to get permission, though, before I do that."

He went to the Dogman. "Bill," he said, "I want a little time off."

"To get drunk? You can't have it!"

"I won't drink. I want to make a visit."

The Dogman looked at Mahan and grinned suddenly. "Yeah, go on," he said. "Go on, and let 'em talk you out of what's comin' to you. Back down. Throw your bet away. You're gonna get a dog, anyway. Ain't that enough pay for you?" He laughed, the snarling laughter of an animal.

Sammy Day went back to Mahan, nodded, and they stepped onto the street together.

So calm and friendly was Mahan that he even paused to say: "That's the finest dog team that I ever saw, Day."

"Ten dogs, all right," answered Sammy. But he felt a little uneasy. He was glad, for some reason, to know that Satan was at his heels. But he was abashed. He felt that Mahan was a bigger man. And his own soul rose up in response to that breadth of spirit.

"Here's the hotel," Mahan said, pausing.

The Joker touched his arm. "Wait a minute," he said.

Mahan turned to him inquiringly. "There's no plant, Day," he said, "if that's what you have in your mind."

Sammy Day flushed to the roots of his hair. "That's all right," he said. "I've let myself in for it. But I'm mighty sorry that you said that."

"I'm sorry, too," Mahan said quietly.

"I've got to tell you this," said Sammy Day. "That's why I stopped you. You look white to me, Mahan. I was wrong the other night." His face burned again.

"Thanks," said Mahan. "I high-hatted you a little, I dare say. I'm glad to forget that evening, Day."

How cool and easy he was about it. There was no threat, no promise that he would find another time to take vengeance. It did not even seem to be in his great, manly soul. Was Goldie like this also?

The Joker cleared his throat. He was speaking with great difficulty. "Another thing," he said. "You went in straight. You're an amateur with your fists. Well, I'm a professional. I mean, I have been. I was good, too. That's why I tackled you, because I guessed that you wouldn't know the game as well as I did."

The big man actually smiled. "Why, Day," he said, "that wouldn't have mattered to you. You would have tackled me if I'd been a mountain and you only a squirrel." He put his hand on the arm of Sammy. "Between you and me," he said, "it's all right. But this is a different matter that's ahead of us. I hope it will turn out as well as our own difficulties." Then he ushered Sammy into the hotel.

They went to the room of the girl. And there, with her, was the dark-faced, dark-eyed man who Sammy had noted in the barroom. He stood up and watched the Joker.

"This is Phil Grant," said Mahan. "Goldie will explain why he's here. I'll stay, too, if you don't mind. Phil, this is Sam Day."

Grant advanced slowly. He seemed to be trying to read the very mind of the young fellow with his dark eyes. He shook hands with a very slight grip.

Then Goldie spoke. The wind was roaring around the building, but that was not the reason why young Sammy Day could hardly hear her voice.

"I want to be let off," she announced simply.

The Joker nodded. Suddenly, the two men were not in the room, so far as he was concerned. There was only the girl.

"I expected that was why you wanted to see me," he replied. "I knew that you wanted to dodge. You'd be ashamed to have me, Goldie, wouldn't you?"

She shook her head. Then she nodded toward Grant. "I want to marry Phil Grant," she said. "That's the reason."

Again the Joker drew a great breath. As it exhaled, he almost laughed. "Did you know you wanted to marry him ten months ago?" he asked.

"No."

"Then …" he began, and paused.

"I thought you were dead. Everyone in Circle City was sure that you would never come back from Bill the Dogman."

The Joker hesitated. "You know," he said, "that there's no law that will make you keep your promise … your bet."

She answered instantly: "I'm not dishonorable, I think. I couldn't break a promise."

"Thank God," said the sudden, deep voice of Rush Mahan.

"Rush," said Phil Grant, "d'you mean that?"

"I mean that. I'd rather see Goldie dead than a liar or a sneak," said Mahan. "You know what I think of you, Phil. I'd like to have you in the family. But not at a price like that. Goldie, I'm proud of you."

She smiled faintly at her brother.

The eyes of Day devoured her.

"Back there, ten months ago," he went on, "did you think it was a joke … that bet we made?"

"Yes," she said. "No girl would be wild enough to do such a thing seriously."

"Wait a minute," he answered. "Remember back to that night. I looked at you, and you looked back at me. You looked at me like the Queen of Sheba at a slave. Now think it over. Were you honestly joking when you made that bet with me?"

She hesitated. Her voice was a moan as she answered: "No, I wasn't joking."

"He'll hold her to it!" exclaimed Phil Grant.

No one replied to this.

"You weren't joking," Sammy went on. "Now, you think back again. When I looked at you, you felt as though I'd laid hands on you, didn't you?"

"Yes," the girl answered. There was an agony in her eyes as she stared at him. She seemed to be seeing his face, and terrible dangers back of it, as well.

"When I spoke to you," he said, "you were insulted, and scorned me. And you looked at Bill the Dogman, and remembered what he had done to other men. In fact, you'd seen Rourke. Hadn't you?"

"Yes," she barely whispered.

"All at once, as you thought of Rourke, you wanted the same thing to happen to me. You wanted me to be broken, to be less than a dog. Am I wrong?"

"I think that I thought that," she replied.

"Think what you're saying, Goldie!" cried Phil Grant. "You're throwing everything away."

"She's telling the truth!" Rush Mahan said sharply.

"Damn the truth!" said Grant.

The Joker smiled a little. "Well," he continued, "ten months have slid under the bridge. Ten months of hell. Now I'm back here. It seems easy, looking back … easy to you. But I can remember every day in the ten months. You understand what I mean?"

"Yes," answered the girl.

"I can remember every day," he continued, his voice rising a little, "by the whip strokes. Not on the skin. I've been chewed up by dogs. But that's not all. I want you to look at something." He pointed to Satan.

She nodded, her eyes dim. But she looked now, steadily, at the big, pearl-gray dog. And the dog looked not at her, but calmly at his master's face.

"Bill the Dogman is a hard man, and he's trained a lot of dogs. This is the best one he ever bred," remarked Sammy. "He tried to handle this one. He was nearly killed. So were his two big buck Indians, one time or another. Finally, he gave up. He called him Satan."

The dog stood up and wagged his tail as he heard his name. With burning devotion he stared at the face of the master.

"He called him Satan," repeated Sammy, "and I went to hell for him, and I came back, and here he is. I don't want to lay it on too thick, but that was only one month out of ten. Take it all in all, it was about the pleasantest month of the lot. Well, now I'm back here, and Satan is with me, but I'm asking you to remember that I've been in hell. Can you realize that?"

"Yes," answered Goldie. "I'm thinking about that."

"Another thing," pursued Sammy. "What kept me going was not just the wish to beat Bill the Dogman. It was the wish to beat you. I hated your pride and your high head. I wanted to drag it down."

"Oh," exclaimed the girl with a strange gesture of appeal, "I'll fall down on my knees and beg if you'll let me go!"

He began to find it hard to breathe. He laid hold of his furred hood at the neck and pulled it loose around his throat. "I've got to tell you another thing," he said, "but it's a secret. Can I whisper it in your ear?"

"We'll leave the room," said Rush Mahan.

"There's no need of that," said the Joker. "If you don't mind me whispering in your ear, Goldie?"

She nodded. "Of course not," she replied. She stepped closer.

He leaned above her. He bowed his head and whispered a short phrase in her ear. Then he straightened.

But Goldie Mahan, burying her face in her hands, was sobbing bitterly, in utter and final despair.

CHAPTER THIRTY-FOUR

The Joker left the hotel at once. Twenty steps from the door, Satan, who was in front of his master, suddenly whirled about. The Joker turned, also, and saw Philip Grant, whose hand was inside his fur coat.

"Don't do it, Rabbit," said the Joker. "If you try it, Satan will get you."

Grant walked straight up and halted with his face hardly six inches from the Joker's. "You blow out of Circle City, brother," he said.

"Do I?" asked the Joker.

"You blow pronto," said Phil Grant. "I've got you in the hollow of my hand, young man."

"Which hand?" asked the Joker.

"Both hands. I know all about that play in Devil Creek. I knew Dan Bray, and I know all about how you croaked him."

"You lie," replied the Joker. "I didn't croak him. He's as much alive as you are."

"He is?" exclaimed Phil Grant. Then he shook his head. "You're lying," he declared.

"No, I'm not lying," answered Sammy Day. "Go ahead and make a squawk if you want to."

"Bray is dead," insisted the other.

"Not out of my gun."

"You're a snaky cheat and a thief, Joker. You can't get away with the bluff."

"I'll break your chin for you, Rabbit," said the Joker. "Back up before you talk like that."

Phil Grant looked him over with a savage interest. "Why don't I slam you now?" he asked, as though to himself.

"Because you're afraid," said the Joker. "You never quite trusted yourself when it came to me."

"I've licked you to within an inch of your life, and you know it," he responded.

"You left me for dead. I was fifteen, then," said Day.

"I can handle you still."

"You start trying, Phil. But you won't. I've got you beaten, and you know it."

"If you knew it, you'd start a play."

"I'll start no play until you begin leading," the Joker assured him. "If I put a bullet through your head, Goldie bursts into tears and starts mourning for you ... and she tries to get me hanged for murder."

Suddenly, Grant began to laugh. "I see," he said. "That ties your hands. Well, I don't mind that. Only, I wanted to tell you this. If you don't back out and stop trying to hold up the poor kid about her promise to you, I'll slam you in jail."

"Will you?"

"Yes, I'll tell what I know."

"You've become a stool pigeon since I last saw you," Sammy observed good-naturedly.

"Your names don't hurt me," answered Grant. "I'll put you in the pen with a rope around your neck."

"Will you?"

"D'you think I'm standing here freezing my feet for nothing?"

"What a cur you are, Rabbit!" Sammy exclaimed.

"All the names in the world don't bother me," replied Grant, unperturbed. "I'm telling you the truth. I'm telling you what I'll do."

"How will you get me?"

"Well, for bank robbery, murder, and a few little things like that. That's all."

"You can't hang a thing on me."

"All of Arizona knows what you are, Joker," pursued Grant in some surprise. "Why d'you try to hold out? D'you think that I won't come across the way I say?"

"You'd poison me, all right," answered the Joker. "But it's no good, son. You haven't been in Arizona for two years, and you haven't been reading the newspapers, either. Where have you been? Doing a little stretch?"

The other blinked. "You can't pull the wool over my eyes," he said. "You're smooth, Joker, but you can't fool me."

"You poor boob," answered Sammy Day with a gesture of contemptuous dismissal, "the governor of the state pardoned me for everything outstanding. He did that nearly two years ago."

"He did what?" shouted Grant.

"I cleared myself of that murder gag. That was only a rap. It never was real. And I paid back to the bank the coin I'd swiped. They were glad to get it. They led me to the pardon by both hands."

"This is a lot of guff," declared Phil Grant.

"All right. Try your rap," the Joker said, shrugging his shoulders.

"I believe you mean it," muttered Grant.

"Sure, I mean it"

"It can't be," Grant said. "If it weren't that you know what I have on you, you'd squeal on me."

Day looked him over carefully. "You don't seem to understand. I never talk," he said finally.

"You never talk?"

"I never talk."

"I guess that you'd let me go straight on with Goldie Mahan, eh? Is that the idea?"

"I'd let you go as far as you could. No marriage, though."

"No?"

"No."

"How would you stop that?"

"With a gun, Rabbit."

Phil Grant laughed cheerfully. "Say, kid," he replied, "d'you think that you can kill me with talk?"

"I'm just telling you."

"What you tell me doesn't matter. What you might tell Goldie is a little different … not that she'd believe you. No, she never would believe anything against me."

Sammy looked him over again with incredible disgust. Yet his voice remained calm as he said: "How did you put it over, Rabbit?"

"Me manly voice and ways," replied Grant. "That's what mattered. Me dark silence, son. That's what turned the trick, and a little thing about a drunk half-breed that started a knife play on Rush Mahan."

"You killed the 'breed, did you?"

"Deader than a door nail."

"Owe him money?" Sammy asked curiously and coldly.

"How did you guess that, son?" asked Grant.

"It might have happened that way. Well, Rabbit, so long."

"You mean that you're walking out like this?"

"Yes, for the present."

"Look here, kid, you don't want me against you. You know I'll poison your soup. Better make a play with me."

"What sort of a play."

"I'm full of it," said the other.

"Full of what?"

Grant snapped his fingers. "The long green," he said. "I'll give you a good cut."

"How much, Rabbit?"

"I'll hand you five grand. I'll hand it now."

"Five?"

"Yeah, I mean it. A lot of money just for turning your back."

"It's a lot, but not enough. You want me to tell Goldie that I'm through?"

"That's it."

"The Mahans have a lot of coin," observed Sammy. "You'd be marrying a soft spot for life. Unless the bad news got this far north before the wedding day … the spoiled news about you, Rabbit."

"The Mahans are a soft spot," Grant agreed, overlooking the last part of the speech. "But I'm talking spot cash, not futures. Five grand is five thousand dollars in anybody's money."

"Let me see it."

"Here. Take it in your hand." He drew out a wallet.

"No," said Sammy. "It's not enough. I can have her. She's promised to me. You can't buy her for five grand."

"I'll raise the ante a little."

"Raise it, then."

"I'll go my limit."

"What's that?"

There was grimness in the eyes of Phil Grant. "I'll make it ten thousand bucks, old son."

"That's a lot of money, if it's real," said Sammy Day.

"Want to feel it?"

"I don't mind. You, lie down, Satan." The dog, which had been stealing closer to Grant, backed up a pace and lay down on the snow. The Joker took off his mitten and bared his hand to the flame-like cold. "Let me feel the coin," he said.

Grant held out a little sheaf of bills that trembled in the wind. "Here you are," he said.

"Thanks," said the Joker. He struck Grant heavily on the point of the jaw. The latter spun about, his hands reaching helplessly before him, and dropped on his face, while the Joker gathered up the money, took the fallen man by one ankle, and dragged him inside the hotel. There he left him, cramming the greenbacks into his mouth like a gag. Then he went off down the street. Satan ran lightly before him, licking his lips.

When Bill the Dogman saw his driver at the end of the half hour, he said instantly: "What's happened?"

"Nothing," replied Sammy. "But I want you to let up on one point of our agreement."

"What point?"

"I want to pack a gun."

The Dogman considered him with the utmost gravity. Then he shook his head. "What for?"

"They're betting on our team," answered the Joker. "And I'll need a gun to keep the fixers away from the dogs."

The Dogman shook his head again. "You're not thinking of the dogs. You're thinking of yourself," he ventured.

"Suppose I am," answered the youngster.

"Somebody been threatening you outside of the little rat, Red?"

"Yes. I'm in danger from other people, too."

"You'll have to keep on inside of that danger, then," replied the Dogman. "I'm not going to let you pack a gun."

"You can't handle that team without me," answered the Joker. "You know that."

"You pack a gun," argued the Dogman, "and you'll be committing murder before the race. You can't mush my dog team while you're in jail, you know."

"Take another think," urged the boy. "They're after my scalp."

"Who?"

"That's my secret."

"Just the same," replied Bill, "you don't get a gun."

CHAPTER THIRTY-FIVE

They went to Nome. By ice, by snow, on the well-beaten trail, they went over the long hundreds of miles to Nome, and the wind never stopped screaming, the cold never abated, and the torment was steady and long.

Bill the Dogman turned blue, but he remarked: "This here is the making of the team. This'll harden 'em."

"Or kill 'em," suggested Sammy.

"You can't kill those dogs except with bullets," replied the Dogman. "Look at 'em! There ain't a limp in the whole outfit." He was right. There was not a limping dog. But when they struck the bad surfaces, they had to keep constantly making and remaking moccasins for the feet of the team. At every halt they were preparing fresh sets. To shoe and unshoe forty feet was no trifle. But that was better than having the pads worn down to the bone.

To show what the surface of that snow could do, one day, through the white, driving snow mist, they passed the silhouette of a timber wolf trying to gallop away from them, but only succeeding in going at a staggering walk. Every step left blood behind him. His paws were worn to the bone.

Bill the Dogman worked valiantly on that trail. It seemed now that he could not do enough to favor his driver. But Sammy was not deceived. He knew that Bill took over the lion's share of the work in pitching camp, not because of any fondness that he might feel for him, but simply because he wished to relieve him of all unessential labors and leave him as fresh as possible for the actual ardors of the race. After they had been for a week on the trail, Bill insisted that the pace, every day, should be increased.

Sammy agreed. He went at such a clip that a dozen times thereafter, Bill the Dogman was left out of sight to the rear, striding valiantly, but far behind the sleds. The team flew. It seemed tireless, gaining in power with the passage of time upon the trail.

At the end of one of those terrific marches, Bill came in two hours late, and fell in a faint on the tarpaulin beside the fire that Sammy had built.

The Joker poured brandy down his throat till he sat up, strangling and coughing.

"Tomorrow you ride half the time," said the Joker, scowling.

"I'll see myself dead first," said Bill the Dogman. He was blue, his face drawn, his eyes rolling. That night he could not eat.

In the morning he was doubled up like a closing jackknife. He refused breakfast, except three cups of steaming tea.

So he got to his feet and took a few slow, grim paces up the trail. As he came to the rear sled, Sammy caught him from behind and downed him on the tarpaulin covering. After wrapping the Dogman in furs, he tied him down.

Bill, struggling with all his might, but feebly, screamed and raved with shame and with fury. He pleaded, finally, to be allowed to march with the team. "You're making a fool of me!" he yelled.

"You were born a fool," answered Sammy. "Shut your face, and take your luck as you find it."

"You've broken the contract!" yelled the Dogman. "I ordered you to turn me loose, and you've gone and refused. The contract's busted. Turn me loose from here now and be damned. You can't travel with my dogs another step!"

Sammy stood over him, watching him closely. He half thought that the wits of the vile old man had forsaken him, but he refused to let the Dogman walk.

So the Joker gave the word to the dogs and mushed them up the staked trail.

But his mind was filled with thoughts of the Dogman this day, even more than with the haunting recollections of Goldie Mahan and her newfound hero, the Rabbit. A strange respect and pity for the Dogman was growing up in him. At least the man had devoted his life to an idea. Of his courage and self-sacrifice on the trail, there was now no doubt.

Through the march to the noon halt, Sammy did not speak to the Dogman, nor the latter to him. But Bill sat erect, staring bitterly before him into the eye of the wind.

Then, at the halt, when Sammy undid the cords that tied him, Bill still uttered no complaint about the treatment that he had received. He merely went grimly about his share of the work in preparing their meal, his old hands wonderfully active and skillful. And he ate for two after his enforced fast.

In the afternoon he marched steadily behind the sleds. He did not speak. Neither would Sammy talk. And he told himself bitterly that Bill would keep to his threat. He would consider that the contract was broken, that he, the Joker, had failed to live up to the letter of it.

What would happen then? Goldie Mahan would be lost, of course. The Rabbit would get her. It seemed to Sammy that his brain would burst into flames, there was such a raging madness in him at that thought, for he had known the Rabbit not long, but too well. Here and there, and again at intervals, he had crossed the path of that gunfighter, trickster, and hypocrite. And never once had he heard anything good concerning that criminal. There was neither kindness, generosity, good faith for his friends, nor any other virtue in him, except those of courage, sharp wits, and all that was necessary to his crooked profession.

Once, when Sammy was still in his teens, he had clashed with the older man and had been shot down. The superior speed and cleverness of the Rabbit had accomplished this. Then the Joker had been unmercifully beaten, until he lay as dead. He had himself thought that he was dying.

But it was not regret for his personal encounter with the Rabbit that mattered, nor did he feel that his personal feud was important. It was the fate of the girl that counted—Goldie, as the wife of the Rabbit!

He could stop it, of course, by saying ten words. But those words he could not say. The loathing that he felt for retailers of news surpassed his hatred of all other things in the world. Whatever harm came to the Rabbit, he knew, would have to be with bullets, not words, so far as he was concerned. That would be the wretched end, then. He would murder the scoundrel and be hanged for it, and Goldie Mahan could mourn for the Rabbit as for a martyred hero. Well, it was a strange world in which he found himself. Yet he might keep her to her promise if Bill the Dogman did not insist that the contract had been broken by his failure to obey.

The whole matter was a ghastly tangle. The Joker could not close his eyes that night. In the morning, when he had harnessed the team, he pointed in silence to the place prepared on the rear sled. The Dogman glared bitterly at him, as though measuring his faded strength against the wildcat energy of the young man. At last, surrendering, he took his place on the load and was drawn by the dogs.

In that way they went to Nome in silence. Not a word was spoken during the last marches. Half of each day the Dogman rode, and half of each day he walked. His face was set and grim.

So at last, across the ice, they saw the gleaming streak of the lights of Nome, like an electric sword through the dimness of the Arctic.

The Dogman suddenly shouted and laughed like a madman. He began to run forward with immense strides. "It's there! It's there!" he screamed. "D'you see it, Sammy?"

The Joker looked at him with a frozen heart. The man was certainly mad.

"It's there!" yelled the Dogman, throwing his hands above his head and then forward. "There I'll be clean, and a man again. I've done my work. I've raised the dogs, and I've brought 'em to the mark!"

He turned and shook his fist at Sammy Day. "Damn you, it's up to you to drive 'em like a man! It's your job to win for us both!"

A whirling, dazzling joy burst upon the Joker. He knew that he had been reinstated. A broken contract would not be held against him now.

CHAPTER THIRTY-SIX

Gold or commerce was not in Nome. The news of the world no longer mattered; the world did not exist. Under the dull sky, and on the white-encrusted streets of the strange city, nothing was of importance save only dogs.

As for men, a few of them also were worth a glance. They were the drivers of the teams, for the great Nome Sweepstakes was now not so very many days away.

If men talked, they talked of dogs. If men fought, it was in argument over the merits of their favorites. When loud voices rose, it was always someone or several proclaiming: "The greatest leader that ever ran a team!" The gambling was on a vast scale.

Reckless life was in the air of Nome when the ten-dog team of Bill trotted down the streets. Men saw them afar, and word went around. How could people have learned so soon about Bill and his formidable team? They had not learned. But one glance was sufficient to tell the story.

While they were finding lodging and quarters for the team, they came by scores—men, women, and children—to watch the dogs.

They looked at the gray beauties, and they looked at one another. But they were quiet. Every grown person, and even most of the children, had placed bets on the great sweepstakes long before. Was this new entry likely to upset all calculations?

"They can move," said one man in a deep voice. And heads were nodded in confirmation.

"They're in the sweepstakes, are they?" asked another.

Bill the Dogman straightened up to his full height. "They're the entry of William Rafferty," he said. "And that's me."

Afterward, when he was alone with Sammy in their quarters, he took out a greasy wallet. On the table he counted out a stack of bills, emptied the wallet, and pulled aside some of the money for himself. "The rest is yours, kid," he said. "It's every penny that I've got in the world. I've blown the rest. But I've created the type, and you'll drive 'em. You'll drive them and me into fame. You'll put us up where we won't be forgotten. I know that. They can't beat those dogs, nor you, either!" He beat his fist on the table as he spoke. Then he said: "There's ten thousand dollars there. I've kept five hundred out for myself. The rest is yours. It's your year's wages."

"The year isn't up," Sammy said, strangely moved.

"The year is up when the race is run," said Bill the Dogman. "And that ain't so many weeks off. It's right on us now."

Sammy counted the money. There was exactly, as Bill had said, $10,000. He shoved it back across the table. "It's a good play, Bill," he said, "but I can't take it."

"Are you batty?" asked the Dogman.

"I don't take money from you," said Sammy. "I'm not working for money. It's something else."

The Dogman scowled ferociously at him. "You worked to beat the game and to get the girl, eh?" he said.

Sammy shrugged his shoulders.

"You worked to get the girl," repeated Bill. "Are you gonna be skunk enough to hold her to a promise like that?"

The Joker said nothing. There was no speech left in him, he was so amazed.

"You blackguard," said the Dogman, "she's a lady. Ain't you got the eye to see that?"

Still the Joker could say nothing.

"You and your money," continued the Dogman. "I don't care whether you take it or not. Or if you murder me afterward, when you're a free man again. Likely you will. I ain't interested. Run the race and win it. That's all I want out of you. But to do that, you gotta go shoppin' here and get yourself the finest, lightest outfit that money will buy for you. Run the race. Then you're free, and you can go and blackmail the girl. Oh, Joker, your soul will rot a million ages in hell if you lay your dirty hands on her."

The Joker at last was able to say: "Talk about the dogs, Bill. But don't talk about the girl, because I won't stand it."

"Every blackguard has his blackest side," said the Dogman, continuing in this unexpected strain. "Well, I wouldn't've thought it of you. Throw that money to the wind if you like, but take enough to buy yourself an outfit."

"I'll not touch it," said Sammy. "It's not money that I want from you, Bill."

"Blood is what you want, eh?" Bill asked with his twisted, leering grin.

"Yes," answered the Joker. "Blood is all that I want from you. You rat!" Some of the concentrated hatred of the long months crept into his voice, though he did not speak loudly.

The other nodded. "Yeah," he said, "I knew it was inside of you, stewin' over a fire. You wouldn't see, you fool, that I had to test you and hammer you and bend you to see whether you'd break, to see whether you was the real steel that I wanted."

The Joker said nothing. He simply watched, taking a curious, savage pleasure in running his eyes over the impossibly ugly face of Bill. There was much to be done between them. There were ten thousand tortures to be repaid.

At last he broke out: "There's only one thing I'd change about you, Bill."

"Tell me what," said the Dogman.

"I'd have you thirty years younger," answered Sammy.

The Dogman stretched his long arms and laughed. "If I was thirty years younger," he said, "I'd break you up for kindlin' wood. I'd drive the dogs myself, except Satan," he added with a curious change of tone. "That's a thing that I never could've done. You say you went to hell to learn how to handle him. Well, you had luck to come back to earth."

"Yeah. I had luck," admitted Sammy.

Then the Dogman said: "Ever wonder why I put you through that torment, kid?"

Sammy nodded. "You don't need to tell me," he said. "I can guess."

"You guess all wrong," said Bill. "It ain't fear of what you'll do to me with knives or guns that makes me talk, but because you've been a man. You've earned an explanation, and here it is. I'd soaked some years into Alaska. I'd struck my gold. I'd brought it out. I was pretty well fixed. Then, on my last trip out, one of my dogs busted a leg, another went mad, and another went dead lame, and one of 'em was bitten to death by the mad dog before it died. And the fifth dog … well, the fifth dog, he seen me through." He paused and tapped on the table. His face grew more hideous than ever. "He seen me through, and he died doin' it, and that kind of got me interested in dogs. I never was none interested in men or women or brats. But in dogs, I got kind of interested. Bing," he added, his voice dropping, "Bing was the name of him that seen me through. He got me clean to the door of the house. That was where they picked me up, and him, too. We poured brandy and things down his throat. It wasn't no good."

He coughed before going on. "After that I said that I'd breed dogs that could stand the cold, stand the gaff. They'd have feet like iron, speed, sense, and brains. Something like Bing. I wanted to make them a kind of monument to him. Something that would last longer and better'n stone. And I been workin' at it ever since." He paused again. "Once I turned out the right kind of dogs, didn't I have to have the right kind of a man to drive 'em?"

Sammy nodded. He was more fascinated than ever he had been in his life.

"I had to have a man of iron. I had to have a man that would work till his soul was on the rim of his lips, ready to blow away. I hunted for men like that. I offered a fat salary. I paid down good hard cash. And I never found a man that would stand what I could do to him." His voice snarled as he added: "Then I found you." He stared at Sammy. "You was small, not a big man, wizened, and no good. But you was mean. You was so mean that you wouldn't go smash. I never thought that you'd march through that first day. But you marched. And then I laughed, because I thought of all the other things that I could do to you. I was gonna smash you to bits. I was kinder irritated, thinkin' of how I had to waste time breakin' a mean brat like you. So I hurried up to smash you quick. I piled on you, inside of a month, everything that I piled on Rourke in three, and more things, too. I turned John and Pete ag'in' you. I underfed you. But on beans and coffee you beat everything that I could do.

"After that I got kinder amused. I was sure, from the size of you, that you wasn't the man that I wanted. I ain't one that ever believed a bit in runts. And you're a sort of runt. So I thought up other things, but none of 'em turned your head. Finally, I got the idea of seein' just what sort of real silk was inside of you, and so I staked Satan out." He stopped again. His eyes grew vacant. "When I seen what you done to Satan," he said, "I knew that you was medicine, all right. And then, for the first time, I had a kind of a hope that I'd be able to hand my dogs to a man able to break 'em, able to drive 'em. The one man in the world. That's what I kinder hoped!" He banged his fist suddenly on the table. "And you're the man!" he exclaimed. "A rotten soul you've got, or you wouldn't try to cheat the girl. But you're a dog man, the same as me!"

CHAPTER THIRTY-SEVEN

The racetrack at Nome is four hundred miles long. It goes over every sort of imaginable country. It includes sea ice and broken snow. But still it is a track. Even on a smoothly tracked turf course, a jockey likes to ride the track a few times in order to gain an understanding of the local grounds, the fences, the turns, the stands, the start, whatever slopes there are to be reckoned with, where the going is deep, and where it is hard.

There was all the more reason why the course of the Nome Sweepstakes should be rehearsed. The day after his arrival, therefore, without a brief interval in which he and the dog team might rest, Sammy Day went out to the Nome racetrack. It was not to be a fast run, and Bill the Dogman went with him.

Bill was in talkative mood. "You see that sled with the eight dogs ahead?" he asked.

"I see it," replied Sammy at the gee pole.

"You think it's another team working the trail, but it ain't. It's a spotter, out to see how this set travels. Watch 'em. They won't never be far away."

He was right. They were never far away. Sometimes they were ahead. On a long up-pitch on the second day they fell behind, and the Joker saw a dark-faced half-breed handling the dogs. He waved his hand, but did not speak to Bill or the driver.

"That 'breed is the spotter," repeated Bill the Dogman. "Watch him throw his eye on Satan."

For Satan was ranging now as a loose leader, scouring along the trail ahead of his master's team, and spotting the stakes, some of them iron, which marked out the way. A well-marked trail it was, and the dog, looking here and sniffing there, was committing all of the important details to memory.

"Will he remember?" asked the Dogman.

"Better than I can," replied the Joker. "Trust Satan and he'll bring us through."

They studied the rest houses along the way, and at every one of these, men came out and looked the dogs over, taking in the two men as well. They knew the Dogman. They had all seen him before, it appeared, and they looked at him without smiling, nodding their heads, as a rule.

"Are you gonna do it, Bill?" they said.

He never answered. Sometimes he would wave his hand at the dogs, as though to invite all strangers to make up their minds for themselves. And certainly every man of the lot seemed to give the team their serious consideration.

"The odds are gonna climb on our side," Bill remarked to the Joker as they pushed forward one day.

And so the Joker agreed. When they had finished the first trip, he remained only two days to rest in Nome. They were busy days. He ordered great quantities of moccasins for the dogs, made of good, tough leather, and he had them fitted well. He tried on a good, light, warm outfit in a store, and left his measurements, so that it could be cut down to suit him.

It was not the Dogman's money that paid for this suit, though he bought the things needed for the dogs, and had under construction a sled light as a feather and tough as gristle. He even used violin strings, at a vast price, to tie together the various parts of the sled. Every ounce would tell in the long run. Brains, legs, and a light weight, Bill the Dogman was fond of saying.

But the clothes were bought by the money of Nagle, from Circle City. He met Sammy in the street as the latter was taking out two of the dogs, Toothwork and Grab, with a small sled for a little special workout. One never could tell. Satan might be crippled, or poisoned, for that matter, and a secondary leader was essential in the team.

Nagle did not give the Joker effusive greetings, but he shook hands and looked deeply into his eyes. "How's things?" he asked.

"Sort of on the up," was the reply. "How's things with you?"

"I'm backing Rush Mahan," the bartender said frankly.

The Joker nodded.

Nagle explained: "You've got the best dogs, to fill the eye. And you're a grand musher, I know. But that won't be the whole deal. You've got people against you that would walk a thousand miles to drop one pebble in your way. That little rat, Red, would stab you in the back if he could. You watch him. He's more poison than you think."

"He's poison," the Joker agreed soberly. "But I've got to take my chances."

"The whole infernal gang knows that the Dogman won't let you pack a gun," Nagle broke out. "They're working with that idea in mind. They'll use bullets on you, son, if that's the only way to stop you."

"All right," replied Sammy Day. "I'll have to take my chance on that, too."

"Tell me," said the other. "D'you think that you'll win?"

"I don't think," the Joker said. "I run in the race, and that's all."

"All right," said Nagle. "You run hard. On second thought, I think I'll do some covering, but it'll cost me a lot of money. They've put you in as favorite, and this is the first time that you've ever covered the course. There's a 'breed here in town that says you've got the best leader that ever ran over the course. But that can't be. I've seen …"

"I don't care what you've seen," said the Joker, yawning. "Quit it, will you, old son? I don't want to talk about the dogs. I want some money."

"Won't Bill finance you?"

"I don't use Bill's money."

The other whistled.

"The Dogman has dirty hands," explained the Joker, his lips curling a little. "I want some proper clothes and some pocket money. What will you do for me?"

"I'm short," said Nagle. "I can't very well give you more than a thousand."

"Two hundred will do for me."

"Bet everything you had?"

"I had fifty cents. They're not betting fifty-cent pieces in Nome. Not on this little race. So I still have my fifty cents."

"The same coin you had back there eleven months ago?"

"The same coin."

Nagle chuckled. "You're living cheap and light, son," he remarked.

"I'm living off the country," answered the Joker. "Give me two hundred, will you?"

The saloonkeeper handed the amount to him, and Sammy nodded his thanks.

"Who's in town?" asked the Joker.

"Everybody. Rush Mahan and Goldie, if you wanna know."

"Yeah. I want to know."

"They're down at the Grand Hotel. Rush is betting his socks on the race. He's got twenty dogs, and he's picking the cream. They're all so good that he might as well shut his eyes and pick at random. How about that number one dog you've got on this man's sled?"

"You'll see him run the day of the race," said the Joker. "So long, Nagle."

Then he exercised the dogs, put them up, and left his orders for the clothes. After that he went to his hotel and slept for two days.

That is to say, he was not up more than three hours a day. The rest of the time, he was relaxed in his bed, asleep or drowsing. He ate one meal a day, and recuperated like an animal hibernating.

After that he left Nome again, and traveled without the Dogman twice around the course. He did not push the team, because they did not need pushing. Satan was no longer a loose leader, but worked between traces, and worked like a horse. The whole line of the dogs responded to his touch. The Dogman could not come along because they were traveling at racehorse speed. He could not run with Sammy at such a rate. Yet the time they made in rounding the course was very bad. It was bad because every day the Joker backtracked for miles, and then came on again. No one was to be able to clock him in his work.

When he had finished the second round, the race was four days off. He took the dogs from harness, fed them well, and turned them into their runs to rest and recuperate again.

Then he went to bed. He ached from head to foot. He had been working for many days under a terrible physical tension, but he knew that he had stripped every wasted ounce of flesh from his body. He was in perfect condition. Now all that he needed was rest, allowing his muscles to grow smooth and soft, until he finally stepped out and made the final effort.

Yet he found that he hardly cared about the outcome of the race, except for one thing. That was the dog Satan.

Satan was not put out in the run with the other dogs. The Joker had tried to put him there, but he chewed his way through two-by-four scantlings and got to the street. He found the trail of his master, followed it through the tangle of a thousand other footfalls and scents, and smashed the flimsy door of the hotel with his shoulder. Then he smashed the door of the Joker's room and quietly sat down by his bed. Bill the Dogman paid the damages without a murmur, but after that Satan was not put into a run. He stayed with his driver.

Nome heard the story. It was a perfect tale to go before a race, and the odds on the Dogman's team mounted and mounted.

The second day the Joker rose from his bed. He had fasted for twenty-four hours and more. Now he ate three pounds of beefsteak, a dozen eggs, and washed it down with six cups of coffee. After that he felt comfortable, and somewhat as a snake must feel after it has swallowed a month's portion. So he went down to the first big saloon, sat in a corner, smoked one cigarette, and went to sleep again in his chair.

No one disturbed him. People came and went softly. The rumbling of voices along the bar did not disturb the Joker. On the contrary, they made rather a soothing harmony.

But many faces turned toward the sleeper. One of these faces was Phil Grant's. Another was the face of the hobo, Red. And finally, as though drawn by an inward sympathy, they drew together and stood shoulder to shoulder at the bar. They began to talk to one another, both of them still looking at the Joker.

CHAPTER THIRTY-EIGHT

"I know a man who'd do it for one grand," Red remarked. "Listen, I don't even ask no commission. I'd pay the coin myself, if I didn't happen to be a little flat just now. You know how it is. But I know the bohunk who'll do the job. He's only got one price. A thousand bucks. It's high, but he takes on anybody. He'd murder King George for the same rate. There ain't no bonuses to throw in afterward."

The hand of Phil Grant, having first made a trip to his wallet, came forth and slid down the bar. The claw of Red closed over it and secured something. His eyes bulged and glistened with pleasure at the feel of the greenbacks. He swallowed hard.

"I'm gonna go get the beauty now," he said.

"Mind you, Red," said Grant. "Tell your friend that he'd better get Satan first and the man second. Tag that dog out before you go on with the game."

"Leave everything to me and me partner," said Red. "So long, Mr. Grant."

He left that saloon and got to another that was warmer, fouler, more dimmed with tobacco smoke. There, in the most sordid corner, he found his bohunk, a man whose face was swollen and whose eyes were starting as though he were about to explode. His complexion was pale, a sickly white, and his eyes were pale, also, as though they were filmed over with gauze. This image of living and breathing death possessed a body swollen like his face, but it was power rather than fat that distended it. He kept his femininely small, delicate hand on exhibition by playing with his glass of whiskey, which he sipped as though it were a liqueur.

Red did not sit down at the table. Instead, he slipped in along the wall until he was behind the shoulder of the other.

"Slade," he said.

The other did not move or answer.

"Slade," went on Red, "I got a job for you. A slick job. Only a kid to bump off, and you pick up two hundred bucks, Slade. Whatcha say?"

"I say go to hell," said Slade.

Red hurried around in front of him like a bull terrier. "Listen to me," he barked softly, furiously, the effort shaking his body, "you ain't gonna turn down easy money like that?"

"Who's the bloke?" asked Slade. "Get me another drink."

Red went to the bar and returned, having paid for another glass of the red-brown poison. "It's only a kid," said Red. "It's the Joker, as they call him, because he's only a joke."

"It's Bill the Dogman's man, is it?" said Slade. "And he's a joke, is he? And you wanna pay me two hundred bucks for socking that beauty, do you?" The expression of his face did not change. His eyes appeared deader than before.

"I'd make it three hundred," Red said, searching the other earnestly, but in vain.

"I'm flush," said Slade. "I've seen the kid. I've heard about him."

"I'll give you your whole price," said Red. "I'll give you five hundred bucks."

"I'll tell you what," said Slade. "I'll sock him for one grand. That's all."

"Hey, you wanna double up on me? You wanna rob me?" moaned Red, outraged.

"Get out of my sight, then," Slade said, "and hire somebody else. I don't like the job, anyway."

Red submitted. He passed the $1,000 he had received from Grant across the table. Slade took the money and calmly counted it in full view of everyone in the room.

"Don't do that," appealed Red. "Suppose they was to see and remember? Suppose they was to ask me what money I brought to you, and where I got it? What would you say?"

"I don't care what questions they ask," said Slade. "For my part, when my day comes, it comes. That's all there is to it. Where's this kid friend of yours?"

Red told him and was waved away. He left in haste. Shuddering fear pursued him, and shuddering joy, also.

So Slade finished his second glass of whiskey, went to the bar for a third, huddled himself into a ragged parka, and left the dive. He walked slowly with short steps. But even that effort made his breath come hard. He was as brittle as an eggshell, and he knew that before long he would break. He cared not a whit.

The point of vantage that he wanted was a deeply indented doorway where he was sheltered from the cold wind. The young fellow would have to pass that way in going back to his hotel. So Slade leaned against the corner of the wall and waited, regardless of the flurries of snow that whipped in against his face, his eyes still bulging. He looked only straight ahead. He saw the dim flurries of the storm, like the beating of ghostly wings above the roofs of the buildings. He felt stifled and cornered. There were fair places in the world. He had seen most of them, but this was his last refuge, as it seemed. However, he had no regrets; he had lived his life; he cared not for the last day. He held out his right hand. It was as steady as a rock. That was all that mattered. Then he slipped his hand out of the mitten and put it inside his coat, until he found the handle of his revolver. There he rested his fingers.

He was there for ten minutes only, but he had begun to feel tired on his legs, when he saw what he wanted—a smoke-gray dog coming up the street, and behind him a man who looked slender even in the swathing of furs, a light-bodied man, leaning against the wind to better resist its pressure.

Slade stepped straight out into the wind. It cuffed him in the back and unsteadied him a little. He wished that he had shot around the corner. Now he was out there; however, he would not change his plan. He raised his revolver and fired.

He saw the young man dodge the whir of the bullet, then the heavy echo of the explosion struck the faces of the buildings and rolled back faintly through the rush of the wind.

I've missed, Slade berated himself. *It's the damned wind.*

He had lowered the gun. He raised it again with more care. But he was amazed. Instead of fleeing, the Joker was running toward him at full speed, dodging from side to side like a snipe flying down the wind.

I could run like that when I was a kid, thought Slade. But he had hardly noticed the dog, and that was his error.

Darting like a shadow, close to the ground, Satan came straight in, silently. Slade caught the form of the young fellow full in the sights for a well-aimed shot. He knew that he could not miss now. He got the body first, but pride made him shift his aim to the head, and it was just as he shifted the aim that Satan rose like a ghost out of the snow and struck at the gun arm.

The bones of the forearm crunched like dead twigs underfoot. The gun exploded, going wild, as Slade was jerked around and flung to his face, skidding on the snow, by the impact of the dog's spring.

The Joker took him by the collar and drew him to a sitting posture.

Slade did not attempt to flee or to speak. With his dead-fish eyes, he looked steadily at the young fellow. Blood was fast crimsoning his right sleeve. The broken arm lay at a crooked angle.

"Who are you?" the Joker asked, panting a little.

Slade did not answer.

"Stand up," commanded Sammy Day. And he helped Slade to rise. "I've seen you somewhere," said Day, "but you've got nothing against me." He looked at the ragged furs. Then he reached inside the breast of the coat and found the wallet. He took it out and glanced at the sheaf of bills. "Who gave you this to snag me?" he asked.

Slade said nothing. His broken arm hung down, and the blood dripped onto the snow. Satan sat close by, curious, intent, licking his red-stained lips.

"Who hired you?" repeated the young man. Still Slade was silent. The Joker looked him over with a revulsion of feeling and yet with interest. "You didn't shoot from behind anything," he said. "And you thought I had a gun, I guess."

Slade watched him with his glassy eyes and made no reply. Then the Joker considered the wounded arm. It was badly smashed by the crunching jaws of Satan.

"All right," the Joker said, nodding. "You'd better find a doctor. Purvis is the best one. I hope he can patch you up." He turned away.

"Wait a minute," said Slade. The young man paused. "I'm Slade," said the gunman. "Red got me. Somebody got Red. That's all." And he walked off down the street with his shortened steps, breathing hard, glad of the wind behind him.

The Joker picked up the revolver that had fallen into the snow. It was small, delicately made, and only a .32, but a .32 will kill as quickly as a .45 if it slides through the heart or the brain. It was the sort of gun that only an expert would use.

Poor Slade, the Joker thought to himself. *He's seen better days.*

He went on back to the hotel, thoughtful along the way. When he got to their room, he found Bill the Dogman making dog moccasins. He threw the revolver on Bill's lap.

"What's that?" asked Bill.

"That's a present," said the Joker. "Fellow tried to tap me. Red hired him. Somebody passed the money to Red. That somebody would be one of the gamblers who've bet against your team, or else it's Phil Grant, the beauty."

"Shot at you, kid?" the Dogman asked calmly.

"Yes. Satan took the game out of his hand before he could plant me, though."

"I see the red on his lips," the Dogman commented, grinning.

CHAPTER THIRTY-NINE

Many things happened during the two days before the great race started. On the second morning before the start, coffee and canned milk were brought to Joker early. The Dogman was already up and out. The Joker lazily regarded the breakfast, luxuriating more in a warm bed than in the thought of food, until the landlord's black cat, which had wriggled through the door, hopped up and began to lap the milk out of the can.

The Joker chuckled and went to sleep again. He was awakened by scratching and piteous moaning. He sat up and saw the cat writhing in death throes. It lay still and dead a moment later. Then he remembered the canned milk. So he smelled it cautiously and detected nothing. He picked up the dead body and took it to his landlord.

"Who's your cook?" the Joker asked.

"I've got no cook," answered the latter, a broad-faced German. "What are you doin' with that cat of mine?"

"Your cook quit this morning, eh?"

"He had a row with me and quit. He's a fool. I pay him more than that …"

"He poisoned my coffee milk," said the Joker. "The reason I'm carrying your cat is because it's dead, and the white of the canned milk is still on its whiskers. Find the cook. And if there's a chemist in town, get an analysis of this milk."

He went out on the street and met Tuckahoe, of all people. The latter started to pass by without speaking, then paused and called: "Hello, Joker."

The Joker stopped.

"Look," said Tuckahoe. "I've had a wrong steer about you. I'm hoping that you win. I'm wishing you luck, Joker."

"Thanks," said Sammy Day. Then he smiled. "What's the matter, Tuckahoe?" he asked. "There's something on your mind."

Tuckahoe hesitated, standing first on one foot, then on the other, swinging his shoulders, frowning bitterly. "I'll tell you," he said, coming closer. "I wanna bet on your team. I've seen the dogs, and I know what you can do with 'em. So does everybody. But the odds are dropping on you all the time. You were the favorite till last night. This morning you're nowhere."

"No?"

"You're in fourth place in the betting, and dropping all the time. If you win on these odds, a dollar on you will bring in seven. You know why?"

"I can guess."

"Guess then, Joker."

"The word is around that I'm to be bumped off."

"Yes. You're due to drop, according to the inside opinion," replied Tuckahoe.

"Who's the inside opinion?" asked the Joker.

"I'll tell you who. It's the Rabbit. Can you beat that? He's up here taking a sunbath. I guess he likes this kind of weather."

"You know the Rabbit?" asked the Joker, interested at once.

"I know the Arizona talk about him," said Tuckahoe, "and I've played poker with him."

"That's about enough," suggested Sammy Day.

"Yeah. He seemed to think so, too. He wanted to be friendly. Bought me a drink. Told me he'd turned over a new leaf. Said he'd been going straight, and hoped I'd believe him. But his eyes were a lot too straight and frank and friendly. It didn't go down with me. Then he gave me a tip. The thing to bet against was your team. He said a lot of the boys were against you … some of them were willing to stop you with a bullet. I'm just telling you."

"Or with poison," added the Joker.

"Poison?" cried Tuckahoe, aghast.

"They've tried a hired gun … they've tried poison on me … and they're not through," replied the Joker. "No, I wouldn't bet on my dogs, if I were you."

Tuckahoe stared at him. "Who's after you?" he asked.

"You ask Phil Grant," the Joker answered genially, and he walked on.

He went in the Elder Saloon and found Grant there. Up to Grant he walked and said, very quietly, so that no one could hear: "You hired Red to hire Slade. You bribed the cook at my place to poison my coffee."

Phil Grant laughed. "You lie," he said.

But there was too much ring to his voice; his eyes were too wide open, too staring, as he uttered the words.

The Joker looked at the purple patch on the chin of Grant, and then left the place.

Grant followed him to the street and called through the half gale that was blowing: "Goldie says that she wants to see you!"

The Joker waved his hand and went on. He decided that he would not see her, but his feet took him of their own independent will to the hotel where the Mahans were staying. He went in and asked for her, and he was told to go into the waiting room.

There he sat down. On the wall were prints of pictures of old racehorses of the 1850s, their legs spread-eagled, their nostrils flaring. On their backs sat tiny jockeys. On the floor of the room, there was a red carpet that trembled as the wind got through cracks in the wall and puffed under it. But there was a good stove in the center of the room, a dull crimson along one side, and the room was warm. It seemed like a dream to the Joker.

And into the dream stepped Goldie Mahan. Rush was behind her, but she turned at the door and said: "No, Rush, I want to be alone."

"Hello, Joker. How's everything?" Rush asked, and went hastily back down the hall, without waiting for the answer.

Then Goldie closed the door behind her and stood there for a moment with her eyes fixed on the floor, as one uncertain whether to go on in or turn back. At last she said: "I had to talk to you, Sammy Day."

"You'd better sit down while you talk," he suggested.

"I'll stand," she replied.

"You're wobbly," said the young fellow. "You better sit down here for a while."

She shook her head and went on: "What's the bad blood between you and Phil Grant?"

His eyes narrowed. He could feel the pinch of the eyelids. He could feel the flare of his nostrils. Suddenly, Satan stepped before him, between him and the girl, and snarled. "Lie down, boy," he said. "Guard this." He threw a mitten on the floor, and the dog sank beside it. He dropped his head on the mitten, but continued to study the girl.

"You haven't answered me," said Goldie Mahan.

"You'd better tell me what makes you think that there's bad blood between me and Grant," he suggested.

"He told me so."

"Were you talking about me?"

"Yes."

He took a long breath. "I'm glad of that," he remarked, "no matter what you said."

"You haven't told me why there's bad blood," she said.

"It's an old story," he remarked. "It's a story that I don't tell."

"Were you at fault? Is that the reason that you don't tell the story?" she asked.

At this he smiled a little. "I'm not talking about Phil Grant," he said. "That's all there is to that. Did he talk about me?"

She admitted reluctantly: "Yes, he did."

"He said I was a gunman, a gambler, an adventurer, a killer," he suggested.

She did not answer. She looked straight at him. "Are you those things?" she asked at last.

"I'm your future husband," replied the Joker.

He saw her quiver, as though a whiplash had been laid on with a strong hand.

"You take a pleasure in torture, Sammy Day," she said.

At this he made an impatient gesture. "You want me to talk," he said. "But I won't talk much. I'll tell you enough, though, if you want to listen."

"I want to listen," she said.

"I'm a bad lot. I don't know that I'll ever be much better," he replied. "And you're in a class by yourself. You're straight. You're good to look at. And I want you. You want another man. You can't have him. The reason is that, no matter what I am, I am better than Phil Grant. Smoke that idea for a while."

She started to speak several times, and the coming and the going of passion in her weather-browned face he watched with a keen interest. He had been keeping the thought of her at arm's length, but after he told her, this day, that she was his future wife, the very word made an intimate passage to his heart. It admitted the hope of her.

Then she said: "Will you tell me what happened between you the other day?"

"We talked," he said, "no matter about what. Then I hit him.

He dropped. I dragged him back to his hotel and put him inside the door. I stuffed something into his mouth … no matter what."

Her chin went up. Disdain and anger filled her eyes.

"You don't believe me?" he asked.

At this she shook her head.

"Can't you see the truth when it's under your nose?" he asked her. "Do you think I'm lying? And haven't you seen the purple patch on his chin where I hit him?"

"You mean the place where he fell against the wall when he stumbled?" she asked indignantly.

He stared at her. Then he went to the door. "You ought to collect some new ideas about men," he said. "You're all woozy about them just now. Good-bye, Goldie. You'll get to know me a lot better when we're married."

"Married!" she cried, all rosy with wrath and contempt. "I'll be dead sooner."

He walked out without an answer and closed the door.

CHAPTER FORTY

Nome was an island of light in a dark sea, and nowhere were the lights so bright as at the start of the sweepstakes. Nowhere was there in all the world a crowd willing to brave such bitter cold for the sake of a sporting event.

The Joker, looking over the faces, missed Red, the rat. He also missed Phil Grant. Somehow the failure of the two men to appear made his heart fall. He was hardly listening to the words of advice from Bill the Dogman, until he heard the latter say: "What'll make you do your best, son? The thought of making Satan famous, or your own pride in not being beat?"

Before he answered, Sammy looked up into the face of the ugly man, and then he said: "Neither of the two, Bill. I'm doing it for you."

"For me?" the Dogman exclaimed, amazed. Then he laughed. "You ain't drunk, are you, kid?" he inquired.

"No. I'll have your heart out of you before I'm through," answered the Joker grimly. "But because you had a big idea about the dogs, and mostly because you bred Satan, I'm going to work like the devil. You'll have one great day if I can give it to you. After that I don't know how long you'll last, Bill."

The Dogman shrugged his shoulders. He was a changed man during the past few days. Since he came to Nome, he had shaved his beard, he had bought respectable clothes that fitted his loose frame. And an unexpected refinement irradiated the ugliness of his face. Now that his unmasked features could be seen, perhaps he was more homely than ever, but he was not repulsive. No man is, when his face bears the stamp of pain. If he offended the eye, in a strange sense he touched the heart, also.

It seemed as though he had lived for this grand moment. He was nervous. His nervousness showed in the suddenness with which his glance shifted from side to side. Then he said: "I dunno, son. I almost wish that anybody but you was drivin' the team, because it's you that so many are out to get. You hear what the chemist said about that milk?"

"No."

"Enough strychnine in it to kill a whole team of horses. They're after you hard. What makes so many folks hate you, son?"

The Joker, hesitating, looked hard and long into the history of his life. Then he said: "I'm not sure, but I can make my guess. It's because I've put on hobnail shoes and tramped on the faces of other people."

"That's a fair reason," remarked the Dogman.

"Yes, it's a fair reason," the Joker affirmed.

"You was a runt, kid, eh? You wanted to show how much bigger you were than you looked?" asked the Dogman.

The face of the young fellow colored hotly. But he answered with honesty: "I guess that was it. I was small-sized. I'm not a giant now, even. I'm only average. I suppose I wanted to seem bigger than I was. I couldn't do it with my hands. So I studied knives and guns. I didn't care about making people like me. I just wanted them to be afraid of me. That is about all I've got from that day to this."

"I was the longest, leanest, lankest, clumsiest kid that you ever seen," said the Dogman. "Everybody laughed at me. Finally, I wanted to show 'em. Just like you. You was helpless, bein' small … I was helpless, bein' overgrowed. Finally, my muscles groomed up to my bone, and I used my size. The harder I could slam a man, the better I liked it. I got mean. You got mean. We're sort of furnished the same inside of the skin."

The Joker listened with bewilderment and interest, and it seemed to him that the parallel was not so farfetched, after all.

Just now came the crash of a gun, a roar of voices, and off went a splendid team of Huskies, all leaning forward at one angle, all pulling straight and true, with a stride that meant miles, many miles, for every hour that slid behind them.

That was the half-breed, Little John. His team was not the most beautiful, but they were all big, rangy animals. They might not be first, but they would not be last, either. A good deal of money, thousands and thousands of dollars, had been invested in Little John by those who liked to pick up fat odds and take the long chance.

Then followed the interval before the next team would start. All through that pause, voices were shouting, and men running here and there, laboring frantically to get down bets at the last minute. There were many takers. Every minute $10,000 was being wagered.

The second team went off, a fine team, but too heavy for the race. Odds of two hundred to one against were freely offered, and there were no takers. The driver, a man of sixty, far too old for this terrible business, had a grim trust in the team with which he had freighted so many thousands of miles. He had wagered the small savings of his lifetime. The money was gone. He would never see it again, but even the loss of the race and his money would never rob him of his faith in his team. In silence the people watched him depart. They knew his type. They could not bet on him, but they respected him all the more, perhaps. Such men had made Alaska.

A great yelling went up next. Men tried to climb over one another, shouting. It seemed that the very lights blazed more brightly. And there was Rush Mahan, kissing Goldie good bye. He, the favorite, stepped to the line with his team, waved his hand to the crowd, and, when the gun cracked, sent his outfit away with a grand burst. The stride of the man as he ran into the dimmer light was a wonderful thing to behold. It made the Joker thrust out his lower jaw a little.

An unknown, a man on whose chances hardly a penny was invested, followed. He had a team of little Samoyed crossbreeds, beautiful as angels, gentle, affectionate. They watched their master with loving eyes. When he came near enough, they licked at his mittens. They barked with a cheerful excitement. And he, a thin-faced, bright-eyed fellow, set off in the grand hunt for glory. He would fail, of course. Those active, intelligent dogs, the most charming in the world, could never hold their pace against the longer-striding teams that opposed them. So he disappeared, with his hope and with his failure before him.

"It's not victory that counts in the world ... it's faith," the Joker said suddenly.

"Now," said Bill the Dogman, "what in hell d'you mean by that stuff?"

Denver Lew went away with a wild Indian yell that lifted his team forward. He carried much money. And Denver Lew would fight to the last ditch to win. There was no doubting his bulldog tenacity. Four times he had run this course, and four times he had failed to win, but every time he was within the money. Now, with far better dogs than ever before, he had a better chance, were it not for that glorious team of Rush Mahan and that equally glorious driver.

Pike Sullivan then went away with the gun. He was second choice in the betting. Another almost unknown team followed.

Then the word was brought to Sammy Day. He waved his hand. Satan took the team forward. He waved his hand again. Satan tossed his head and stopped. The long line of dogs behind him came to a halt.

The crowd acted as it had not acted before. It stood still. There were no voices raised above a murmur. There were no wagers made. All stood hushed, as though some tragic event were taking place.

The Joker looked calmly around him. Well, he knew what was in the minds of these people. But a sudden, hiccuping, drunken voice cried out: "Hey, all of you, what's the bets on the Joker? Who's gonna bet on him?"

People turned and stared. It was Tuckahoe who strode out in front of the closely packed crowd. He was more than half drunk, and as he stood there, he called out again: "Come on, boys! You tell me who's gonna bet on the Joker. I don't mean on whether he's gonna win or not. We all know that he's got the best dogs. Look at 'em, if you got any doubt. Dogs like that never mushed in Alaska before. Bill the Dogman made the breed, and the Joker has made 'em into sled dogs. But what I'm asking for is bets. Who'll make 'em? Here am I, Tuckahoe, offering ten to one that the Joker is a dead man before this here race is finished."

He paused. He was smiling widely with a drunken amusement. That smile was not mirrored by the faces in the crowd, and the Joker noticed Goldie Mahan standing with a frown on her face.

"Who takes me?" exclaimed Tuckahoe. He added: "Here's several thousand dollars of easy picking. I got 'em in my hand. I'll pay ten for one against the kid. I know he's as tough a puncher as ever drove dogs over snow. I know that he's got the best team that ever pulled a sled. But I'm offering ten to one against him, because I know that he'll be a dead man before the race is ended. Come on! Talk up! You all know the same thing. You know that the cards are stacked against him. Why don't you talk money, you boys, if you got any other idea? You talk about this being a country too cold to be crooked. Then why don't you talk up and tell me what you mean? You know that the kid is slated for murder before this game is over. You're all betting against him. Why don't you stand out in public and admit it?"

A single voice rose. "Who knows that Sammy Day is going to be murdered?"

It was Goldie Mahan who spoke. And Tuckahoe laughed richly, with much meaning in his laughter, then went on: "If you want to know, ma'am, you ask that crook out of Arizona, or some of his kind. Ask the Rabbit, the guy who calls himself Phil Grant up where it's too cold for his hot past to foller him. Ask Phil Grant, I say. Know him, ma'am?"

Before the girl could answer, before the Joker could look into her face, the word was given, the revolver spat fire and sent its boom through the icy air. The Joker called to Satan, and off went the team at a smooth trot, not too fast, unlike the melodramatic speed of the other teams, and he found himself running through the well-iced dimness of the Arctic with the Nome lights well behind. The race had begun, and his life was worth—well, perhaps the fifty cents that he still carried in his pocket!

CHAPTER FORTY-ONE

When a team is overtaken in the Nome Sweepstakes, it pulls out a little from the staked trail, if the dog-puncher is a gentleman, and lets the challenger go by. The Joker had never driven in a race before. He knew that the dogs were strong and true. He knew the pace that they would stand and that he could follow. But he did not know what that pace would do to the other teams against him.

The first thing he did was to pick up Denver Lew, traveling leisurely.

Denver called to him: "Is that you, kid? Is that you?"

"I'm Sammy Day," answered the Joker. "Is that the name you want?"

"You're a fast starter, kid," said Denver Lew, "but you'll rest a long time in hell before the finish!"

Sammy Day went on past Denver. He was working without friction, easily. It seemed to him that the snow was a medium in which he had spent all his life. Where it hindered others, it merely helped him. There was no pride in him, because he knew better how to wield snowshoes than other people do. It was because he had had one lesson from a master, and because he had had to apply that lesson to the utmost.

Yet he was a little surprised when his team overtook Pike Sullivan. For Pike was known as a rusher from the start of a race to the finish. He ran fast at first, while he and the dogs were fresh. He tapered off toward the finish. And yet the Joker passed Pike early and easily. As he went by, he judged the dogs with a keen eye, and he saw that the cloudy-gray team, undoubtedly, was running with far less effort, was far less spent than the team of Pike Sullivan.

He had admired the breed of the Dogman before. Now he understood easily that they were indeed worthy of the work of a lifetime. They had more strength than the solidly built Huskies. Their coats, though far lighter and less clumsy, were warmer. In addition, they had more spirit, more length of leg, more power in the stride, and in every way they outclassed the other teams on the trail. The race became a joke to the young fellow from that moment.

Pike Sullivan saw it, too. He called out, in an honest burst of admiration: "All right, kid! If they don't put a plug in you, you'll win. But I'm gonna get second in spite of Rush Mahan and high water."

The Joker laughed and went on. Then he saw that he had more than enough dog power in the traces. So he turned Satan loose and let him range ahead. It was worth the diminution in power, for the great dog read the very mind of the trail. He knew perfectly well to what points they were traveling. Not in vain had he been three times around the course. Therefore, he did not hesitate to take his master on shortcuts. They might be slow, through unpacked snow, but they were always worthwhile. A few hours of steady lugging might cut off hours of hard running. Besides, it gave the team a change of pace, and nothing is more important than that. A dog's wind may be gone for hard running when it is still able to lug a burden at a steady walk.

So the smoke-gray team of Bill the Dogman ate up the mileage and gradually crept up on the leaders. So sure was the Joker of the result that he did not push at all. For two days, one by one, he picked up the strong and pathetic members of the race. He passed the rest houses. He was greeted everywhere with amazement and scowls. Half through the second day, he knew that only one team was ahead of him, and that was Rush Mahan.

But Mahan would not stay before him. They were off the ice. They were in the broken country when he got to Rush Mahan. They stopped their teams side-by-side, and the loose leader, Satan, came back and stood by his master and laughed with a red tongue in the face of big Rush Mahan.

The giant stared at the team ahead, at the sled, and then at the man and the master dog. "It's not possible, Day," he said. "I've pushed to the limit all the way, and here you are up to me, and these infernal dogs of the Dogman's are as fresh as daisies. You've even got one out of harness for luck. Is that Satan?"

"That's Satan," replied Sammy.

Mahan nodded. He sat on his sled with his chin on his palm. "I'd quit now," he said, "except that so many people have put up their thousands on me. I'd quit now, but I can't. I've got to fight it through and come in as close on your heels as I can. What a dog Satan is! What would you do with him in the traces?"

"He goes in tomorrow," said the Joker. He looked at the magnificent shoulders of Mahan, at the lines of his closely bearded face, and thought that he never before, in all his days, had seen such a man, such a clean-cut athlete, such a clean-hearted hero. "Mahan," he said suddenly, "suppose that I live through it, what will you think if I marry Goldie?"

"I don't think of it," Mahan replied wearily.

"Neither do I, much," answered the Joker bitterly. "I think of something else. I know that they'll get me sooner or later, while I'm running on this trail."

"Then why do you run on it?" Mahan growled without lifting his eyes. "I've heard the same thing."

"I run on this trail," said the Joker, "because I want to prove that these dogs are the best, and that I have the best leader that ever walked in Alaska. Understand?"

"I understand," Mahan said still more wearily.

"I want to ask you one more question," said Sammy. "About Phil Grant. If he married Goldie, would you approve?"

"That's a question that I can't answer," Mahan said very shortly.

"Maybe you can't," replied Sammy, "and it's a question that I wouldn't ask, if I were not a dead man that still happens to be on his two feet. Only, after I'm bumped off, before Goldie marries, find Tuckahoe and ask him what he knows about the … about Grant. You might even tell him that I told you to ask."

"What d'you mean by that?" demanded Mahan.

"I don't tell you meanings. I tell you facts. That's all. I ask you one other thing. It's not likely that I'll finish the course. A bullet through the head will finish me first. But when you get in, I want you to say that I started behind you and that I passed you fair and square. Will you say that?"

"If you're dead," asked the other, "what does it mean to you?"

"It means something to the Dogman," Sammy responded. "So long, Mahan. You're a white man … you try to keep on being white." And he sent the gray team down the trail.

* * * * *

The next morning he knew that there were only bullets to fear. At the rest stations, the men came out gaping. A hard wind had been blowing straight in the teeth of the team, but still they were making time. From those stations, reports were being sent back to Nome.

"How's the betting now?" asked the Joker of a stalwart, gloomily bearded man at one of the stations as the dogs were being fed.

In a surly tone, the answer was: "What d'you expect? Folks thought that dogs was to run in this race, not long-legged horses.

And now the odds are even on the Dogman's team, in spite ..." He paused abruptly.

"In spite of what?" asked Sammy.

"In spite of bullets," the other said, and looked straight into the Joker's eyes.

"Yeah. In spite of bullets," murmured the Joker. He went on to the next station.

It was bitter weather. He had to check his breathing and make it small and short, for fear of freezing his lungs. The snow, under his snowshoes, crackled and popped like dry twigs. It flew up in powdery puffs now and then. Where the snow struck his face, it ate against the skin like flame. Now and then, even when the wind was not blowing, quick gusts of the cold rose up against him, and it seemed that he was frozen as deep as the marrow of his bones. He thought sometimes that he was sustained only by the thought that others along that long trail were as hard hit as he. There were four hundred miles of that trail. It was the extreme test of man and dog.

Leaving one of the stations, he went on until a strange thing happened. A stiff wind was blowing now. It did not increase the cold, but it drove it through clothing and flesh. It stilled the very heart. Sometimes the dogs paused, as if moved by a single impulse. Only Satan kept on. He was in harness now, and when the team behind him halted, he glanced back over his mighty shoulder and, with one growl, told them to strike ahead. They never disobeyed.

But now a miracle happened. The dog, Satan, who never went wrong, left the staked trail and cut across the country.

The Joker could not believe his eyes. He turned the dog back with signals of the hand, and then with shouted orders. Back to the staked trail they went, and yet again Satan insisted on turning to the right, across unstaked country. What madness was in him? Finally, Sammy was forced to go ahead himself, and then Satan followed. Once he sat down and howled long and loudly, as though in protest.

"You're named right. You're Satan," was Sammy's comment. He forced the dog along the staked trail. Then it ended!

Yes, the stakes were no longer to be seen. A mile ahead the Joker scouted, but he could find no stakes, no matter how often or how deep he turned. So he veered about and went grimly back to the station. They told him there. There had been new stakes driven. The instinct of the dog had been more sure, in spite of such marks. Who had driven the stakes? Who had thrown him out of the way? That could not be said. The right trail was again marked clearly enough.

Then, turning, through the small crowd, the Joker saw Red cringing into a corner.

CHAPTER FORTY-TWO

Three teams had passed him in the meantime. The leader, as a matter of course, being Rush Mahan. They might be overtaken, with a bold push, but what really counted was the long distance that the Dogman's team had mushed in vain, and the effort that they had expended for nothing. Why should such rats as Red exist on the face of the earth?

The Joker took a small nip of brandy and went ahead on the course, the right course, and he could hear Satan yipping joyously on the trail before him. The dog knew when the trail was correct. Well, he would never be challenged again. His way would be accepted.

He took the Joker through three shortcuts over ground that the fiend had contrived, but they reached the next station in the lead.

It was a leaden morning. The air, the sky, the ground were all of one gray color. A clear run lay ahead of them, and, though the dogs had been taxed by the extra mileage, still they seemed fresh and full of vigor. The Joker wondered how they would have been timed over this course when weather was good and false trails were not laid down by such reptiles as Red.

Again he was greeted by hostile scowls. Odds had changed again, the telephoned reports from Nome said, and he was now the favorite to win. Two to one was being bet that he would come in first.

But the last day would be enough to ruin all. He knew that. There was no great sense of triumph in him as he pulled out with the dogs again and looked at the red laughter of Satan, running in the lead.

What made him turn Satan loose? A loose leader was hardly needed now, but Toothwork knew the rest of the trail home well enough, and, if he were challenged along the final stretch, Satan would then be a reserve to put in the traces. Besides, the sled was light, and the work would not be very great. On this final run, he felt that the team would profit more by the inspiring sight of their great leader roaming up and down, making them confident of the trail.

This was the condition of the team as the Joker sent it through a ragged defile, not deep, but dangerous with ice-encrusted rock, a difficult place to make headway with a team.

However, the weather for the moment promised to clear, and the Joker was now so sure of his ultimate success that he almost enjoyed the labor of hauling the sled through the gap. Now was the time to show the brains of Satan, and the big dog pulled and mauled and hauled according to where his master told him to fix his teeth. The powerful sled dog Pat was also a tower of strength and help on this occasion.

Now they were through. There needed only an instant's pause, since the harness of Grab was twisted too crookedly. As the Joker leaned to rearrange the webbing, a bullet struck him. He dropped flat in the snow under the impact.

* * * * *

When consciousness did return, long lancing pains worked from the pit of his right arm through his shoulder and up to the skull. In a moment, sitting up, he knew what had happened. They had got him, well enough, and the prophecy that was in the air had come true—he would not finish that race!

Indeed, if he could cling to life until he was able to reach the next station, the only one between that point and Nome, he would be doing well indeed. The rifle bullet had whipped cleanly through the shoulder; it had slid upward, and what had knocked him flat was the impact as it struck the side of his skull. Blood trickled steadily from that hurt.

Who had done the thing? He looked about him, stunned, and there sat Satan, before him, busily cleaning his red-stained vest. A red trail ran behind him into a tangle of rough ground. The Joker blundered along that path with its ghastly markings, and there among the rocks, he found a huddle of clothes, face downward in the snow.

No, not dead. As he leaned over the wreckage—clothes ripped into rags and blood oozing at every pore of the body—the man stood up. He was more than half-blind. And his torn and unspeakably mutilated face showed why the wolf dog might well have left the carcass for dead.

No one could recognize him now. No one would be able to recognize him thereafter, either. It was merely a new face that would appear in the world. Seeing the Joker dimly with the half-obliterated vision of one eye, the mutilated man screamed out: "Don't shoot, Joker! Don't shoot!" Then he turned and ran staggering away, his footmarks being pools of blood behind him.

The very voice of the man was stifled to a caricature of what it had been, but the Joker felt certain that he had recognized the accents of Philip Grant. That was the end of the Rabbit, then. He might live, but he would never live in the world of real men. He would be an outlaw even among outlaws. From ambush he had shot an unarmed man!

How had Satan got at him in spite of the rifle? Well, the Joker could well remember how even with a club in his hand, he had failed time and again to stop the swift, tricky rushes of the beast. And well might both bullets and clubbed gun fail.

He stood now at his master's side, sniffing at the blood that trickled out over the fur, and whining a little.

"All right," the Joker said huskily. "I'll do what I can, Satan. Good old boy."

He made a fire and stripped his right shoulder bare. Rush Mahan whooped his dogs through the pass just then, and, seeing the brushwood fire, he paused and sang out. Then he came running over. He stood, immense, powdered with snow, within the grip of the ruddy fire, and groaned with sympathy and with anger.

"The infernal cowards! The low curs!" Mahan exploded. "They've done it, have they? Here, Joker. Let me get at that. You can't make a bandage for yourself … you have to have that right arm bound tight against your side. Then lie flat on your sled. You're losing enough blood to kill you. I'll see you safely to the station. The devil take the race."

Sammy looked up finally, and said in a solemn voice, staring at Rush Mahan: "Rush, you get on down the trail. I won't have help. I don't want it. I'm going to get straight on to Nome. I'm going to win this race with these dogs. And I won't have a finger's weight of help from you or anyone else. Understand me?"

Mahan exclaimed: "Whatever else you do, let me tie up that arm for you! The head wound is not bleeding so badly. That'll stop before long. But that arm will drain the heart out of you. Let me bind it up, and then you can do as you please and be damned."

"Mahan, get out of my sight, or I'll send Satan at you," replied Sammy, "and he's worse than killed one man already today."

Mahan, with a loud exclamation, half-despairing, half-enraged, finally turned back to his team and mushed them down the trail.

A shoulder at the best is a difficult thing to bandage. Twice, thrice, and four times the completed bandage slid at the very moment of completion, and Sammy had to begin over again. All the time that trickle of blood, he knew, was taking the life out of him, just as Mahan had explained that it would. And the molten steel of the torment burned into his very soul.

At last he discovered a better system. It was while he sat with his head resting on his knees, almost fainting, his shoulder gleaming in the firelight, that the thought came. Then he started to work, and the story that Little John, the 'breed, told when he got to Nome later on was a perfectly true one.

"I seen this feller settin'. Then I seen the team and knew it was Bill's outfit. So I went over and had a look, and it was the kid. He'd been got. They'd socked him through the shoulder and cracked his head for him. He was bandagin' himself up, and while he worked with one hand, that leader, Satan, he stood by and takes the one end of the bandage and gives it a pull. Then the kid makes him walk around him, pullin' the bandage tight all the time. The kid was groanin', and the dog was whinin' like he was taking a beatin'. I offer to help, and the kid says that he'll send Satan at me if I touch him. So I come along down the trail."

CHAPTER FORTY-THREE

Two others, Pike Sullivan and Denver Lew, went through that valley, also, while the young fellow still worked to get his wound dressed, and finally to put it inside the furs of his coat. But at last the thing was done. He had lashed a chunk of wood under the pit of his arm to shut off the flow of the blood, and now, swinging one arm only, he ran down the trail, behind his sled, with Toothwork leading the dogs valiantly and Satan back at his master's side.

At that steady stride, the Joker passed Pike Sullivan. He went by Denver Lew, whose team was beaten by exhaustion to a walk. He picked up Little John, who began to curse and rave and dance like a madman.

But the great Rush Mahan was not overcome so easily. Hours and hours went by, and the wounded Joker kept to his dogtrot or walked. Only on good downslopes did he treat himself to a ride on the sled.

As for the pain, his right arm had turned numb. There seemed no torment whatever from the surface wounds, but there was an inward fire eating at his heart. Swooning moments of weakness came over him. Once, when the sled stuck, instead of directing the team and working at the jammed runners, he simply sank down on the snow and watched Satan, like an inspired fiend, snarling, struggling, and fighting until, with the more or less blind help of Pat, the sled was free again. It was the short, high, snarling bark of Satan that launched the team on its way again, while Satan ran back to his master. The Joker caught him by the collar with his left hand and spoke, and so the dog drew him up to his uncertain feet.

"That's not so wonderful," the Joker heard his own voice saying, as though in a dispute. "An ant or a bee could do as much as that."

Strength flowed back into him, and he submitted once more to the infernal pounding of that trail until, far before him, he saw a wavering image, larger than human, larger than any beast, like a mountain—except that mountains do not move, and this image was moving.

It dissolved in parts. It was a man with a team of dogs and a sled. It was Rush Mahan, who cried out with horror and amazement as the Joker went by.

"You're killing yourself, Day! You're bleeding to death right now!"

"You lie!" the Joker cried out, and whooped his dogs ahead.

A few miles farther on, however, a sudden profound faintness came over him. He laid himself flat on the sled, his eyes closed, a swimming dizziness, a revolting nausea seizing him. Then he felt better, but still he was not well enough to stand when he reached the last station before Nome.

Many men had sledded out that far in order to see the race at this point, from which the homestretch began. And they never would forget the picture of the Joker as he pulled by. He did not stop. He could not stop. He felt that his life was dripping away from the tips of his fingers like lukewarm water out of a sponge, and he had to get to Nome.

They would have taken him from his sled by force, but, when he called, Satan came running between and headed them off. They could only run alongside and look at the bloodstained face, locked in determination and sodden with agony, and at the telltale right side, where the blood was fast freezing the clothes to the flesh.

But they dared not challenge the teeth of Satan. So the Joker went on and called faintly to Toothwork, and Toothwork valiantly led on the team.

Yet it was Satan who did the hardest job of all. For he divided his time, often running far in the lead to pick out the best way along the trail, then running back to the side of the sled to watch his master.

Finally, the time came when the Joker felt that he was living no longer. He was simply enduring a long death. He saw before him, then, a blur, and knew that it was Nome. With that knowledge, he collapsed. He fell half off the sled. Satan stopped the team with one sharp bark and fixed his teeth in the hood of the Joker and pulled him back onto the sled again. It was hard work, but the strength of fury was in the dog. He knew that loads must lie straight on that sled, and he knew that the voice of the master had gone out. The absence of that beloved voice left Satan in a dark room, cut off from light. But he knew that the trail must be completed, and yonder were wise men to be found. That was how they came into Nome.

People ran out and met them. Among them was long-striding Bill the Dogman, and it was he who dropped to his knees and discovered that the heart of the young man still beat. Then he warned back the others.

For the finish line had not yet been reached. Far down the trail loomed the great bulk of Rush Mahan and his splendid team, struggling furiously from behind, and though the Joker was so near to victory, yet it was not his, and if a finger's weight of help were given to him, he would be disqualified, as a matter of course. A runner who faints cannot be carried over the line. That was why the Dogman had quickly warned the curious crowd back.

"If the Joker lives," he cried, "he'll have the heart out of the fool that lays hands on him now! Leave him be, and let Satan manage him to the line."

That was what Satan did. He sent the team ahead until a bump tilted the sled and the Joker rolled quite onto the snow. He was five yards behind before the barking of the dog stopped the team.

All those frantic hundreds and hundreds of spectators saw the dog scurry back and drag the Joker by the nape of the neck, like a loosely filled sack drawn by one ear, up to the sled again.

It was only a matter of a few rods to the finish line now, and Mahan was coming up fast. His voice could be heard cheering on his staggering team. There was no stagger in the team of the Dogman. But the driver had to finish with them, and only Satan could see to that.

He could drag and pull the body of the man, but he could not make the sheer lift to the top of the sled. Yet he struggled frantically, until the vibrations caused by his tugging worked the sled down into the snow. Then the dog managed to get the head and shoulders of the master on the sled. Then he had to pause and rest.

Rush Mahan was close by! And the Dogman, on his knees in the snow, his face and eyes terrible to see, watched the labor and uttered no sound, when the very heavens were splitting as the men of Nome groaned and shouted.

Someone called for police to interfere. But the Dogman pulled out a long-barreled revolver and warned back all hands.

Then the big leader, shifting his grip, changed his tactics, took a firm hold on the clothes of the master near the hips, and suddenly that weight was rolled loosely onto the sled. Only one foot trailed, and still trailed as Satan howled to his team, and Toothwork, growling also, dug in his claws and helped to make the start. A shudder and then a lurch—the sled came free and started for the finish line just as Rush Mahan came abreast.

Mahan was running with a stagger, too, and well past the Dogman's team he ran toward victory, when the left runner of his sled snagged against a jagged projection of hard snow. It was only a jerk, a moment's pause, but in that moment the Dogman's team won the sweepstakes.

They wondered, then, how they could get at the young fellow without killing Satan. But to their amazement, he allowed the Dogman to pick him up in his arms. Only now Satan ran alongside, supervising, leaping up high now and then, to make sure that all was well with his master.

But if Satan was convinced of that, the doctors were not quite so sure. Between a half-frozen body, utter exhaustion, and a terrible lack of blood, they had little to work with. Then the young fellow opened his eyes.

"How are you?" the Dogman asked.

The Joker growled like a bulldog.

"He'll live," the Dogman announced. "He's gotta live to carve the heart out of me, eh? Whatcha think, Goldie?"

She was there with her brother.

She was there, though another sled had brought in Phil Grant from the spot on the trail where he had collapsed. That torn and ragged face the doctors patched, but it was not his repulsive appearance that filled them with revolt. It was the story that was spreading like a foul poison through the mind of Nome.

He was the gunman who had stopped the Joker on the trail! The whole story might never have been known had not Red told. Red was suspected of having run ahead up the trail and of lying in wait for the Joker. He was suspected because it was known now that he had run out the false line of stakes. Then he confessed the plan that he and Phil Grant had worked out together. He was to work the stakes. If he failed to stop the Joker, Phil Grant would do that later on with a rifle bullet. So much for that.

So Goldie Mahan stayed by the side of the Joker that day, that week, that month, while he battled for his life. And Rush was with her.

He told her what he knew of the story of the trail. Gossip floated to her here and there, and when Phil Grant left Nome under escort, he sent no farewell message to the lady of his heart, nor she to him. His very name had become a sign and a symbol of horror. As the Dogman said, however, there was too much bulldog in the Joker for him to die.

He lived, and he sat up at length, with his weak head sunk in a pillow, and his thin hands feebly crossed upon his lap. He looked straight before him at the gray, statuesque form of Satan, which lay across the foot of his bed. The head of the dog was toward the girl, and when Goldie, from time to time, leaned to straighten the sheet or make the head of the Joker more comfortable, the eyes of Satan turned green.

Yet he made not a sound. Nor did he stir until he saw the girl lean lower and still lower, until her face was touching the face of the master. Then the great dog leaped up with a roar. Between them he sprang and stood towering, bristling. Goldie had drawn back with a cry, but now she laughed.

"It's all right," she said. "I know that I'll never have more than second place. And it's right that Satan should come first forever. God bless him."

The first time, it is said, that a devil was ever blessed.

THE END

ABOUT THE AUTHOR

Max Brand is the best-known pen name of Frederick Faust, creator of Dr. Kildare, Destry, and many other fictional characters popular with readers and viewers worldwide. Faust wrote for a variety of audiences in many genres. His enormous output, totaling approximately thirty million words or the equivalent of 530 ordinary books, covered nearly every field: crime, fantasy, historical romance, espionage, Westerns, science fiction, adventure, animal stories, love, war, and fashionable society, big business and big medicine. Eighty motion pictures have been based on his work, along with many radio and television programs. For good measure he also published four volumes of poetry. Perhaps no other author has reached more people in more different ways.

Born in Seattle in 1892, orphaned early, Faust grew up in the rural San Joaquin Valley of California. At Berkeley he became a student rebel and one-man literary movement, contributing prodigiously to all campus publications. Denied a degree because of unconventional conduct, he embarked on a series of adventures culminating in New York City where, after a period of near starvation, he received simultaneous recognition as a serious poet and successful author of fiction. Later, he traveled widely, making his home in New York, then in Florence, and finally in Los Angeles.

Once the United States entered the Second World War, Faust abandoned his lucrative writing career and his work as a screenwriter to serve as a war correspondent with the infantry in Italy, despite his fifty-one years and a bad heart. He was killed during a night attack on a hilltop village held by the German army. New books based on magazine serials or unpublished manuscripts or restored versions continue to appear so that, alive or dead, he has averaged a new book every four months for seventy-five years. Beyond this, some work by him is newly reprinted every week of every year in one or another format somewhere in the world. A great deal more about this author and his work can be found in *The Max Brand Companion* (Greenwood Press, 1997) edited by Jon Tuska and Vicki Piekarski.